What they're saying about *Widow's Walk: The Reckoning*

"First time novelist Ken Spillias has the unique ability to take a common thread in a story line and weave it into an intricate, exquisite mosaic. The symbolism he has crafted, especially in the Widow Chiever's enigmatic character, will keep your mind twisting with salacious nuances, God-fearing intrigue and allegorical imagery."

Suzanne Niedland
Award Winning Documentary Filmmaker

"*The Reckoning* is an excellent series finale with mystical intrigue at every turn of the page. While Donovan attempts to find seclusion in Paradise, S.C., he is led to the ultimate realization that "Paradise" is anything but what its name implies."

Chuck Elderd
Palm Beach County Film Commissioner

Praise for *Widow's Walk: The Precipice*

"Hooks you from the provocative opening to the powerful and unexpected ending."

Paulette Cooper Noble
Author of 19 books

"*The Precipice* embodies the depth and breadth of a major motion picture. Its characters, from Jim Donovan to Dr. Pe're, personify the ever changing faces of good and evil and the power that raids the souls of both! Page turning mind candy . . ."

Mel Maron
Film Producer Representative

"Ken Spillias brilliantly develops a thought provoking tale of temptation, lust, and greed in *Widow's Walk: The Precipice*. This fantastic new author takes you on an emotional roller coaster that follows the main character's chaotic journey in a life fraught with dark secrets and a yearning for redemption. Every turn of the page is rich in characterization, description and impossible to put down! Five Stars!"

Bruce Merrin
Bruce Merrin's Celebrity Speakers & Entertainment Bureau, Inc.
Celebrating 40 Years

Wow!

"Couldn't put the book down! I found myself wanting to reread certain parts to let them echo more deeply, as the words were stated in such deliciously eloquent ways. Can't wait for part two!"

Aura Baltrusaitis
Songwriter/Musician
Gaia

GREAT READ!

"From the very first page, I couldn't put it down. Just when I thought I knew Jim Donovan's next move, I was completely side-swiped as the turn of events unfolded. He went through many scenarios questioning his moral character, yet his conscience always got the best of him. In the end, it felt like I was left hanging ... I look forward to reading the next one!"

Samantha L. Arvanitis-Santini
Author
Letters to Mom and Dad (And Things That Happened Along the Way)

Widow's Walk

Part 2: *The Reckoning*

Kenneth Spillias

abbott press®

A DIVISION OF WRITER'S DIGEST

Abbott Press books may be ordered through booksellers or by contacting:

Abbott Press
1663 Liberty Drive
Bloomington, IN 47403
www.abbottpress.com
Phone: 1-866-697-5310

The Music Of The Night
From THE PHANTOM OF THE OPERA
Music by Andrew Lloyd Webber
Lyrics by Charles Hart
Additional Lyrics by Richard Stilgoe

ISBN: 978-1-4582-1301-3 (sc)
ISBN: 978-1-4582-1302-0 (hc)
ISBN: 978-1-4582-1300-6 (e)

Library of Congress Control Number: 2013921197

Printed in the United States of America.

Abbott Press rev. date: 12/12/2013

Acknowledgements

I owe a continuing debt of gratitude to all who have contributed to the development of the Widow's Walk story.

To those acknowledged in the Foreword to *Widow's Walk: The Precipice*, I repeat my expressions of thanks and gratitude.

My children continue to be a constant source of support and love, teaching me that even the wisest of parents needs technology for their voice to be heard.

In addition, for getting *Widow's Walk: The Reckoning* ready for publication, I would like to express my sincere appreciation to Heather Ebanks and Chris Blackwell for their editing of the manuscript; to my law colleague, Howard Caplan, for his sage advice and assistance regarding legal and copyright issues; and, once again, to my sister-in-law, Robin Spillias, for her indefatigable efforts in shepherding me through the sometimes labyrinthian process of getting both books to print.

To Monica, my lovely and loving life partner.

Where and how a journey must end,
Oft clouded 'ere it's begun,
To eyes opened wide comes sure and ordained
As viewed in the morrow's sun.

Journey's End

Preface

Sooner or later, every man reaches a point where he knows that it's time to take stock of his life—to create an inventory of the choices he's made, good and bad, and decide whether to stay on the same path or change course. Sometimes he reaches that point gradually, as a result of a number of consequences or occurrences that cumulatively lead him to a recognition that he is drifting, with no real purpose or goal—at least not one that is likely to lead to joy or fulfillment. Some have an epiphany, an "aha" moment, triggered by a bolt of enlightenment or, more frighteningly, by a sudden tragic loss or event that scares him into introspection and self-realization.

For Reverend Jim Donovan it was a convergence of the gradual and the sudden that brought him to the present point in his life, as well as a frustrating sense that not all of his choices—especially the bad ones—were decisions made only of his own free will.

His triggering event was his forced sexual encounter—his rape—by a young African girl in Togo at the hands of her sinister and mysterious giant of a father, just a few yards away from his wife, Renee, who was strapped naked to a wooden pole inside a ring of fire and surrounded by hostile natives.

But as sudden and traumatic as this single event was, Jim saw it as the culmination of a lifetime—a young lifetime to be sure—of choices and events that had prevented his seemingly idyllic life—a beautiful and devoted wife, two darling children, work of a higher calling and the respect of most who knew him—from being anything but.

Like most men, his life had been a combination of good and bad. He had successfully completed college, met and married the love of his life, graduated at the top of his class in his study for the ministry and had proven himself to be a dynamic and charismatic clergyman at a small church, a large church and as a missionary. But he also suffered loss—the unexpected and premature deaths of his father, whom he idolized, and his best friend, Tony Scarlotti—and painful betrayals by people he had loved and surrendered his soul to.

So the struggle within was joined. There would always be a powerful force for good within him. His strict Catholic upbringing and his conscience, in the ever-present voice in his head of Father McTighe, would see to that.

Yet, a new voice, or force, had been introduced when he crashed and burned and found himself in a mental institution under the care of Dr. Pe're—the strange psychiatrist whose unorthodox methods lifted the cloud of depression from Jim's mind and boosted his self-esteem. But the price of the successful treatment was steep—the implanting within him of a seed of narcissism that would engage in a constant battle with his conscience for primacy in every important decision he would ever again be called upon to make.

Jim knew there was more, something outside himself. But what, and why him, he could not know. His rape was not a product of his inner struggle between right and wrong. It was evil, pure evil, supernatural evil. So too with the attempted seduction of him by Melanie Lee, the seventeen-year-old daughter of his powerful benefactor, Richardson Leigh, and the brutal Charles Manson-like murders of Leigh and his wife by the cult their daughter belonged to.

One's entire life, all of his experiences and all of his choices, brings him to each new point in his life, and new choices to be made. At this point in his life, Jim Donovan needed a new beginning, a righteous start. He hoped he had found it, in Paradise.

Chapter 1

It was a small town. "Population 942" the sign at its boundary line stated. It appeared to be an old sign that hadn't been changed in quite some time seeming to indicate that the town's number of new births and arrivals were in constant equilibrium with its deaths and departures. The water tower announced the town as Paradise, South Carolina. *What a great name for a small town,* Jim thought. As he drove by the water tower he could see that a portion of the name of the town had been covered over and repainted—as if its name had at one time been shorter. *Pretty sloppy job.*

As soon as he passed the water tower he was in the heart of town. The main street, which in most northern towns of similar size and character would most likely have been named Main Street, was called Dixie. Not Dixie Road, or Dixie Highway, or Dixie Street. Just Dixie. It was a two traffic light town—one on either side of a central square sitting precisely in the center of town, through which Dixie quietly made its way.

When he reached the square he asked an elderly gentleman strolling slowly along the sidewalk how to get to the church where he would soon have his interview for the open pastor position. It took a good five minutes for him to get the directions, what with the elderly gentleman's polite curiosity about this potential newcomer to their fair town and his slow Southern cadence. It was of no matter to Jim. The interview was at two o'clock and it was clear that in this small town the fifteen minutes he had left to get to the church was going to be more than enough.

Once there, Jim stood before the building he hoped would house his new mission, and his new spiritual home. "Paradise Community Christian Church" was neatly painted on the curved white wood at the top of the church sign. Behind the glass covering of the body of the sign, white tack-on letters on a black background announced:

ALL SOULS WELCOMED
SUNDAY SERVICES 10:00 A.M.
BIBLE STUDY WEDNESDAY 7:30 P.M.
PASTOR: REV. LUCAS CARTER

The church building itself was modest in size. It was painted white and had a steeple at the front end of the roof, seeming to rise directly up from the light tan double doors leading into the sanctuary. In front, on either side of the doors, azalea shrubs extended to the ends of the building, their pink and white flowers in full bloom lending a soft feminine air to the façade seeming to welcome all comers to enter this place of warmth and peace. On the front lawn, about twenty feet from the church itself, and to his right as he looked at it, was a single magnolia tree. White blossoms settled in its branches like the heavenly bodies in a starlit night and filled the air with their sweet fragrance.

It was a simple, nineteenth century style church building, not unlike the thousands of similar houses of worship that dot the rural American landscape. It bore no particular markings or indications of any particular Christian denomination since it was, in fact, a non-denominational parish.

I love it, Jim thought as he stood admiring the church's simple beauty and drinking in the aroma of the magnolia blossoms. *I've got to get it. I just have to.*

He took a deep breath and entered through the unlocked front doors. To his left was a stairway leading downstairs. It was downstairs in the basement, in the church's community center, that he would have his interview.

When he entered the hall he noted that it was quite small. This was not particularly surprising given that it served a relatively small church in a similarly small town in the heart of South Carolina. Yet he did find that his first impression was that he wished it were a bit larger.

In the middle of the hall was a long, rectangular folding table. On one side of it was an empty folding chair. On the other side sat three men. They were talking to each other and didn't seem to notice that he had entered the room. Suddenly the two men on either side of the third man broke out laughing. It was the hard and hearty laughter of men who truly appreciated a good joke, and each other.

Jim walked up to the empty chair. For the first time the three men noticed he was in the room. The laughter began to tail off. Not waiting for it to end completely, he introduced himself.

"Hello, I'm Jim Donovan," he said to no one of them in particular.

The man in the middle—a slight, white-haired gentleman in his sixties—stood up and extended his hand.

"Yes. Yes. Reverend Donovan," he said, taking Jim's hand in a firm handshake. "Welcome. Welcome to Paradise. I'm Ned Ferguson. I'm . . . I guess you could say I'm the chairman of the Parish Board, though I can't say that title gets me anything hereabouts. I reckon I have more clout because of being the town's only barber for . . . oh my . . . must be over forty years now."

The man finally released his grip on Jim's hand that had begun to turn white for lack of circulation.

"Pleased to meet you, Mr. Ferguson," Jim replied politely.

"This here" Ferguson said as he pointed to the man on his left—a stocky, dark-haired fellow, maybe in his early forties, sporting a small scar over his right eyebrow—"is Charlie Bruener. Charlie's our chief of police."

Bruener stood up and shook Jim's hand. Bruener's grip was stronger than Ferguson's and Jim began to wonder whether his hand would survive one more friendly greeting.

"Actually, he's our Director of Public Safety," Ferguson continued. "Runs our police and our fire. But Charlie will always be a cop first, so that's just what we call him—chief of police."

"Happy to meet you, Reverend," Bruener said, mercifully letting go of Jim's hand much more quickly than Ferguson had. The police chief struck an imposing figure but his manner was warm and friendly.

"Happy to meet you as well, Chief."

"And this," Ferguson said, pointing to the rotund, middle-aged man standing to his right, "is Harold Riggins. Harold owns the town's only bakery. Wouldn't do to say he was the town's only baker.

That would get most of the women-folk mighty upset." Ferguson chuckled. Jim chuckled too at the barber's attempt at humor. It wouldn't do, he figured, not to acknowledge the humor of the parish board's chairman who was about to interview him for a job (not to mention the town's only barber). Bruener and Riggins, having no such need to curry favor with their colleague, issued weakly swallowed harrumphs.

Jim and Riggins shook hands briefly, much more softly to Jim's relief, and nodded to each other.

"Please, sit down Reverend," Ferguson said, pointing to the empty chair. "Would you like something to drink?"

"A Pepsi, if you've got one."

"Sure. Harry . . ."

"Got it." Harry Riggins went to a refrigerator behind a counter that separated the main portion of the hall from a small kitchen area as Jim and the other two men sat down. He brought back a twelve-ounce can of Pepsi which he placed in front of Jim.

"Glass?" Riggins asked as he sat down.

"No. This is fine," Jim said, chuckling to himself as he opened the pop-top and took a sip.

"Now Reverend, as I'm sure you've figured out," Ferguson continued, "the three of us sort of make up the church's . . . well, we're called a board officially. Most folks refer to us as the elders. Anyway, it's our task, our *responsibility*, to select a new pastor for our church."

"Yes. I understood that from your letter."

"Good. Good." Ferguson folded his hands together and pointed his two index fingers at Jim. "I've got to tell you Reverend, we are *real* excited that a man with your credentials and your references—you know, Dr. Westin from the Bible College in Florida wrote just wonderful things about you—well, anyway, we're just thrilled that you would even consider becoming the minister of our little church here in Paradise."

Dr. Westin had been very helpful to Jim in landing this interview. When he first contacted his mentor for help, he had worried that Westin might have heard about what had happened in West Palm Beach, in the way Richardson Leigh would have told it. But Westin had accepted the official explanation. And why not? Given his fondness for his former student, it wouldn't have been hard for him to believe that Jim would want to minister to the spiritual needs of poor Africans.

"But why a small parish, in a small town when you clearly have the ability to lead a large congregation?" Westin had asked. Jim's explanation that his experience in Togo had changed his view of who he wanted to minister to, and how, had the ring of believability, as well as the benefit of being the truth.

Jim looked squarely into the eyes of the chairman of the board, folded his hands, placed his elbows on the table and leaned forward. "Mr. Ferguson," he said, "it is I who am thrilled that *you* would consider *me* to be your spiritual leader."

He looked at all three men's faces. He knew he had them where he wanted them. The job was his, unless he did or said something to blow it.

The questions about his work in Africa were, emotionally, the most difficult for him to address, as he knew they would be. Even as he talked about his accomplishments, memories of the terror-filled night intruded. It was a struggle to remain attentive and focused.

Riggins was talking now. Jim wasn't quite sure what he was saying. His mind was going in its own direction by its own force of will.

It's ironic, he thought. *I'm actually beginning to feel . . . grateful, yeah,* grateful *that I was sent to Togo—even if it* was *because of the coercion of a crazed father accusing me of molesting his child. Maybe . . . maybe even that night, maybe I'm supposed to get something good out of that. Maybe that had to happen to bring me here—to these good and kind folks in a small town in South Carolina. What else would have brought me to a place like this?*

Mr. Riggins' questioning voice brought Jim back. "Reverend?"

"Yes. Yes, Mr. Riggins. I'm sorry. My mind wandered for a moment, back there."

"I can understand that," Mr. Riggins politely replied. "I hear a great deal of excitement and self-satisfaction in your voice as you talk about your missionary work."

"Yes sir. It was an experience I'll never forget, and one I'll always be grateful for."

"Reverend?" It was Chief Bruener's turn. "I would also like to ask you about your missionary work, but from another angle."

Another angle? Jim took a big swig of Pepsi.

"You had only been at the church in West Palm Beach one year when you left to do your work in Africa. If we were to hire you, what's to say you won't up and leave us in a year's time, or even less, to go do something else that interests you more. You know, lots of folks get pretty bored in a small town like this one, especially if they've worked in glitzy and exciting places like you have."

Got that one. "That's a very fair question, Chief. I can't guarantee anything. It's God's will, not mine, that will determine where I'm to do His work. What I can tell you is that this is precisely the type of church and community I want to serve. And Paradise is just the kind of town I want to raise my family in. So I won't be looking to leave anytime soon—that is, if you offer me the position."

Jim smiled. *Nailed it.* He leaned back in his chair and draped his right leg casually over his left.

"Charlie? Harry? Any more questions of Reverend Donovan?" Ferguson asked his partners. Both men shook their heads.

"Well Reverend Donovan," Ferguson continued, "there is one more very important question."

Money.

"And that is money. We know you made a pretty good salary in Florida. And a foundation of some sort paid your way in Africa. But we're a small church and we can't afford . . ."

"I'd be willing to start at twenty thousand a year with a housing allowance that would allow me to find a decent home for my family," Jim interrupted, already having given the matter a great deal of thought. "Then, if I can help grow the church and you can afford more, we'll deal with it then."

He was convinced he wouldn't be at that income level very long. He knew his willingness to start so much lower than what he made in West Palm would seal the deal.

The three men looked at one another. They all nodded.

"Well, Reverend Donovan," Ferguson said, "we would like to officially offer you the position of pastor of the Paradise Community Christian Church at a salary of twenty-thousand dollars a year. Now, as far as a housing allowance, we can do better than that. Old

Reverend Carter—our minister who passed away two months ago, God rest his soul—the man you'd be replacing—he had no wife, no kids. He had an older sister who passed away years ago and that's it. No other family and no heirs. So he willed his house to the church to serve as a parish home for the pastor. I think you and the Missus will like the house just fine. If you don't we can discuss an allowance then."

"I'm sure we'll like it. I haven't seen anything in this town so far that I don't like. You're very generous, and I gladly accept your offer."

"Wonderful!" Ferguson gushed. "Wonderful! When do you think you can start?"

"We've been staying with my mother-in-law in Illinois since we returned from Africa. We should be able to be here in about two weeks."

"Great. Then your first service would be two weeks from this Sunday."

"That should work just fine," Jim said.

Chief Bruener, who had apparently been content to let Mr. Ferguson do most of the talking, spoke up. "Let me ask you Reverend, is there anything else about the church or the town that you need to know before you get here?"

"Nothing I *need* to know," answered Jim. "But there is one thing I'm curious about."

"What might that be?"

"As I drove into town I noticed that the town's name on the water tower seemed to have been painted over another word or name. It seemed like I saw the letters "H" and "O". Was Paradise—which, by the way, is a perfect name for the town—but was it always the town's name?"

Ferguson leaned back in his chair and crossed his legs. "Now *that's* an interesting story," he said. "You got some time?"

"All the time in the world."

"Harry," Ferguson said, looking at his fellow committee member, "could you get me an orange soda while I fill our new minister in on the heritage of our name?"

Harold Riggins the baker said nothing as he got up and headed to the kitchen to get Ned Ferguson an orange soda. It was clear to Jim that Ferguson liked to tell this story, which only made Jim more interested in hearing it. Besides, if he was going to be making this small town his and his family's home, the more he knew about it the better.

"So, Reverend Donovan," Ferguson began, "as you've guessed, Paradise was not always the name of our fair town. Its original name, from the 1700's until 1865 was Weston, named after our founder, Nathanial P. Weston."

"Westin?" Jim asked. "W-E-S-T-I-N?"

"No sir. Weston. W-E-S-T-O-N. Oh, I see. Similar name to Dr. Westin, from the Bible College. Now ain't that a coincidence."

Yes, of course. An interesting coincidence, Jim thought. *I'm beginning to wonder anymore—is* anything *a coincidence?*

"Anyway," Ferguson went on, "the town was renamed in 1865 in honor of one of our native sons, whose name is no longer spoken aloud. As the story was told, this young man fought courageously in the War of Northern Aggression and was wounded real bad at the Battle of Gettysburg. When he got home, not long after, he told everyone he had been commended by General Robert E. Lee himself for his bravery in trying to take a key Yankee position known as Little Round Top. The war was going badly for the South. Everyone was looking for heroes, and hope. It was a small town and most of its menfolk who went off to war didn't return, or returned with fewer limbs than they left with. And here was a genuine hero. Everyone was so proud, and so happy he come home in one piece, that no one thought to check his story. Right after the war ended the town was named in honor of our brave young Confederate soldier."

Ferguson paused to take a swig of his orange soda.

"So it stayed for over one hundred years," he continued, "until some university professor doing research on what he called 'Civil War facts and myths' came to town asking all kind of questions about the town's namesake. He told us that his research so far showed that our Confederate hero was no hero at all; that in fact, during Pickett's Charge he had actually turned and run in the face of the Yankees' firepower and that he had hid in the woods near Seminary Ridge until Pickett's suicide charge had ended. The professor said there was even some indication he might have shot to death a lieutenant who come to take him back to the front lines, though there was no solid proof of that.

"Well, of course, no one believed this pointy-headed Yankee professor, coming into our town and trying to tell us that our greatest Confederate war hero was . . ."

Ferguson hesitated as if he was having difficulty getting the next words out. He took another sip of his orange soda.

" . . . was a coward. 'What about his commendation from General Lee,' we said. 'Has anyone ever actually seen such a commendation?' he asked. 'Is it in your town hall, or wherever you keep the town's historical papers?' We had to admit that no one had ever actually seen it, not even then. The story was that he had lost it on his trek back home.

"The professor told us that our soldier had in fact met General Lee, but it was when the great general told him he would be court-martialed for desertion. And he was, in the field after the army's retreat, and the professor had the papers to prove it. But the battle at Gettysburg had taken its toll, even on General Lee. When the young soldier was found guilty of desertion, instead of the firing squad, he was mustered out dishonorably and sent home."

Ferguson paused again, this time for effect Jim surmised. He guessed that Riggins and Bruener had probably heard Ferguson tell this story a hundred times, but they seemed as interested as Jim, who was hearing it for the first time. *The mark of a good storyteller,* he thought.

Ferguson took another sip from the orange soda can and then returned to his story.

"This news was devastating to the town. No one knew what to do about it, given that the town's name—which no one has since said aloud—well, it was founded on cowardice, not courage. The mayor at the time was Heath Marton. Everyone called him Butch. Winnie Lowe, our present mayor's wife—his name is Andy Lowe— was Mayor Marton's wife at the time. Her name had been Winnie Picklethorpe. She and Butch met when they were both working at the Piggly Wiggly. Then, after Butch Marton died, Harvey Handley became mayor, and not long after he married Winnie, so she was still the town's first lady. And then . . ."

Chief Bruener coughed a loud, dry cough. Ferguson looked at him and chuckled.

"You're right, Chief." He turned and looked back at Jim. "That's a story for another day. You'll get to meet Winnie in due time. She's close to my wife, Belle, the biggest gossip in Paradise—Belle, that is." He leaned closer to Jim and said in a loud whisper, "But I'll deny ever having said that."

Ferguson leaned back into his chair. He crossed his left leg at the calf over his right thigh near the knee and grasped his left knee with the interlocked fingers of both hands. With a smile and a wink, he went on.

"So, anyway, Mayor Marton suggests a contest to come up with a new name for the town. The town council agreed and gave the mayor the authority to make the decision. Mayor Marton was a strong mayor and there was no doubt he would control that decision, but he always let the council feel like it was an important part of the process.

"Of course, so many of the town's residents had ancestors or relatives who had fought bravely in the War of Northern Aggression, the Great War, WW two and Korea; others whose bloodlines had been giants of business or politics in the town—to try to come up with some kind of consensus was, well, just doomed from the get go.

"Soon, the renaming of the town had become the most divisive issue we had ever faced. Neighbor fought neighbor. Friendships exploded. Even families were being torn apart. Mayor Marton's grand idea which, to her credit, Winnie was totally against from the beginning, was destroying the town. Finally, on the fourth of July, the appointed day for naming the winner—the grand prize was being the grand marshal of the fourth of July parade—the mayor couldn't select anyone's suggestion without pissing everyone else off. Oh, excuse me, Reverend, I meant to say . . ."

"That's perfectly all right, Mr. Ferguson," Jim said with a smile. "That's not high on the list of objectionable language."

"All the same, my apologies. So, faced with certain rebellion from almost all of his constituents—in other words, all of the voters—the mayor, during his usual fourth of July speech, made the long-awaited announcement. I remember it like it was yesterday."

Ferguson stood up and hooked his thumbs into his suspenders, mimicking a politician's speechifying pose.

"Friends, neighbors. As you all know, today's the day for announcing the name of our great town. Many of you all have answered our call for suggestions and ideas. All of your suggestions are great suggestions and any one of the names submitted would bring honor and dignity to a town which has just gone through so much heartbreak and shame. In fact, all of your suggestions are so darn good that it's downright unfair to just pick one. So, I decided the only fair thing to do is pick a name that has nothing to do with any of our kin, and yet speaks to the pride we have in our heritage and our history. A name that symbolizes the beauty of our town and the enduring love we have for the land. You have all seen *Gone with the Wind*. And whatever may have happened to her, whatever her faults may have been, no one can doubt the beauty of Scarlet O'Hara, and her love and devotion to her beloved home. I know what some of you are thinking. But no, Tara isn't what I have in mind. After all, Tara didn't fare too well. Neither in fact did Scarlet. But someone who did fare very well from the movie, and whose beauty and grace brought Scarlet O'Hara to life, was the actress who played her, Vivian Leigh. So, my fellow citizens, I declare that our fair town shall be known as Leighsburg."

Leighsburg?! You've got to be kidding! Jim continued to look at Ferguson, who was still telling his story, but he wasn't hearing a thing being said. He was too stunned at this second apparent coincidence, this second reminder of people and events from his past—this one a most unpleasant reminder. *What's going on? What's the connection between this town and Richardson Leigh? There is no connection. I'm being silly. What kind of connection can there be between Richardson Leigh, Vivian Leigh and a town named Paradise? I've got to get a hold of myself. Get a hold of yourself, Jim!*

Not having taken his eyes off Ferguson, Jim strained to push thoughts of Richardson Leigh out of his mind so he could again focus on the storytelling barber, and so he wouldn't blow the job he had already been offered and accepted. *Focus. Focus and listen, now!*

" . . . and talk of a recall election. And citizens spoke at town council meetings for the next two months about the absurdity of naming the town after a movie actress, and one that wasn't even an American at that."

Ferguson took up his orange soda can and drank the last of it. He looked at Jim and said nothing. Jim guessed that this pregnant pause was designed to elicit a question from him. He actually had one that he did want to ask.

"So, was the town called . . . Leighsburg?"

Ferguson smiled.

"Not on your life," he said. "It became Paradise."

"And how did that come about?"

"Well, as I understand it, having been told the story by my wife Belle, at some point Winnie Marton looked at her husband and said, 'That's the dumbest thing you've ever done. You ever do something that dumb again, it's going to get you a quick one way trip to Paradise—or more likely, Hell.' That's when the light went on in Winnie's head. At the next city council meeting, Mayor Marton suggested Paradise as the town's new name. Now that's a name we could all get behind.

"And I'll tell you, Winnie Picklethorpe Marton Handley Lowe has never again let one of her mayor husbands do anything big in this town without running it by her first."

Ned Ferguson sat down. He looked satisfied at his telling of the story. Jim suspected that he had told it so many times that it had become rote, though he told it in a way that sounded new and fresh. Jim's mind was clear again. He knew it would be wise to acknowledge Mr. Ferguson's tale and show interest in the history of the town.

"And this Confederate soldier . . ."

Ferguson put his finger to his mouth and interrupted Jim. "Shh! His name is never mentioned in this town. And except for telling how the town got its name, his story is never talked about."

"Understood," Jim said.

The interview was over. The job was his. He stood and shook hands with the three board members he would be working with. He had truly enjoyed the interview and found that he genuinely liked these three men. Ned Ferguson's story about the naming of the town, and the tidbits it included about the town's seemingly all powerful first lady, endeared him even more to what appeared to be a quaint, if somewhat quirky, slice of down home America.

He felt silly about his reaction to the Vivian Leigh part of the story. *After all,* he thought, *Leigh is a fairly common name. It's not as if we were talking about a name like Papanicolou or something.*

As he walked up the stairs of the community center to the

sanctuary above, he looked at every nook and cranny of the building. He stopped and looked at every pew in the church and the lectern he would give his sermons from. He was excited about making Paradise his new home. He knew Renee would like it too. It was as close to the perfect place as they were ever likely to find.

Chapter 2

He didn't think he would be so nervous that first Sunday in Paradise. After all, he had preached dozens of sermons, and to larger congregations. Perhaps it was his concern over how they would react to a Yankee minister preaching to them. Or, he thought, maybe it was just that he wanted so badly to be accepted by this small town that he had already accepted totally into his heart. Whatever it was, the butterflies in his stomach didn't stop the incessant flapping of their wings until the soft "Amen" of his sermon.

As the chairman of the Parish Board, it was Ned Ferguson's responsibility—his "privilege" he called it—to stand by the new pastor at the chapel doors at the end of his first service to introduce Jim and his family personally to the parishioners as they filed out. Renee, as always, was resplendent in that modest way of hers. She wore a simple white dress with matching shoes and purse and a necklace with a small diamond that had once been her grandmother's. The twins—also dressed in white as if to match their mother (who they clearly favored)—sat calmly in a double stroller, talking to each other in a language only they could understand.

"Don't worry about remembering everyone's name," Ned reassured them. "I'll give you the skinny on who would be offended if you forgot theirs, at least those who you should care about being offended."

The parishioners began to file out, family by family, and Ned went to work. Everyone was pleasant. Everyone seemed very pleased with

Jim's first service. And, of course, everyone just *loved* the beautiful twin girls.

After the first few families had passed, Ned softly jabbed Jim's arm with his elbow and nodded toward a middle-aged couple walking out the door.

"Reverend. Mrs. Donovan," he said, "let me introduce you to our mayor, Andrew Lowe, and his lovely wife, Winnie."

Jim clearly understood these were names to remember.

"What a pleasure to meet you," Jim said, softly shaking Winnie's hand first and then the mayor's more firmly. Renee gracefully followed suit.

"It's our pleasure," said Winnie as the mayor smiled and nodded. "And Mrs. Donovan . . ."

"Please, call me Renee."

"Thank you Renee. What lovely children you have."

"Thank you Mrs. Lowe."

"Now, now. Please call me Winnie. No one calls me Mrs."

"Of course."

"You must come over for tea tomorrow afternoon. I'm having some members of the Women's Club over and it would do you good to learn as quickly as possible about what we do."

Winnie bent down and looked into the stroller.

"And of course you can bring these wonderfully behaved darlings with you," she said.

"Thank you, Winnie. I'd love to."

"Wonderful," Winnie said, straightening up and taking her husband's arm. "See you tomorrow then."

With that, Paradise's first couple moved on, the mayor never having said a word.

As the rest of the congregation passed through the mini-receiving line, Ned Ferguson only jabbed Jim's arm one more time.

"Reverend, this is Norma Hutchins. Mrs. Hutchins was Paradise's only seamstress for over . . . how long Norma?"

Norma Hutchins was elderly, at least in her late seventies Jim estimated. She was slight, with thinning white hair and she walked slowly with the aid of a wooden cane.

"Fifty years," she answered. While talking to Ned, she kept her eyes focused on Jim.

"Over fifty years," Ned continued. "Just retired six months ago. I swear she must have sewn just about every prom dress and wedding gown ever worn hereabouts for them fifty years."

"What an honor to meet you Mrs. Hutchins," Jim said as he bent over slightly to gently shake her hand.

"Likewise, I'm sure," she said. But, unlike all of the other parishioners they had met that morning, Mrs. Hutchins' response was not accompanied by a smile; and Jim felt little warmth in her otherwise polite and proper greeting.

"Ma'am," she said, turning to Renee. She nodded towards the kids in the stroller. "Your children are lovely. Keep them close."

Jim looked quizzically at Ned.

"I'll tell you about her later," Ned whispered in his ear, "after everyone is gone."

"Thank you," Renee said. Jim could hear a touch of confusion in Renee's voice. "Of course I will."

Renee glanced at him and raised her eyebrows. His instinctively darted up and down in acknowledgement.

"Good day," Mrs. Hutchins said as she slowly walked away.

After the church emptied Renee immediately took the girls home. They would ordinarily go straight home together and have a pleasant family brunch. But this first Sunday, there was much for Jim to do, and much yet for him to learn about his new position, and his new town.

"Let's go downstairs," Ned said to him. "I'll put some coffee on and we can chew the fat awhile."

They went down to the community center and Ned put on a pot of coffee. The two men sat at the folding table in the middle of the room where Jim had been interviewed less than three weeks before.

"So," Jim said, "tell me about Norma Hutchins. I felt a decided lack of enthusiasm from her."

"I got to admit Reverend, that's not a good sign. You're going to need to do some work on warming her up to you. There's no telling what she's thinking, or what her issues might be, but I noticed some coolness too. And people here do look to Norma for guidance."

"Why is that?" Jim asked. "She was just a seamstress."

"No sir. Not just a seamstress. Norma Hutchins is the most revered, and most feared, woman in Paradise." Ned leaned back in his chair and locked his hands together behind his head. "Like I told you, she was the town's seamstress for over fifty years. Few years back she got rheumatoid arthritis, real bad. It deformed her hands and finally caused her so much pain when she sewed that she sold her shop six months ago to the Widow Chievers. But for those more than fifty years she spent five or six days a week in her shop, looking out on the town square, watching every child in town sprout, every teenager grow, every adult turn into his or her own parent, then to age, some gracefully and with dignity, some not."

The coffee had quit brewing. Ned got up and walked over to the coffee pot in the center's small kitchenette, talking as he went.

"She also learned everything there was to know about almost every person and every family—not so hard to understand when considering that at one time or another she had spent countless hours fitting just about every woman and girl in town. My how those women loved to gossip about others and talk about themselves as they stood there waiting on Norma's needles. And Norma has never forgot one single thing she's heard."

Ned returned with two cups of coffee. He place one in front of Jim, sat down, and continued.

"Not only does Norma Hutchins know everything there is to know about everyone in town, she also seems to . . . to sense things that others don't."

"What do you mean?" Jim asked. "Like clairvoyant?"

"I don't know how to describe it. It's not the ability to tell the future. It's more like . . . like being able to see right through people, to cut through the crap in your mind, see inside your soul, to know who you *really* are and what you're *really* up to. Everyone in town has a Norma Hutchins story—a story of how she's caught them in a lie, or counseled them because she knew what they were thinking and feeling when no one else did."

Jim leaned back in his chair to the point that its two front legs were off the ground—exactly how his mother always ordered him not to sit for fear of tipping over. It was, for him, a subtle sign of rebelliousness.

"You make her sound like some kind of seer," he said to Ned. "You don't really believe all that do you?"

"I sure do," Ned answered. "She's done it to me—looked right through me to the truth. And seen it many more times. Truth be told, parents come to use Norma as a foolproof human lie detector, to uncover their kids' deceptions. Not only can she detect lies, but she would fix on the offender of the truth a glare of such intensity and foreboding, that those who've experienced it swear that they were struck with a chill wind, even in the sweltering heat of summer. It's come to be that just the threat of going to see Mrs. Hutchins is enough to convince the most hardened youthful liar to confess—anything to avoid 'the stare'."

"So you're saying I'd best behave myself around Mrs. Hutchins." Jim said this with a hint of sarcasm. If Ned noted it he paid no attention to it.

"I'm saying you'd best behave yourself as long as you're in this town. With most people, she has no interest in messing in their business, unless they ask. But she takes her religion, and God, serious . . . real serious. You're the minister, God's primary servant and . . . and well, like his agent. She'll take any shortcomings she sees in you personally. You can count on it."

"And how did she get along with Reverend Carter?" Jim asked.

"Got along right well with him. Reverend Carter wasn't what you'd call an inspirational leader, but he was a good man, and he did a right good job as our pastor."

Jim set his chair back down on its front legs. He took a sip of his coffee which had grown a bit cool.

"Thanks Ned," he said. "I appreciate the information . . . and the advice."

"Anytime Reverend. Both the information and my advice are free." Ned raised his coffee cup as if offering a toast.

"That being the case," Jim said, "tell me a little bit about the Widow Chievers."

"Ah, you noticed her, did you?" Ned said with a naughty twinkle in his eye. "She's a stunner, ain't she?"

"She is attractive Ned. But that's not why I asked. You said she bought Mrs. Hutchins' business six months ago. I assumed that meant she was new in town and I just want to be able to separate the natives from the newcomers like me."

The only part of his response to Ned's comment about the Widow Chievers that was true was that she was attractive. In fact, he couldn't help but notice when he was introduced to her after the service that she was just what Ned called her—a stunner. She stood a statuesque five feet eleven inches—just one inch shorter than Jim. She had wavy auburn hair worn to the shoulders, emerald green eyes and a well-formed body. He guessed she was probably in her early to mid-forties, but she had the body of a twenty-five-year-old, and on that morning she was wearing a clingy pale blue dress that accentuated every inch of it. Jim had noticed her all right, but it wasn't because she was new in town.

"Okay," Ned said, "what can I tell you about the Widow Chievers? Like I said, she bought Norma Hutchins' seamstress shop about six months ago. It's right off the town square between Harold's Men's Store and the Old Towne Dress Shop. Actually lives upstairs from the dress shop in a kind of loft apartment.

"From what I hear, she's an excellent seamstress. Not as good as Norma mind you, but pretty good. No one's really complained yet."

Ned rubbed his chin as if in thought.

"Let's see. What else? Um . . . don't know where she came from. Norma might know, but I haven't heard anything. Don't know what happened to her husband. Haven't heard any talk about that either. And mind you, if there had been any talk, my wife Belle would have heard it and passed it on. I reckon that's all I know, except that every man in town drools when she walks by, and gets beat with a rolling pin by their wives when they get home. Oh, and her first name is Sandra."

Ned had now more than once told Jim that his wife Belle was the town's biggest gossip. His experience of Ned told him that he could probably hold his own with Belle in the gossip game, although Ned would surely think of himself more as the town's historian. Of course, Jim thought, this was almost an occupational necessity for barbers, just like bartenders.

He took another sip of coffee. It was completely cold now.

"Thank you Ned. And I will be asking you about other people in town as we go along. I'm sure that your information and insight will be very helpful to me; that is, if you don't mind continuing to share it with me."

"Not at all Reverend. We have a fine little town here. We're proud of it and of its people. Anything I can do to make your job easier, and make you feel comfortable—feel like one of us—I'm happy to do."

Jim knew that Ned would want to talk more church business. That's why they had agreed to meet after the service. But he needed to find a way to end the conversation now. His mind had locked in on the image of Sandra Chievers. She had said nothing, had done nothing to cause it, other than just being beautiful. He needed to get out of the church and get home quickly so he could be with Renee and the twins and get this woman, a stranger to him, out of his mind.

He stood up abruptly.

"Thank you again Ned. I really must be getting home to help my wife with the unpacking."

Without waiting for a reply he bounded up the stairs and out of the church for the short walk home. The entire way his mind was troubled by the strong attraction he had felt toward the Widow Chievers. He knew that if he let it, it could ruin what was otherwise a wonderful first day and a wonderful start to his new ministry.

If he let it. But he wouldn't let it. He would hurry home to his wife and children, all of whom he loved dearly. They were his protection— his protection against . . . against himself. They would stop him from ruining his first day as pastor of the Paradise Community Christian Church.

Chapter 3

"**S**eventy-nine!" Jim said as he hung his golf cap on the old hat rack by the front door.

"Is that good?" Renee asked innocently.

"Good? Best round I've had since we moved here. And given the weather and the brown fairways and rough greens, that's a *great* score! Maybe I should just always play in February."

"Wow!" Renee lovingly mocked him. "Look out Jack Nichols!"

"Huh? Jack Nichols? You mean Nicklaus."

"Who?"

"Nicklaus. His name is Nicklaus."

Renee shrugged her shoulders. "What do I know?" She reached up and kissed him on the cheek.

"Anyway, it let me and Charlie Bruener take twenty bucks each off the hands of the mayor and Fred Baker, the investment banker who just opened up that new Merrill Lynch office." Jim put his arm on Renee's shoulder as they walked towards the kitchen. "Now that guy's a pretty good golfer. Beat him too."

"That's wonderful dear," she said, "but do you think you should be gambling on golf? You know how some people are."

"Yeah, I know. But Charlie and Andy are discreet, and this Fred guy seems to be okay. Besides," Jim went on, kissing Renee lightly on the top of her head, "I just don't see the good Lord getting all in a twitter about a harmless, friendly wager. By the way, it's awful quiet. Where are the girls?"

"Taking a nap. They had a big day. I took them shopping today."

"You mean, we have some time . . ."

"By the way," Renee interrupted, not seeming to have heard him, "you got a postcard today."

They entered the kitchen and Renee retrieved a card from the kitchen table with a picture of Big Ben on it. She handed it to him.

"From London," she said.

"London? From who?" he said as he looked at the world's most famous clock. He turned it over and checked the signature. "It's from Dr. and Mrs. Westin."

He read the short note to himself.

> Dear Jim and Renee,
>
> Greetings from London! Finally decided to do the European tour we've talked about for years. From here Paris, Lucerne, Rome and Athens. Having a great time. Be back in the states in two weeks. WRITE SOON.
>
> All our best,
> Robert and Maribel Westin

"Hmm. That's nice," Jim said. He placed the card back on the table. He opened the refrigerator and reached for a Coors.

"Well, are you going to?" Renee said. He felt like he was being scolded, but he didn't know what for.

"Going to what?" he asked as he popped open the can of beer.

"To write, to Dr. Westin, soon. Except for Christmas cards we haven't written to them since the first week we were here, when you wrote to thank him. Jim, it's been over two years."

She's right, he thought as he stood against the kitchen sink drinking his beer. *It* has *been a long time since I've written to Dr. Westin. Or even talked to him. I wonder why? It hasn't been intentional. Maybe because things are just going so well I haven't felt the need to talk to a mentor. That's not a very good reason, though. After all he's done for us. And he's not just a mentor. He's a friend too.*

"You're right hon," he said. "It has been too long. I'll write to them tonight. It'll be there waiting for them when they get back."

"Good."

Renee walked over to him and kissed him gently on the lips.

"Now why don't you go take a shower so you don't gross the girls out when they wake up."

"Why? Am I grossing *you* out? It was in the fifties out there today. I hardly sweated."

Renee slapped him on the shoulder.

"Get upstairs."

"Okay, okay," he said laughing. "Down the hatch." He chugged the rest of the Coors, tossed the can in the garbage under the sink and headed to the shower.

He sat at the desk in their bedroom. He pulled some paper out of the right lower drawer and removed one of the two pens in the marble (or fake marble—it didn't much matter to him) pen holder at the front of the desk. He stared at the paper. As it was, Jim wasn't much of a letter writer. After a tremendous dinner of roast lamb and potatoes, he was much more interested in sleeping than he was in writing. But he had promised Renee he would do this tonight. After a few minutes he got started. Once he did, the words came quickly and easily, just like his best sermons.

Dear Dr. and Mrs. Westin,

Thank you for the postcard from London. I'm sure you are having a great time in Europe. Renee and I envy you. It has been a long time since I've written, and for that I apologize. While this may be a small town, and the church is quite small too, I seem to be constantly on the go. I know that's not a good excuse, but it will have to do. I can't begin to thank you enough, Dr. Westin, for helping me get this opportunity. Actually, for all that you've done for me and Renee. I wouldn't be where I am today if it weren't for you. And where I am is great. In the time we've been here, the people of Paradise (what a great name, huh; remind me to tell you some day how it got its name) have been wonderful to us. The church is great, too. It broke off years ago from the First Baptist Church here, but there have been no ill feelings or competition of any kind. We actually work together quite often. Our church has remained small. All in all there are only about 100 members. But some of the town's most respected citizens are parishioners. They include the mayor, the police chief and Norma Hutchins—"the most respected and most feared woman in town"—as she was once described to me. And there is no real pressure on me to grow the church. I think they'd be happy to stay just the size they are forever. But, as you so often told us, if a church isn't growing, it's dying. To that end I have expanded the youth and outreach programs. At first I was worried about the reception the outreach program would receive, especially from First Baptist. But it is a testament to the goodness of the people of this town that there has been no problem whatsoever. I've rambled on long enough about work and me. How are the two of you doing (aside from becoming world travelers, of course)? I trust that things are well with the school and that you are still turning out well-educated, dedicated "Westinite" theologians. One thing I can attest to is that once Dr. Westin has entered our minds and our souls, we are never truly free of you.

Renee and the girls are doing just great. The girls are 4 now. They're growing so fast. I never realized, until we had them, just how much children change your perspective on life and how much they come to mean to you. Renee has fallen in love with Paradise. She's very active. She's joined a sewing club (hooray!), the church's women's club and a regional literacy organization. She is a great mother to Carly and Jessica and has become the penultimate minister's wife.

Well, you asked for it. You said WRITE SOON— and I have. I'm sure neither one of us expected it to be this long. Now that you're world travelers we expect

you to visit us soon. Until then, with warmest regards,
I remain

Yours truly,

Jim Donovan

He signed the letter and reached into the bottom left drawer for an envelope. As he did so, his eyes were drawn to one phrase he had just written in the letter—"the penultimate minister's wife." He hadn't given particular thought to what he was writing about Renee as he wrote it. But looking at that phrase now, he wondered what he meant by it.

The penultimate minister's wife, he repeated to himself. *I know I must have meant them as words of praise. But they sound so . . . so insincere. No question, she is a truly exceptional mother. She doesn't read the child-rearing books by the so-called experts. She's not constantly on the phone seeking advice from her mother. She just seems to come to it so naturally. When it comes to the girls she always seems to say and do just the right thing.*

He looked at the words again.

The penultimate minister's wife. And she is, too. She makes sure that life for me at home is easy and comfortable. The house is always well kept. I couldn't find a speck of dust if I looked for a week. And meals-she's such a fantastic cook. And she takes such good care of the kids so I don't have to be worrying about them. When I come home I can let the troubles of work, which there aren't too many of, but still, I can let them drift away.

And I couldn't ask for a better partner at work and in the community. Everyone likes her, even old Norma Hutchins. I still don't know why I haven't won her over. I wonder what I've done to tick her off?

Renee, you're the perfect wife, the perfect mother, the perfect partner. I just wish . . . I just wish you could be the perfect lover. Not even the perfect lover, just . . . just a little more passionate. Why do I think that way? Why do I feel less than satisfied and fulfilled in our marriage? It's nothing Renee has done. After all, eighty or ninety percent perfection ought to be enough for a good and stable marriage. Yes, she's a minister's wife, and a good one too. There's plenty of reason for this marriage to last a good long time.

He looked again at the letter. As he had described it to Dr. and Mrs. Westin, everything was perfect in Paradise. Paradise. *If the town wasn't named Paradise,* he thought, *it should be named Brigadoon.* Brigadoon—the legendary perfect Scottish village that only appeared for one day each one hundred years and then disappeared into the mist. But here, he had a Brigadoon that was there every day.

Jim's thoughts were interrupted by a sudden feeling of something happening within him. It wasn't pain or illness. He focused on his stomach in particular, trying to figure out what was bothering him. Something . . . unsettled, uncomfortable, even fearful; like a simmering pot of water on a hot stove, getting hotter and hotter and just starting to form the first bubbles of boiling. It hadn't reached the boiling point yet, but he knew it was coming.

What is it? What is this . . . fire? What's causing my insides to feel like they're boiling? What is this—out of nowhere?

For more than two years now he had seemed at peace with himself and the world. He had felt in control. The traumas, humiliations and betrayals he had experienced were all behind him. Somehow he felt they were all boiling to the surface again.

Why? What's changed? he wondered. *And why now? This particular moment? What's happening?*

"DAMN!" he shouted.

Writing the letter to the Westins, telling them how well things were going for him had made him feel good, satisfied, even fulfilled, or close to it. But before he could even get the letter in the envelope, it was as if it turned on him like a rabid animal, leaving him pained, forlorn, afraid, and not knowing why.

The penultimate minister's wife, he thought again, looking at the words on the paper. *The penultimate minister's wife. The penultimate minister's wife.* Over and over he repeated the words in his mind. He tried to stop them from forming. He looked away from the letter. He thought about ripping it up, but something stopped him. The words wouldn't stop. Over and over, louder and louder. *THE PENULTIMATE MINISTER'S WIFE. THE PENULTIMATE MINISTER'S WIFE.*

He realized that even though the thoughts were his, he had no control over them. *THE PENULTIMATE MINISTER'S WIFE.* *THE PENULTIMATE MINISTER'S WIFE. Wait! What's that? That . . . that's not my voice. I'm thinking in someone else's voice! But whose? It's familiar. I know it. I know I know it. But I . . . I can't place it!*

THE PENULTIMATE MINISTER'S WIFE! THE PENULTIMATE MINISTER'S WIFE! Over and over, louder and louder still. *THE PENULTIMATE MINISTER'S WIFE! THE PENULTIMATE MINISTER'S WIFE!*

The voice—it was becoming more familiar, but he still couldn't place it. He put his hands over his ears, but the voice and the words wouldn't stop. Boiling water was scorching his stomach while the incessant shouts—*THE PENULTIMATE MINISTER'S WIFE! THE PENULTIMATE MINISTER'S WIFE!*—were pounding his brain.

The pain was becoming unbearable. He stood up from the desk and rolled his head back and forth, side to side, trying to make the words, the voice and the pain go away. It was a futile effort. Shooting pain in his stomach caused his hands to instinctively leave his ears and clutch at his gut. The pain became too much. He collapsed in his chair, his head slamming down on the desk.

His whole body hurt. The chanting continued. *THE PENULTIMATE MINISTER'S WIFE! THE PENULTIMATE MINISTER'S WIFE!*

"Please, stop," he whimpered, his head still resting on its right side on the desk top.

It didn't stop. Instead, it was joined by images, brief images. They were like snapshots, like the tricks used by brainwashers and advertisers—subliminal messages that, at first, he knew were there but didn't know what they were showing. Then he started to see them—young Jimmy getting beat up; his father's funeral; screwing Veronica in a tree house; running naked through a dark, frightening forest; standing naked before snickering adolescent girls.

The pain grew stronger. He broke into a full sweat. He wanted to call out to Renee for help, but he couldn't even open his mouth. He was frozen, in that place. A prisoner of . . .

Of what? Of who?

The images continued. In quick succession now—every girl he

had bedded in college. His mother. Random, seemingly unconnected events and people now. Tony. Billy. Richardson Leigh smoking like a fiend. Richardson Leigh throwing him up against a wall. Katy naked next to Professor Roderick. Melanie Leigh, standing naked before him sneering at her father. Car accident. Hospital. Lanie standing naked over him. Dr. Pe´re drawing on his pipe.

"Dr. Pe´re!" he shouted as his head shot up from the desk and his lips and tongue seemed to come unfrozen.

The voice. The voice repeating over and over the mantra, "the penultimate minister's wife," was Dr. Pe´re's! He blinked his eyes several times. *Or was it?* He closed his eyes and kept them shut hard. He tried to concentrate on the voice, on how it sounded. It stopped. He continued to listen. He tried now, contrary to all of his pain avoidance instincts, to call the voice back up, to listen to it one more time, to identify it for sure.

Was it Pe´re's voice? he wondered. At the instant Pe´re's image had come into his mind he was sure the pounding, painful voice was his. But now, he wasn't so sure. Perhaps, he speculated, it was just because of the image in his mind, and how much time, concentrated time, he had spent with Pe´re. He had been certain, for an instant, but now he just couldn't be sure.

He looked around the room, trying to re-focus. He noticed that the pain had stopped. He wasn't sure exactly when that had happened. *Could it have been the image of Dr. Pe´re that made it stop?* he wondered.

He looked down at his clothes. They were completely soaked with sweat. He was completely exhausted, as if he had just run the Boston Marathon.

What the hell just happened? he wondered. *What on earth could have caused what felt as intense . . . no, more intense, than my nervous breakdown that sent me to Pe´re? I don't know. All I did was write a letter, an unremarkable letter. How could that have triggered so much pain . . . such feelings of, of foreboding? Those words . . .* He was afraid to think them for fear of triggering a new attack. But trying to avoid thinking of them made them impossible not to think of them. *The penultimate minister's wife. How could those four words have conjured up those images, those unpleasant memories. I don't know. But if I don't figure it out, soon, I know. . . I don't know how, but I know . . . there's going to be a . . . some kind of big explosion. And I won't survive it. And it's going to destroy everything and everyone I love. I just know it.*

He slowly lifted himself from his chair and went into the bathroom. He splashed water on his face. He took the hand towel from the towel rack and wiped his face dry. He didn't bother to replace the towel on the rack, dropping it into the sink. He went back to his desk and sat down again. He looked at the letter. He began to fold it to place it in the envelope. He thought about how he had told Dr. and Mrs. Westin that everything was great when, obviously, it wasn't; and how Dr. Westin had always been there for him.

He unfolded the letter, picked up his pen, and wrote a postscript:

> P.S. Dr. Westin—There is something I would like to talk to you about when you return to the states. I'll call you in a few weeks.
>
> Jim

Maybe Dr. Westin can make sense of what's happening, he thought. *Maybe it's time for some spiritual counseling. I don't know. Maybe my principles, my character, maybe they need some shoring up too. Maybe this was some kind of warning . . . or a sign of some sort. Dr. Westin will know. And he'll know what to do about it.*

Jim folded the letter, placed it in the envelope, addressed it and placed a stamp on it. Then, without bothering to say goodnight to Renee, he undressed and went to bed.

Chapter 4

That Sunday's service was unremarkable, though Jim did feel that he had given a good sermon. He couldn't wait to get out of the church and over to Millie's Home Style Kitchen to have brunch with Renee and the kids. Millie had the best meat loaf and mashed potatoes in the tri-county area. Actually, it was her homemade country style gravy that made it so good. *Just what the doctor ordered,* he thought as he and his family walked the short two blocks from the church to the modest, diner-style family restaurant.

After brunch Jim took Renee and the girls home. He then set out on his Sunday afternoon house calls. It was a custom that Reverend Carter religiously followed and one that Jim happily continued. On Sunday afternoons he would visit parishioners who were unable to attend services because of illness or infirmity. He would bring them news of the community, pray with them or, sometimes, just sit with them.

On this Sunday he first went to see Emma Morningside, the late Dr. Adam Morningside's widow. The previous Monday she had fallen in her tub and broken her hip. It would be a while before she could attend church, even with help. He spent about twenty minutes with Emma, reading a Bible passage, praying and asking after her health.

Next he proceeded to Calvin Potter's home. Mr. Potter's lung cancer had spread and he didn't have much longer to live. He wouldn't likely see the inside of a church again until his funeral. Until then, this would be a regular Sunday visit for Reverend Jim.

His last call that day was on the Widow Chievers. He had been informed—by whom he couldn't recall—that she was suffering from a bout with bronchitis. It wasn't serious, but enough to keep her from church. He had never been to her modest loft apartment. Yet as he climbed the outer stairs overlooking the alleyway along the side of the building, a warm tingle of familiarity touched him. *Déjà vu,* he thought.

He reached the top of the stairs and knocked on her door. There was no answer. He knocked again, a little louder.

"Just a minute," came a raspy-voiced reply. It was followed by two foghorn coughs. "Let me throw something on."

He found the Widow Chievers just as attractive as did every other man in town. Since that initial Sunday service when she first came to his attention, he had had very little contact with her. Her total participation in the life of the church was Sunday service. This was good, he had decided early on. The ability to avoid temptation, he had learned, was in direct proportion to its geographic and temporal distance from him. But now, her request that he wait while she threw something on created within his mind the image of the unclothed widow. He shivered briefly.

The door opened a crack, just enough for him to see a sliver of her face and one eye.

"Oh. Reverend Donovan." Her voice betrayed her obvious surprise.

"Good afternoon Mrs. Chievers," he replied cheerfully. "You weren't in church today and I understand you're under the weather. I thought I'd call on you for some Bible reading and prayer. I do make house calls, you know."

"But I'm such a mess."

"Now Mrs. Chievers," he said reassuringly. "You know I'm married with two young daughters. I can assure you that the sight of women without make-up and fancy clothes is a normal state of affairs to me. No need to be embarrassed."

Her one visible eye seemed to look down at the ground. A few seconds passed. Then, slowly, the door opened and the Widow Chievers stood before him. She was wearing a white, terry cloth robe. It had no belt so she held it with her left arm wrapped before her. Her auburn hair, usually shining and hanging smoothly and wavily down and over her shoulders, was dull and unbrushed, hanging out and down in various directions. She wore no make-up thus revealing a few wrinkles and crow's feet which he was probably the first man in Paradise to see. She stood before him plain, natural, unglamorous and older. Contrary to what he would have expected, he found the unaccessorized Sandra Chievers strangely even more alluring.

"Please come in," she said. She looked mildly embarrassed despite his admonition not to be.

He stepped into her living room and passed by her as she closed the door. There was an early twentieth century feel to the furnishings and décor, similar to those he had experienced as a youngster when visiting his grandparents. As he quickly surveyed the room he particularly noticed the absence of any photographs, memorabilia or mementos of her late husband.

"Please, sit down." She motioned towards an old, antique couch with exquisitely embroidered cushions. He walked over and sat as gently as he could, almost afraid of soiling the couch which, if it had been in his mother's home, would certainly have had a clear plastic covering over it.

"May I get you some tea?" she offered. "Or perhaps a cold drink?"

"No. No thank you."

"I apologize for my appearance and the condition of my home. As you've obviously heard, I've not been feeling well."

"So I understand. Are you feeling any better today?"

"Yes, actually. But for an occasional nasty cough, I seem to be over the worst of it. I experience bouts of bronchitis every few years. Especially when I don't get the proper rest."

She sat down in an old rocking chair with a handmade cushion on the other side of a coffee table that was located between the chair and the couch. She continued to hold her robe closed with both hands but its hem now rested above her knees. It was a struggle for Jim to keep his eyes on hers.

"If I do say so myself, Mrs. Chievers, you missed one of my better sermons today. It was on the raising of Lazarus from the dead."

"Oh dear," she chuckled. "I certainly don't think I'm in need of that sort of miracle quite yet."

They both laughed nervously.

"No, I don't think you are. I thought a brief visit might simply lift your spirits and expedite your recovery. Would you like to pray together?"

"Quite frankly Reverend, I've been praying a lot lately to get rid of this damn . . . oh, excuse me . . ." She stopped, with a devilish look on her face. ". . . this *darn* cough. I don't want to overdo my asking of the Lord."

"You can never overdo your asking of the Lord," he responded in his most pastor-like manner.

"Yes, I suppose you're right. But what would really make me feel better is if we could just visit for a spell and talk about . . . things. Anything and everything, *except* religion. Would that be all right with you Reverend?"

Her tone seemed entirely innocent, but for some reason Jim found himself looking for a hidden meaning or motive in her request.

"Certainly Mrs. Chievers. I'd be glad to visit for awhile."

"Please Reverend, call me Sandra. Mrs. Chievers sounds so . . . so old."

"Okay. Sure. Sandra."

He felt almost as if bait had been set and that he had bitten on it. It only remained to be seen if she chose to reel him in.

They chatted for awhile. He talked about his schooling, his first congregation, his mission work (though not too much), and Renee and the twins. He was surprised at how easily he opened up to her. But when he asked her questions about her background and her late husband she managed to avoid answering by skillfully changing the subject and turning it back to him. If he wasn't so distracted with trying to suppress a growing infatuation with her, it might have annoyed him.

They had become so relaxed in each other's company and so engrossed in their conversation that the Widow Chievers had stopped clutching at her robe and had rested her arms naturally on the armrests of the rocker. He hadn't particularly noticed, but what he did notice was that the longer he spent with this woman, the more enamored he was becoming. He knew that if he stayed much longer, he would do or say something that would greatly offend her or, worse, get him into a dangerous and compromising situation. Either way, he had much to lose.

What he was beginning to feel in this cozy living room was a threat to all he had accomplished. He knew he had to leave. Immediately.

Exercising great self-discipline, he stood up, smiled his best preacher's smile, and begged his leave. "Well, I've truly enjoyed speaking with you Mrs. . . . ah, Sandra. But I'm afraid it's getting late and I really must go."

"Yes, of course, " she responded politely. "It was very generous of you to spend so much time with me. It's made me feel much better."

She began to rise to see him to the door. As her arms pushed off the armrests at her side, her unbelted robe fell open revealing flaming red undergarments so sheer they fully exposed her entire feminine anatomy.

Jim's eyes froze on the scene before him. Sandra likewise froze in place. Aside from the sheer eroticism of seeing her so scantily and sexually clad, his stimulation was further enhanced by the thought that, absent the robe, this was how she dressed when hanging out at home alone. He took a deep breath, as if to avoid drowning. His heart and mind both told him to turn and run, as fast and as far as he could.

What exactly happened next he could never really remember. What was certain was that Reverend Jim Donovan and the Widow Sandra Chievers found themselves naked and passionately embraced on her living room couch, with its expertly embroidered cushions, engaged in lovemaking so intense, uninhibited and unrestricted by any rules of modesty or propriety that he knew something had started which they couldn't easily end.

When it was over they remained on their sides, exhausted, in each other's arms. She kissed him gently on his forehead.

"What now?" she whispered.

"I don't know."

"I've wanted you since I first laid eyes on you."

"Sandra, I'm married. And I'm a minister. I can't do this."

He tried to comfort himself with the thought that this could be a one time fling, a momentary lapse, something to be forgotten and not repeated.

"I know what you are, Jim." It was the first time she referred to him by his first name. She paused. "I want you anyway."

"Sandra, I . . . there's no way we could get away with it. You know that. This is a small town. Everyone eventually finds out everything."

She ran her index finger softly over his lips.

"It was *really* good, wasn't it?" she said, her eyes moving slowly from his lips to meet his eyes.

"Yeah . . . it was . . . it was really great." Indeed it was. It was the greatest sex he had had since Veronica. And it was everything he had wanted with Renee, but couldn't seem to find.

"I can't remember the last time a man made me feel so good, and so . . . so absolutely sexy." She had fed his passion. Now she fed his ego. "You were *sooooo wonderful!* I'd hate to think I'll never feel like this again."

As it was, he was having trouble enough thinking about never again feeling what he had just felt with Sandra. Her psychic massage of his pride made the thought of this liaison being their last virtually unbearable. Still, he resisted.

"Sandra, you . . . you were just . . . just incredible. I felt things today that I . . . well . . . I . . . I . . . I don't even know how to describe it. It's like . . . if everyone could always feel that way . . ."

"I know baby. I know what you're trying to say. And I want us to keep making each other feel that way."

"I know. And I do too. I mean . . . no. No I don't. I can't. I've got too much to lose. My family. My position."

"We'll be careful." She had the look and sound of someone about to close a deal. "You'll be able to come here without being noticed. And the only time we'll do it is when it's not dangerous. I won't make any demands on you. I understand your situation, and I'm not asking you to leave it all behind for me. But I know we were meant to be together, at least some of the time. You fill a big need in my life, Jim. And I think I fill a big one in yours too."

Whether by luck or prescience, in this last remark she had hit the nail on the head. She did fill a big need in his life, a need his wife, his loving, caring wife, was not meeting. His willpower quickly weakening, he turned to her to save him from himself.

"You don't know what you're asking, Sandra," he said, his voice quivering.

"I'm not asking anything," she replied softly, compassionately. "I'm offering."

Chapter 5

The mid-day summer sun beat down unmercifully. It was a much hotter day than Jim expected, even for mid-June. As he walked up the stairs to Sandra Chiever's apartment, he was tempted to remove his jacket, but thought better of it. Something as simple as that, he knew, could start tongues wagging in a small town like Paradise.

He was apprehensive about meeting with Sandra again in her apartment. Since their sexual encounter four months before, Jim had managed—though the struggle within was titanic—to avoid another liaison with the most desirable, and mysterious, woman in town.

But now he *had* to visit her. For two days the sign in her shop said it was closed due to "Illness of Proprietress" and she had not been in church that morning. To not include her in his Sunday afternoon visitations would be much too suspicious—more suspicious, he thought, noting the irony, than not going to visit a sultry, beautiful, widowed woman alone in her apartment.

As he reached the top of the stairs his heart was racing. He hoped, with a sense of guilt, that she was really ill. Then, with an equal sense of guilt, he hoped that she wasn't. Whichever it was, he had no choice but to play it out.

He knocked on the door. For a few seconds there was silence. Then the door opened a crack. Like the first time he visited she wore no make-up and wore her terry cloth robe held closed by her hand.

"Hello Sandra," he said through the cracked door.

She smiled.

"Hello Reverend. Just a minute."

She closed the door and Jim heard the chain lock being undone. The door opened.

"Come in, please," she said softly, almost timidly.

He walked in and past her. The room looked exactly as it had on his first visit. He heard the door close behind him and then the chain being placed into the slide lock on the door.

"How are you feeling?" he asked as he turned to look at her.

By the time he faced her, the robe had come off and lay in a heap on the floor behind her. She hadn't bothered with underwear this time.

"Sandra . . ."

Before he could say anything else she was in his arms. He knew there was no way to resist. He didn't even try. He lifted her naked body in his arms and carried her into the bedroom.

"I missed you so much," she said, her head resting on Jim's chest. He didn't know what to say. He didn't think it was possible, but the sex was even better than it had been the first time. So much so that he was fearfully certain that someone must have heard their passionate groans and screams.

"I . . . I . . ."

All he could do was stammer.

"It was good, wasn't it baby?" she asked her fingers pulling the hairs on his chest ever so gently.

"Yes . . . yes. Of course. It was . . . it was incredible."

She smoothly moved her hand over his right nipple sending a chill through his body.

"Are you willing to give it up?" She softly kissed his left nipple. Another chill. "Forever?"

There, he thought. She had put the question to him directly—as directly and starkly as it could be put. The question he had refused to think about. The question he had known since the first day with her that he couldn't answer "yes."

"Forever?" she asked again.

The only way he knew to answer was by making love to her again.

He dressed quickly.

"Must you go?" Sandra asked as she lie naked on her bed in a Marilyn Monroe — like pose.

"Yes," he answered, trying mightily, but unsuccessfully, to avert his gaze from his seductress. "I've already been here too long. I don't spend nearly this much time with anyone else. It's too suspicious."

"But I'm really sick," she purred, smiling. "Love sick."

"I've got to go, Sandra," he insisted.

"I know."

She slid out of bed and walked over to him. She kissed him. Before he lost control and ripped his clothes back off, she took him by the hand and walked him to the front door. She picked up her robe but didn't bother to put it on. She kissed him again.

"When will I see you again?" she asked.

"I don't know. But we've got to find another way."

"I know." She kissed him again. "I can't just keep getting sick every Sunday."

Jim hugged her firmly.

"I've got to see you again," he said softly into her ear. "Soon. And somewhere . . . somewhere private, and safe."

"I know baby," she said. She kissed and gently bit his neck. "Let's think on it. We'll come up with something."

One final passionate kiss and Jim left her apartment, making sure she stepped away from the open door so as not to be seen as he let himself out.

Wednesday evening at seven o'clock had been set as the regular meeting time for the church's Annual Bazaar Committee meeting. The Annual Bazaar was always held in October. It wasn't big by church bazaar standards. But all the same it still took a good deal of planning and work to make it successful.

On the Wednesday after his second encounter with Sandra Chievers, Reverend Jim was surprised to see her seated at the long table in the Community Center with the rest of the committee members. Since he had become pastor, she had never been actively involved in church affairs other than attending Sunday services.

He could feel the blood begin to flow more swiftly through his veins. As he walked up to the table, he noted that Sandra appeared to be getting a quiet earful about something from Norma Hutchins who was seated at her right. It stopped when Winnie Lowe said "Good evening, Reverend Donovan."

Everyone's attention turned towards Jim as he approached his chair at the head of the table.

"Good evening everyone," he said. "What a pleasant surprise to see you, Mrs. Chievers." He did his best to be as nonchalant as possible given the excitement he felt at her unexpected presence. "Are you going to be working at this year's Bazaar?"

Before Sandra could answer, Norma Hutchins, who, for the fifth straight year, was the overall Bazaar Committee Chairman, spoke up.

"Yes she is. She's volunteered to run this year's thrift sale. Don't you find that interesting, Reverend?"

Just as Ned Ferguson had told him on his very first day in Paradise, Jim had the distinct feeling that Mrs. Hutchins' words held a greater meaning than they appeared to on their face—a meaning letting him know that she saw something that no one else did.

"Interesting?" he answered, not really knowing what to say.

"Well, maybe interesting isn't the right word," she said. "Wonderful. And helpful, perhaps. Wouldn't you agree, Reverend?"

"Very much so, Mrs. Hutchins. Very much so. We can use all the help we can get and it's always a pleasure to see parishioners get involved in the work of the church."

Jim sat down.

"Welcome Mrs. Chievers," he said, looking at her and nodding politely. "I think you'll enjoy working on the committee. And, of course, at the Bazaar."

"I'm sure I will," Sandra said, giving a quick glance at Mrs. Hutchins.

The committee went about its work, planning the Bazaar activities and menus, assigning various tasks to the appropriate subcommittees and individuals. By eight-thirty they had wrapped up their work for the evening.

As the committee chair, Norma Hutchins declared the meeting adjourned. The committee members rose to take their leave. As she did so, Sandra turned and looked at Jim.

"Reverend Donovan," she said in a voice loud enough for all to hear, "do you have a couple of moments to spare—to talk to me about . . . about something personal?"

She was asking to have a few moments alone with him and trying to find a way to cover it up. His heart began to race both at the prospect of being alone with her, even for a few moments, and at the surreptitiousness of it.

Jim intuitively glanced at Norma Hutchins. He saw no look of suspicion on her face, but he certainly felt that she was suspicious. *Damn*, he thought. *Got to get rid of my paranoia.*

"Of course, Mrs. Chievers," he said. "Why don't we go into my office." He held out his arm in the direction of his small office next to the hall's kitchenette.

"Thank you," she said. "I won't keep you but a few minutes."

"Be sure you don't tarry long, Sandra," Mrs. Hutchins broke in. "The good Reverend's wife and children are certainly anxious for him to get home soon, dear."

What is that *supposed to mean?* Jim wondered.

Sandra smiled.

"I won't, Norma," she said. "I need to get home soon myself. You know I haven't been feeling well lately."

Everyone else had left. Mrs. Hutchins' eyes shifted back and forth between Sandra and Jim.

"Then I'll be taking my leave," she said. "Good night, Reverend. Good night Sandra dear."

"Good night," Jim and Sandra said in unison. They watched the elderly woman use her cane to negotiate her way to and up the stairs leading to the church proper where she would exit the building and walk home.

Once Mrs. Hutchins was out of sight, Jim led Sandra into his small office and closed the door behind them. Before he could say anything Sandra threw her arms around him and locked her lips on his. The kiss alone generated such passionate feelings in him that it was all he could do to avoid ripping her clothes off and doing it on his desk.

"I missed you so much," she said, releasing the lip lock only long enough to get the words out.

"Me too," he managed to mumble through their re-locked lips.

He was about to totally lose control. Summoning up all of his willpower he managed to gently push her away. She looked at him with a beguiling smile.

"Surprised to see me?"

"Of course," he said, taking her hands in his. "I wish you had given me some warning. I have a face that is too often easy for others to read."

"You hid it well."

"When I came in," he said, "you and Mrs. Hutchins seemed to be in a rather . . . vigorous discussion. What . . ."

"Oh, that was nothing," she interrupted. "Just some stuff about the shop."

She began to swing their clasped hands outside and in.

"I've got a surprise for you," she said.

"What kind of surprise?"

"A *big* one."

She kept swinging their hands like they were little kids.

"Well, are you going to let me in on it?" he asked.

She gave him a short and sweet kiss.

"I rented a cabin for us."

"You what?"

"I rented a cabin for us. For a week, a whole week. So we can spend some real time together without having to worry every minute about being caught."

"Where?"

"Nags Head. North Carolina. On the Outer Banks." She started swinging their hands again. "I was really lucky. This time of year it's hard to get a nice place. But there was a cancellation and . . ."

Jim interrupted her. "Sandra, how can I get away for a week without Renee and the kids?"

She let their hands drop. She let go and sat down in his office chair behind his desk.

"Can't you say you're going to some religious convention, or . . . or some kind of retreat or something?"

Her idea actually wasn't that far-fetched. Jim had been thinking of taking some time and going off on his own. He needed time to recharge his batteries, and for some introspection, both professional and personal. He felt that Renee probably wouldn't object. He had taken her and the girls to Disney World in Orlando just last month and hadn't had any real time to himself for as long as he could remember. *Yes, that could work,* he thought.

"When?" he asked.

"What?"

"When would we go?"

Sandra leaped eagerly out of the chair.

"In August. The middle of August!"

The prospect of a full week with Sandra had gotten hold of him. But he was still worried. He walked over to the chair in front of his desk and leaned his hands on its back.

"It sounds great Sandra. But . . . but I can't help thinking what a big risk it is."

"No it's not baby." She walked around the desk and the chair and put her arms around his neck. "We'll be far away. No one will know."

Another soft kiss.

"Won't people be suspicious if we're both gone the same time."

"Thought of that," she answered. "I'll close the shop for three weeks. Family business in Atlanta. I'll be gone the week before you and the week after. No reason for people to put anything together."

Another soft kiss, only this one much longer and accompanied by the pressing of her body hard against his.

Jim fought to come up with every reason, of which he knew there were a multitude, to say no. But midway through that kiss, he knew he was a goner.

"Okay," he said. "Let's do it."

"Really?" Sandra squealed like a child being told by her father that they were going out for a hot fudge sundae. She jumped in the air. Jim caught her and gave her another long kiss as he held her suspended above the floor.

"Really," he said, then kissed her again. He put her down. "It's late. It's time to go."

"Will you walk me home?" she asked. "It's dark by now. No one will question it. After all, even Norma Hutchins would say a proper gentleman wouldn't allow a lady to walk home alone in the dark."

He offered her his arm.

"My lady, may I escort you home?"

They both laughed as she took his arm.

The night air was humid. Sandra had let go of Jim's arm and they walked with a proper and respectable distance between them. They were both silent. Jim's mind was already racing ahead to the week they would spend together, as he expected hers was.

It dawned on him that he was making plans to spend a week—to again commit adultery—with a woman he knew virtually nothing about. A widow who had never talked about her late husband—who, in fact, didn't have a single photo of him in her home. He knew he wouldn't have much time alone with her before August, even though she was on the Bazaar Committee now. It was time to learn more about her.

"Tell me about your husband," he said.

"What?"

"Tell me about your husband. I've made love to you and I'm going away with you and I don't know anything about you. Why don't you have any pictures of him in your apartment?"

She remained silent, her eyes staring ahead and then up to the stars, as if she was searching for just the right words. After a minute or so she looked at Jim.

"I'm not really a widow," she said.

"You're not?"

"No."

"Then why . . ."

"It's a long story. You don't have the time."

"I'll make the time. I want to know why the . . . the charade, the deceit? There's nothing wrong with not having a husband. Or not having been married."

"I *was* married. I'm divorced."

Jim softly put his hand on her back.

"Tell me about it Sandra."

Sandra took a deep breath.

"I've never talked about my divorce because it's . . . it's just so embarrassing. I just couldn't face the prospect of either explaining it or politely refusing to talk about it. I figured that moving to a small town as a widow was less stigmatizing and provided more opportunities than doing so as a divorcee."

She nervously picked at her fingers as she talked.

"His name was Raymond. Raymond Chievers. We were married for fifteen years. He was very successful, and very influential. He was a commercial developer in Atlanta. He provided me with a very comfortable life. We belonged to the best clubs. We were welcomed at the classiest restaurants even without reservations. We lived in a large and magnificent house. We were invited to Atlanta society's toniest events." She chuckled. "I even learned to use words like 'tony'. We were even named one of Atlanta's up and coming 'power' couples—he as one of the area's great builders and me as owner of one of the city's most exclusive women's clothing boutiques. The one thing we couldn't have, which we both desperately wanted, was a child.

"For years we went to doctors. We tried every fertility treatment and drug available."

"What about adoption?" Jim asked.

"We discussed it, but our hearts were set on creating our own child. I know it's silly, but . . ."

"No. Not at all Sandra. Go on."

"The doctors said there was no reason, no physiological reason, we couldn't have kids. So, for some reason, I determined that the only explanation for our inability to bear children must be our lack of religious devotion. We were churchgoers but I decided that wasn't enough. So I re-avowed my Christian faith. I was born again. And then I set out to convince Ray that only if both of us rediscovered and accepted Jesus as our savior would we have any hope of having children of our own."

"Did he?"

"Ray resisted. He had a secular life that had been very successful for him, for both of us. But I wouldn't be denied. Every meal began with a prayer of thanks. I prayed before we made love, then after we made love. Then I began to pray even while we made love. I became very involved in church activities and took every opportunity to interact with other born again Christians. Religion overtook my life, and I was making every effort to help Ray see, as I had, that since our childlessness was not a physical problem, it had to be a spiritual problem."

"How did he take that?" Jim asked.

"At first, he looked at my new-found spirituality with . . . I guess you'd call it bemused tolerance. But as time went on, and as my devotion persisted, Ray found my enthusiasm for Jesus infectious. He finally began to find hope and solace in a more Christian life. He began to understand that despite all of his success, only through Jesus could he hope to find salvation. Unlike me—I was raised Baptist—Ray had been raised a Roman Catholic.

"My rediscovery of my faith and roots, as I saw it, held the promise to me of a spiritual unity between us so powerful and unbreakable that it would assure us of conceiving our first child."

Sandra lowered her head.

"His held the seeds of our . . . of our final separation."

She lifted her head and looked at Jim.

"I did too good a job, Jim. Too good a job, if you can believe that, of imbuing Ray with the spirit of Jesus Christ. He . . . he returned to the strict Catholicism of his childhood. Eventually, religion so dominated his life that . . ."

She put her head down and rubbed a finger over her right eye.

" . . . that he left me. He . . . he got an annulment of our marriage. An annulment?!" she choked. "After fifteen years of marriage? On the grounds that we were too emotionally immature to understand the nature and consequences of the marriage vows! After having consummated our union at least a thousand times! Call it what it is damn it, a divorce!"

She was angry. So much so that she was shaking and crying at the same time. They were nearly at her apartment and the streets were deserted. Jim took a chance and put his arm around her.

"It's okay, honey." It was the first time he called her anything like that. "It's okay." He gave her his handkerchief. She wiped away the tears smudging his white hanky with her running mascara

"Why?" Jim asked. "Why would he want an annulment? It's not like there was another woman he wanted to marry. Or was there?"

"Another woman? Heavens no. Except the church. He gave everything he had to the church. All of his property and money. I didn't fight for much of it. I was too devastated. Then . . . then he entered a seminary and became a Catholic priest.

"Well, I decided that if I had created this 'new man of God' I had the power to un-create him, at least as far as the rest of the world, or my world, was concerned."

Her voice was becoming firm and strong once again.

"And that is just what I did. I became the Widow Chievers."

They had reached the stairs leading to her apartment. She handed the handkerchief back to Jim.

"So," she said, "does that make you think less of me?"

"Less of you? No. Not at all."

He gently squeezed her left hand with his right.

"Thank you," he said. "For confiding in me."

"Can you keep my secret?"

"Of course. I'm a minister, remember?" He smiled at her. "It's your private business. No one needs to know."

She smiled a weak smile.

"Thank you. Thank you, Jim."

They each puckered their lips and sent a phantom kiss. Jim watched as the Widow Chievers climbed the stairs and entered her apartment.

Then he walked home.

Chapter 6

He paused. A long pause. He intended it to seem like an eternity to the congregation gathered before him. He often did this for dramatic effect, and it almost always had its intended impact. The Reverend James Donovan was just about to get into the heart of his sermon, and he wanted to make sure he had everyone's attention. He grasped the edges of the lectern and leaned forward, as if trying to get close enough to speak personally, one on one, with every person in the room.

"So, in a world of sins and sinners, where each and every one of us is the first among sinners, and where each and every one of us knows that he or she will continue to sin, what hope is there of joining our Lord? Where is our salvation? Why, dear brothers and sisters, do we even ask this question, when the answer has been provided to us over and over again by our Lord Jesus?"

Extending his right arm before him he thrust his hand up and down, as if he was splitting a log, for added emphasis.

"Did he not say to his disciples at the Last Supper as the Bible tells us in Matthew twenty-six, verse twenty-eight, 'For this is my blood of the new testament, which is shed for many for the remission of sins'? Did not John the Baptist preach the baptism of repentance for the forgiveness of sins as we are reminded in Mark one, verse four? And why do we not look in Luke twenty-four, verse forty-seven where he gives us the words of Jesus when he appeared to the disciples after the Crucifixion: 'And that repentance and remission of sins should be preached in his name among all nations, beginning at Jerusalem.'"

He folded his hands before him on the lectern and lowered his voice. The softening of his tone provided a contrasting emphasis, again just as he intended.

"Do we forget the teachings of the Apostle Peter in Acts two, verse thirty-eight, as he spread the word of Christ: 'Repent, and be baptized every one of you in the name of Jesus Christ for the remission of sins, and ye shall receive the gift of the Holy Ghost.' And again, as we are told in Acts five, verse thirty-one: 'Him hath God exalted with his right hand to be a Prince and a Savior, for to give repentance to Israel, and forgiveness of sins.'"

Another, shorter pause. Then, with enthusiasm, pointing his right index finger toward the assembled worshipers, he delivered to them what he had built them up to wait for.

"The answer, my friends, the answer is and always has been with us, right before our sometimes blinded eyes, in the Holy Bible." He picked up his Bible from the lectern and held it before his audience. "The Good Book. It tells us—baptism, faith and repentance! *These* are the keys to the forgiveness of our sins. *These* are the keys to the Kingdom of Heaven!"

For almost three years Jim Donovan had inspired his small congregation. He knew that at just over six feet, with his dark, neatly trimmed hair and Paul Newmanesque crystal blue eyes, he struck an imposing figure from his elevated lectern. He was also keenly aware that he was silver-tongued, with the ability to convince everyone in an audience that he was speaking directly and personally only to that one person. And, of course, there was his beautiful family—his lovely, dedicated wife and two gorgeous young girls—to seal the deal. The Paradise Community Christian Church had certainly found the perfect spiritual leader.

He stepped out from behind the lectern and stood in front of it at the edge of the raised stage that served as his alter. Being without a microphone really made no difference to him. He folded his hands before his chest.

"'But Reverend, you ask, can it be so simple as a matter of believing, going to church every Sunday and asking for repentance?'"

He paced back and forth from one side of the seated congregation to the other as he continued.

"'Does that mean that I can live my life any way I want, fornicate and commit adultery when I want, murder those who offend me, break any or all of God's commandments at will, knowing I will simply ask forgiveness each Sunday, or even every day, and that that's all I need to do to be absolved of my sins?' What an important question."

He stopped at center stage.

"Especially now, in 1999, a time when many believe that Armageddon and Judgment Day are upon us. Unlike some, I do not pretend to know when Judgment Day will arrive. But I will tell you, woe to him or her who plays loose with the language of the Lord and selects passages from the Holy Bible to rationalize sinning and debauchery! Yes, the Lord promised us forgiveness of our sins. But Jesus also warns us against being hypocritical worshippers. Turn in your Bibles to Matthew six, verses one through eight, and read along as Jesus speaks directly to each and every one of us."

As his followers read along in their Bibles, Jim recited, from memory, the eight verses of Matthew where Jesus instructs his followers how to pray, without fanfare, in secret and not by rote. Another lesson well learned from Dr. Westin—that demonstrating superior knowledge of the Holy Book, being able to quote it without reading it, would itself be a powerful tool for establishing credibility as a religious leader. And in Jim's experience it was not always *what* he said in a particular sermon, but *how* he said it that most often made the difference.

After completing the recitation from Matthew, he returned to his spot behind the lectern. He folded his hands and rested them on it. He leaned forward again toward his flock and shifted from a preaching delivery to a conversational, almost friendly one.

"So, what is our Lord Jesus telling us about sin and forgiveness? Do we go about living our lives however we want, rather than how God wants us to, confident in the knowledge that our faith and prayers for forgiveness alone are enough to earn God's favor? Do we just recite our magic prayers before, during and after sinning and, of course, right here on Sunday mornings, and that way earn our grand invitation to God's Kingdom? You don't need me to tell you that it's not that easy. You know that it's what's in your heart that makes the difference—that God 'seeth in secret' what is in your heart, and it is upon what he sees there, not what you say here in church, at home or anywhere else that decides whether salvation is to be yours. God's love is eternal for those who love Him with all their heart. His wrath is just as certain for those whose hearts are hard. Amen."

The congregation responded enthusiastically as one—"Amen!"

He felt that he had delivered a very good, maybe even great, sermon. The delivery was powerful and the subject, forgiveness, was one that everyone in the building, including himself, could relate to and needed to hear.

Good job, he thought to himself as he looked down at the front pew where the Widow Chievers usually sat.

One by one the members of the congregation exited the church. The mid-August sun beat down on them incessantly. Even on this hot summer day Reverend Jim was clad in black trousers, a blue collarless shirt, a white clerical collar and a black dress jacket. As was his custom after every church service he stood to greet the parishioners one by one at the church doors.

"Wonderful sermon Reverend," said Crystal Stevens, grasping his hand with both of hers as she went through the receiving line. "And I should know, being an expert about forgiveness and all," the thrice-divorced beautician said with a wink and a smile.

"Lovely, lovely sermon, Reverend Jim," said First Lady Winnie Lowe. "How do you manage to be so inspiring every Sunday?"

"It's the Lord who is inspiring," Jim answered as he gently took Winnie's hands between his. "Not me."

One by one they filed through, congratulating him, sometimes chatting a moment, always being gently stroked by him. Eventually, though, he knew it would be time to greet Norma Hutchins.

"Good morning, Mrs. Hutchins," he said as she walked through the chapel doors. "How are you this fine morning?"

He reached his hands out to hold hers. Mrs. Hutchins kept her hands folded to her chest as she walked by. She muttered a simple, and none-too-cheerful, "Morning."

So what else is new, he thought as she passed by and Fred Blakely, the pharmacist, walked up.

"Wonderful sermon," Fred said shaking Jim's hand vigorously.

"Thank you, Fred. Thank you."

Jim loved this quirky little town. It was a good town, with good people. In return, he felt loved and respected by everyone in Paradise—everyone, that is, except Norma Hutchins. For nearly three years he had done nothing but good things for his church and the town. But she had never warmed up to him. Not that she was ever nasty or rude. She just remained cool, and distant. It was clear to him that she was suspicious of him. She had been from the beginning. Why, he didn't know. And he doubted that she would tell him even if he asked, which, of course, he had no intention of doing.

Ned Ferguson's words kept coming back to him—"It's like she looks right through you to the truth."

That's one thing, he thought, *that I wouldn't want her to be able to see right now—the truth.*

After the last parishioners exited the church Jim went inside and turned off the lights. He stepped outside, closed and locked the doors and turned to walk home where Renee and the twins were waiting for him. As he walked down the two stairs from the doorway to the sidewalk into the hot August air, he suddenly felt a chill wind. He looked up at the dead still leaves in the trees and the brilliant noonday sun.

Funny, he thought.

Chapter 7

"**A**re you sure you won't join us for lunch, Norma?"
"No thank you, Belle. Don't seem to have much of an appetite today. Don't know why. But I'd just be a burden, tagging along and all. You and Ned run along. I'll be thanking you for the ride though."

Norma Hutchins slowly exited from the back of Ned Ferguson's old four door Oldsmobile Cutlass sedan, pulling herself up off the seat by bracing herself on her ever-present walking cane. On her good days she would walk to and from church. But on this Sunday her arthritis was acting up and she had gratefully accepted Ned's and Belle's assistance in driving her to church and back home again.

"As you wish, Norma dear," Belle said. "You take care of yourself now, you hear?"

"Oh hush, Belle. Ain't nothing wrong with me that needs taking care of. I may be a might aged, but I'm healthier than most folks half my age."

"Of course, dear. Anyway, have yourself a good day."

"God willing. Now y'all get yourselves out of here."

"Bye Norma," Ned called out from the driver's side of the car as he began to slowly pull away from the curb.

The old former seamstress haltingly made her way up the front porch steps to her front door. It was unlocked. She had lived in this house for fifty-seven years, the last twenty-five alone since the premature death of her husband George from a sudden and unexpected heart attack. And in those fifty-seven years she had never seen cause to lock her doors when going out, especially when going to church on

Sunday mornings. "God would never let evil enter my home while I was worshipping Him in His house," she would say.

She opened the door, stepped in, and stopped. She looked down the hallway and listened intently in anticipation. She saw and heard nothing. She clucked her tongue several times. Still nothing.

"Cat!" she called. "You playing games with me again? Where the tarnation are you?"

Just then, down the stairs from the second floor, bounded a white and gray Persian cat. When it reached the foot of the stairs, it sat, looked up at its mistress and, with typical feline indifference, began to lick its left paw.

"All right, Cat. I know you're hungry. Don't have to be uppity about it. Sermon went a little long is all. Come on and I'll fix you some tuna."

Norma headed towards the kitchen at the back of the house, followed closely (but not too closely lest it give an impression of dependence) by her proud Persian friend, Misty Velvet Cezanne the Third, otherwise known as "Cat." This was Norma's third Persian over the course of forty-five years, each given the patrician name Misty Velvet Cezanne, and each called by the common moniker "Cat." She couldn't remember why anymore.

She opened a can of tuna and filled Cat's bowl. As Cat feigned finickiness by picking at the white chunk meat, Norma began to boil some water.

"Going to make me some nice cold mint julep tea." Norma would never be seen drinking any kind of liquor, except for the splash of Bourbon necessary to make her mint julep tea legitimate. "Just don't feel much like eating. Must be the heat. Sure don't seem to be bothering you none."

By now Cat had set aside her finicky act and was wholeheartedly digging into her Sunday afternoon treat.

"Quite a sermon the pastor gave today."

Cat stopped eating, looked up briefly at her elderly owner, then buried her nose back in the tuna.

"All about forgiveness and redemption. Might powerful it was."

The water had come to a boil. Norma completed preparing her ice cold concoction before continuing her one-sided conversation with her companion. She sat down at her kitchen table and took a sip.

"Yep, might powerful all right. That man can sure work up a crowd. Strange though. Almost seemed as if all of us folks in the pews weren't even there; as if he weren't speaking to us; like his message was meant for someone else—someone real important just to him."

Norma knew that she was probably the only person in the congregation who didn't feel that Reverend Donovan was speaking right to her during his sermon. But Norma understood she was different, more perceptive. She had always reveled in her special, unique gift. And never questioned it. What God willed, would be.

"Because he sure did speak with the spirit of the Lord today," she continued. "He sure did. But it just didn't seem to be for us Cat. Cat?"

She looked down at her furry friend.

"You listening? You all done with your lunch? Good. Let's go set a spell in the sitting room. These kitchen chairs are just too darn hard for me anymore."

She got up from her kitchen table, took her glass of tea in one hand and her cane in the other, and walked slowly towards her sitting room. Cat followed a respectably aloof distance behind.

Though it was mid-day, the room was relatively dark. When alone, she always kept the shades in her sitting room drawn and lights off. This is where she could do her best thinking and it seemed to help not having the rays of the sun shining in on her or the glow of artificial lighting surrounding her. The dimness of the room brought peace and relaxation which, in turn, seemed to enhance the clarity of her mind and thoughts.

Norma seated herself in a rocker made for her by hand over fifty years before by her husband George. She laid her cane on the floor next to her and placed her glass on an end table next to the rocker. She softly patted her lap. Cat, who had set herself down in front of her mistress, looked up as if seriously considering the pluses and minuses of the offer that had just been extended to her. After waiting long enough to be sure that Norma understood that acceptance of the invitation was not a foregone conclusion, Cat sprang up onto her lap, laid across it and began to purr contentedly.

Norma rocked silently for awhile, stroking Cat's head and back, drinking her mint julep tea, ruminating about Reverend Donovan's sermon and her sense that it held even more meaning than he had intended. What was it, she wondered, about this man—this hard working, friendly man with the lovely family—that caused such uneasiness within her? Was it her general discomfort about him that, perhaps, caused her to read more into his sermon than was really there? She had always trusted her instincts, had always had supreme confidence in her ability to read people and what truly lay behind not only their actions, but their character as well. For the first time in her life, she found herself questioning those very instincts and abilities by which she had always defined herself, and which others had always admired, and often feared. Reverend Jim Donovan had managed to work his way into her being in a manner she was certain he had never intended, nor was even aware of. And in a way she would have cursed if she ever allowed herself to stray far enough from God's admonitions to do so.

"What do you think Cat? Am I being too harsh on our handsome young pastor?"

She continued to stroke her pet whose motor-like purring increased in velocity, yet who otherwise feigned indifference to anything her master was saying or doing.

"Ain't no question he's been good for the church. And for the town for that matter. Sure has more energy than old Reverend Carter had them last few years."

Her eyes followed her aching hand as it stroked Cat from the top of the animal's head down along its back. Sitting and petting her beloved companion often served as a sort of therapy that would bring her temporary relief from the pain of her arthritis and the loneliness of her solitude.

"But I just can't seem to get this gnawing feeling about him out of my bosom. Know what I mean Cat? I've been trying. Sure been trying. For three years now I've been trying. Ain't seen nothing to cause it. Just can't get rid of it."

Cat stirred slightly.

"What do you think that means, Cat? What do you think of our esteemed Reverend Donovan?"

At this mention of the minister's name Cat let out a hiss, followed by a guttural meow, and quickly sat upright in Norma's lap. Her feline eyes—the left of which was blue, the right one green—looked up at the wrinkled face of her mistress. Norma looked down at her cat's whiskered face and when her eyes met Cat's they stopped. There was something unusual, out of the ordinary, about them. It was nothing she could see, just something she felt. Her eyes became transfixed by Cat's. It was as if she was supposed to see something in them—something more than irises and pupils.

Then it happened. She did begin to see something. And hear something, too. It was faint at first. But it grew. And as it grew she realized that what she was hearing, she wasn't hearing with her ears. And what she was seeing, she wasn't seeing with her eyes. It couldn't be described as a sense, or sensation, nor a vision or dream or any other product or creation of an active and vivid mind. She couldn't place it, or describe it, even to herself. She was simply *experiencing* it. She would go where it would take her. She knew she had no choice.

The sound was clearer now. It was the sound of a man—a man groaning—groaning in what sounded—no, what *felt*—like despair. The voice had a familiarity to it, but she couldn't identify it. The groans got louder at first. Then they began to fade, until they were no more than a whimper. At the same time, she felt there was something to see, but she could see nothing.

Then, a long, loud cry. It jolted her, but not a muscle in her body moved. It was a strange cry, like nothing she had ever heard before. It was a man's cry, but it wasn't. It was a cry of anguish and, she didn't understand, but at the same time a cry of joy. It contained no words, yet seemed to be a communication of some sort—with whom, and about what, she didn't know. Its tone was contemptuous, and at the same time conveyed respect and humility.

Norma was awash in a sea of auditory contradictions, confused and frustrated at her inability to understand it all when, suddenly, she no longer felt the sounds. She didn't know how long it had been since they had started, but neither she nor Cat had moved during the episode. Then, as quickly as the groans and cries had ceased, she began to "see." It was a meandering river, a river with no banks, no rocks, nothing around it. Just a winding river surrounded by cold, empty black space. As it came more into focus she could see that its current was strong and though it seemed to exist within no scene or context, her sense of it was that it flowed variously downhill and uphill like some sort of amusement park roller coaster.

It came closer into view. As it did, she could sense the turbulence of the water, not only as it raced quickly along, but as it bubbled up from beneath. She started to sweat profusely. She reached her hand out as if to touch the water, then recoiled it in pain. It felt as if she had burned it. The water in the river was boiling.

As she continued to "look" at the river of boiling water she could see there was something on top of it being carried along with the swift current. It came ever so slowly into focus. It was something lying on the water. A board, or a large log perhaps? Then she could see it was neither a board nor a log, nor any other inanimate object. It was a man. He was lying totally still, seemingly unaffected by the scalding liquid that he was lying on or the turbulent waters roiling under and around him. She couldn't make out how he was dressed, though she was sure he was. Her attention was being drawn only towards his face.

She felt a sense of familiarity again. The picture was coming into focus, but again ever so slowly. Then it was clear. It was Reverend Donovan. She was sure of it. His eyes were closed and his body was still, but it was him. He appeared lifeless, yet there was clearly life within him. His expressionless face masked intense emotion stirring within him, now stirring within her, as if they were one with the boiling water of the river.

What was that? she thought. A whispering. She was sure of it. She felt herself drawing nearer his face. Again, now a definite whispering. His lips didn't move, but he was saying something, talking to her. She moved still closer, until she could hear. And she listened. As she listened, she could feel even more what he felt. The contradictions, at first, confused her—the heat of the boiling water and the cold of the surrounding space, the void of the dark and the comfort of the light, the fear of life and the hope in death. She listened intently and strained to understand.

Then, silence again. Reverend Donovan's expressionless face had not changed, but the whisperings had stopped. The emotions, too, had gone. It had all ended just when Norma believed she was about to grasp what was happening, what he was trying to tell her. A great disappointment fell over her. Then, a sense of foreboding, of sadness to come which, if only she had had more time to understand, to figure it out, she might be able to prevent. She looked at the pastor again, hoping to hear and feel more. She moved her face as close to his as possible, to see or hear something, anything.

Suddenly, his eyes shot open. They were incredibly large and blinding white. Norma was so startled that she screamed out, her body jerking and her arms flailing so forcefully that she knocked Cat, screeching, off her lap.

It was over. She knew she would learn no more, at least not now. It would happen soon, whatever *it* was. Perhaps she should warn Reverend Donovan, she thought. About what, she didn't know. But she expected he would.

Yes, that's what I should do, she thought. *As soon as I take a little nap. I'm so tired. So very, very tired. Yes, I'll go see him, right after I take a little nap.*

Norma Hutchins closed her eyes and fell asleep in her rocker. She would sleep where she sat for the next twenty-four hours.

Chapter 8

As Jim walked into the house, Renee walked toward him coming from the kitchen with Carly and Jessica fast on her heals yelling "Pancakes! Pancakes!" She reached up to him on her toes and kissed him lovingly. Each twin grabbed one of his legs. They changed their shouts to "Daddy! Daddy!" He kneeled down and took one in each arm kissing each in turn on the cheek.

"I know you heard this from everyone at church," Renee said as Jim stood back up, "but you were wonderful today."

"Well, that's special praise coming from my toughest critic," he said with a smile as he kissed her lightly on the cheek.

"I'll fix lunch while you pack," she said.

"Let me guess. Pancakes?"

Renee patted him on the butt as he started up the stairs. They wouldn't be going out for their usual Sunday brunch because Jim was looking to get as early a start on his trip as possible. He had broached the idea of the trip a month and a half earlier. He was nearing burnout, he had told her, and needed to get away from everything and everyone for awhile. At first, Renee was cool to the idea of her husband leaving her and the kids for a whole week. But Jim Donovan was nothing if not persuasive and once Renee had accepted the idea, she did so wholeheartedly. Or at least that's how Jim saw it.

He pulled down his brown travel bag from the upper shelf of the bedroom closet. He packed enough clothes to last the week. Everything he packed was casual. There would be no occasion to dress up during this trip. He finished quickly and headed back downstairs.

He arrived in the kitchen just as the first stack of pancakes was being placed on the table.

"Pancakes!" he shouted out in mocked surprise.

The girls laughed. Jim sat down in his usual chair which, at their small round table, took on the character of the head of the table only because he was the one who sat there. The family held hands and said grace. With the children leading the way, they then dug into the stack.

"So where have you finally decided you're going?" Renee asked as she poured maple syrup over her three-high stack of golden brown hotcakes.

Jim had just placed in his mouth a forkful of pancake smothered in honey. He chewed slowly and deliberately. He swallowed and began to cut another forkful.

"I thought I'd head west, towards Columbia, and just stop wherever it seems I'm meant to stop."

"When you get there, wherever 'there' is, call me and give me a phone number so I have some way of getting in touch with you," she said.

"Darling, it's a week. Actually, less than a week. I'll be back Saturday, and I'm sure the Lord will provide for you and the kids while I'm away. If you need anything you can always call Ned or Charlie. I really need this time to myself, uninterrupted. I'll call and check in, okay?"

"Okay," Renee said, agreeing unconvincingly.

This was one time Jim was glad he didn't have a mobile phone. He had intentionally refused the church's offer to provide him one. Paradise was a small town and in a real emergency he could always be quickly reached. To have his own phone would have meant having absolutely no time for himself and his family. And for the upcoming week, it would have meant not having the solitude he wanted *from* his family.

Jim and Renee spoke no more to each other during brunch. They spent the rest of the meal being entertained by their girls and, on a couple of occasions, interceding to prevent pancakes and maple syrup from ending up on the floor or in the girls' hair. When they had all finished, Jim pushed his chair back from the table and stood up.

"It's time to go," he said. "Come here girls, and give Daddy a big hug."

His daughters jumped out of their chairs and ran to their father's arms giving him farewell hugs and kisses.

"Bring me something! Bring me something!" they shouted in unison.

"I will," he promised. "I'll bring you something."

He and Renee, followed by their twins, walked into the foyer. He picked up his bag and walked to the front door from where he could see his old white Chrysler LeBaron waiting for him in the driveway. He turned to kiss Renee goodbye. Before he could, the phone on the side table in the hallway began to ring.

He hesitated to answer. What if it was a parishioner who demanded that he address an emergency that could clearly wait a week but which the parishioner insisted be dealt with now? Against his better judgment, and knowing he was risking his immediate escape, he decided he should answer. He looked at Renee, raised his eyebrows and walked over to the table. He picked up the receiver.

"Hello," he said.

"Reverend Jim? Is this Reverend Jim?"

Just as he feared. It was a distraught woman's voice on the other end. It sounded like Clara Doyle.

"Yes. Clara?"

"Oh thank God I got you!" Her voice was trembling and she was in obvious distress.

"Clara, what's wrong?"

"Reverend Jim. It's Missy. She's run off with Tommy Nobles. And . . . and Frank's gone looking for them. He's got his shotgun, Reverend, and I'm scared out of my wits what he's going to do!"

Jim knew Clara had a right to be frightened. She had come to him before about the situation with her fifteen-year-old daughter, Missy. Two years earlier Missy had taken up with Tommy Nobles, who was now nineteen. Clara's husband, Frank, who owned Doyle's Auto Body Shop—the best body man in town, though there were only two to choose from—had never approved of the relationship. He considered Tommy Nobles a shifty ne'er-do-well who, as far as Frank was concerned, would turn out just like his old man, Nate Nobles, who had always been in trouble with the law and was serving a fifteen year prison term for armed robbery.

Frank had forbidden Missy from seeing Tommy almost from the

beginning of the relationship. But for almost two years Missy and Tommy had sneaked around and managed to see each other despite Frank. It was a small town, so they could never be seen in public. It would get back to Frank right away. So their entire relationship consisted of Missy sneaking out of her bedroom to see Tommy late at night, and secret rendezvous in his house or hers when his mother or her parents were gone.

This manner of seeing each other had the effect of pushing Missy and Tommy closer together. They began having sex two months after they started seeing each other. Clara became aware of it about a year later when she came home from shopping one afternoon and caught Tommy and Missy naked in Missy's bed. Missy told her mother everything, and said she wouldn't stop seeing Tommy.

This created a tremendous dilemma for Clara. If she didn't tell Frank, she would be keeping something from her husband that he had a right to know. On the other hand, if she did tell Frank, she knew he wouldn't hesitate to take his shotgun to the young punk. Clara had opted for life instead of honesty, but had been sickened by it, and by the knowledge that Missy was continuing to see Tommy, and continuing to have sex with him. Now, they had run off, and Frank knew.

"Slow down, Clara," Jim said. "Settle down." He sought to calm her down and get some information. "How do you know they've run off?"

"When I got up this morning, Missy wasn't in her bed. I went and woke my thirteen-year-old, Penny, and asked her where Missy was. Penny didn't want to say nothing but I threatened to take the belt to her and she told me that Missy snuck out last night after midnight and went somewhere with Tommy. Then Frank come in and heard what Penny was saying and went and grabbed his shotgun and took off himself."

"Does Penny know where they went, Clara?"

"No. She swears she don't know. Missy just told her to keep her mouth shut about her having gone with Tommy. Didn't say where she was going to or when she was coming back or nothing. Reverend Jim, you've got to help me find her before Frank does. He'll kill that boy for sure. I know he will."

"Okay. Okay, Clara. I'll be right over. You call Chief Bruener and tell him what happened so he can get his deputies looking for Missy right away—and for Frank."

Jim placed the receiver back in its cradle.

"What's wrong honey?" Renee asked having heard only his half of the conversation.

Jim looked up from the phone and turned his head to face his wife.

"Missy Doyle's run off," he said. "Looks like with Tommy Nobles. And Frank Doyle's taken after them with his shotgun. I've got to get over to the Doyles' place."

Renee stepped around Jim and picked up his travel bag.

"I'll put this in the closet until you get back," she said. She kissed him on the cheek. "Be careful."

"I will. Thanks baby." He kissed her back with a peck on the lips.

When Jim Donovan arrived at Clara Doyle's house, Charlie Bruener was already there with two of his officers. He was sitting on a rocking chair in the Doyle living room facing Clara and Penny who were seated on the couch opposite him. The two officers, who were in uniform, stood behind the Chief, their arms folded in what Jim suspected was an intentionally imposing fashion. As Jim walked in it appeared to him that the Chief had just about wrapped up his initial questioning of the obviously distraught mother and the intimidated, wide-eyed little girl.

"Afternoon Reverend," Charlie greeted him as he entered the living room through the unlocked screen door. On the golf course and in private Charlie referred to Jim by name. But in public, he always referred to him respectfully by his title.

"Afternoon Chief," said Jim, equally respectfully.

"I understand Clara has pretty much told you what's going on," Bruener said.

"Yes Chief, she has. Any idea where the kids might have gone?"

"Not from what Clara and Penny have told us. We're headed over to the Nobles place to see what Ginny Nobles or her other boy, Petie, can tell us. You're welcome to join us."

"Thanks Chief. I think I will. I'll be right along. I'd like to talk to Clara for a moment."

The Chief stood up.

"We'll see you there then," he said as he started towards the front door flanked by his two loyal soldiers. As soon as they walked out onto the front porch Jim sat down in the rocker just vacated by the Chief.

Clara's eyes were red and still moist with tears. Jim moved his chair right up to the edge of the couch and took Clara's hands in his.

"We'll find them Clara. And we'll find Frank too before he does anything foolish."

"I pray you will, Reverend," she said, wiping tears away with an already wet tissue she had been holding in the ball of her hand. "I pray you will."

"Clara, is there anything else you can tell me that might help us figure out where the kids went? Anything Missy may have said recently or anything she may have done that might give us a clue?"

Clara glanced quickly at Penny, then looked back at Jim. She seemed about to say something, then looked down at her hands folded on her lap. She looked up at him again.

"No, Reverend. Nothing else I can think of."

"Okay," Jim said. "I'm sure Chief Bruener already went over all of that with you. I'm going to join him over at the Nobles' house. You just stay here and take it easy. If you hear from Missy or Frank you call the police station right away so they can let the Chief know. Okay?"

Clara sniffled, and nodded her head.

"Okay," she said.

"And if you need anything you feel free to call my wife, you hear?"

"Yes. Yes, I will," she answered, nodding her head again. "Thank you. And God bless you."

Jim grasped her hand in both of his and squeezed gently. He got up without saying anything further and left the house knowing there was nothing further he could say to bring the worried mother comfort until they found Missy, and Tommy Nobles, alive and well.

As he walked briskly up the sidewalk and approached the Nobles house Jim could hear Ginny Nobles yelling at Charlie Bruener.

"That's right Chief!" she screamed. "Blame Tommy! It's always *my* boys who's to blame! Anything goes wrong in this shitty little town, go find the Nobles boys! It must be them that's done it, whatever it is!"

He turned up the Nobles sidewalk and negotiated the four steps onto the porch in two paces. He stopped to listen through the screen door to get a feel for where the conversation might be headed. He already had a pretty good idea where it was at that moment.

"Now settle down Ginny," the Chief said in a firm yet much softer voice than that of the angry woman. "No one's blaming anyone for anything yet. All we know is that Missy Doyle and Tommy went off somewhere last night and no one knows where they're at. And we just want to find them, that's all. Before Frank Doyle does something stupid."

"Well, *that's* who you should be looking for," she said, her voice still angry, but a couple of decibels lower. "That good for nothing Frank Doyle. His little Missy is too good for my Tommy. She sees the good in my Tommy and that fucking grease monkey wants to take after my boy. It's him you should be looking for."

"We are Ginny. We're looking for Frank too. But you've got to help us find out where the kids went."

The Chief was using his best diplomacy to calm Ginny Nobles' anger so he could get some information from her, anything that could give him a clue where the missing kids were so he could find them before Frank Doyle did. So far it didn't seem like he was getting too far. Jim decided it was time to enter the conversation, such as it was. He opened the screen door without knocking and entered the house. The first thing he noticed was how much more clutter and mess there was in the Nobles' living room as compared to the Doyles'.

"Afternoon Mrs. Nobles," he said smoothly as he entered the house.

Ginny Nobles turned her gaze towards Jim at the sound of his voice. She looked at him with an expressionless face.

"Afternoon Reverend," she replied in a voice devoid of any emotion.

At least she's not screaming at me, Jim thought. *That's a positive.*

"I see Chief Bruener has told you of our little problem," Jim said. He had remained standing in front of the screen door. Even a few feet away from the seated Ginny Nobles this caused him to appear to tower over her. The fact that she had to look so far up for her eyes to meet his created the impression of a worshipper praying to her Lord. "We would certainly appreciate it," he continued, " . . . I would appreciate it if you could tell us if you know anything about the kids' whereabouts."

Ginny Nobles was not a churchgoer. Jim had never seen her in his church anyway. Nonetheless, she showed respect towards him presumably, he thought, because he was a man of the cloth. As she looked at him her anger seemed to dissipate. These few words, spoken by Jim in the most calming, reassuring manner he could muster, seemed to have put her at some ease.

"I . . . I don't know where they could be. I ain't seen Tommy since before I went to work yesterday." She appeared to have focused on the fact that her son was missing too, and that he might be in danger. "I worked three to eleven shift at the diner. When I got home I was so tired I went straight to bed. Never even looked in his room to see if he was there. Ain't seen him at all today, but that ain't unusual. He don't always tell me where he's going to or when he's coming back."

Jim took over the questioning with the Chief's tacit assent.

"Has Tommy said anything to you recently to give you any idea that he might be planning to leave, or run away?"

"No. Nothing I can think of."

"Has he been acting strangely, or different in any way?"

"Well, now you mention it, does seem he's been going out less lately. And asking for overtime down at the bowling alley. Been saving his money more than usual, too. Do you think that might have something to do with him running off with that Doyle girl?"

"Don't know Mrs. Nobles. It might."

"Ma! Ma!"

Jim turned to see Ginny Nobles' fourteen-year-old son, Petie, running up the front porch steps calling out for his mother.

"Ma!"

Petie burst through the front door and into the living room. He stopped suddenly at the sight of the minister, the Chief of Police and two uniformed officers basically surrounding the living room couch upon which his mother sat alone.

"Ma, what's going on?" Petie asked as he looked around at the group with suspicious eyes.

"It's all right, Petie," she said, extending her hand out to her son inviting him to sit with her on the couch. He moved immediately to her and sat at her right side. "Tommy's run off somewhere. Apparently, with that Doyle girl. And the police is looking for them, that's all. Anyway, what are you all up in a dither about?"

Petie's eyes darted from his mother to the minister to the cops and back again to his mother.

"Come on," Mrs. Nobles urged. "You got something to say? Spit it out. You know something about where Tommy's gone to?"

It was clear that Petie knew something. It was just as clear that he was frightened of something.

Jim took one step towards the couch and spoke to the young boy softly.

"Son, if you know something it's important to tell us. Your brother might be in danger."

"He is! He is in danger!" the boy blurted out. "That crazy Mr. Doyle's got a shotgun and he's looking for Tommy! Says he's going to blow his head off!"

"How do you know this?" Chief Bruener asked the boy.

"Cause he came up to me just five minutes ago. Put the barrel to my head and told me he'd blow my head off if I didn't tell him where Tommy and Missy was. At first I didn't think he'd do it so I didn't say nothing. But then he got this look in his eyes, a crazy look. He says, 'Tell me boy, or I swear I'll blow your fucking head off. I don't care how young you are or what they do to me.' And I sure as hell believed him then. He would have shot me, sure thing, if I didn't tell him."

"Tell him what, Petie? Tell him what?" There was urgency in Jim's voice now.

Petie looked at five pair of adult eyes watching him with eager and impatient anticipation. His own eyes dropped to the floor.

"Tommy took Missy to get an abortion," he said in a low, weak voice.

"A what?!" Ginny Nobles exclaimed.

Petie looked up at the incredulous face of his mother.

"An abortion, Ma. Tommy done got Missy pregnant and they gone to get her an abortion."

"Holy shit," said Bruener. "And you told this to Frank Doyle?"

"Didn't have no choice, Chief. He'd a shot me if I didn't."

"Jesus Christ," Bruener said. "Forgive me Reverend. But Frank Doyle *will* shoot Tommy if we don't find him first." Bruener turned back to the boy. "There ain't no place close to here where anyone will give a fifteen-year-old girl an abortion. They must be heading pretty far away. Petie, do you know where they're going to?"

"Yeah, Chief." The Chief's confirmation of Petie's fears about what Frank Doyle would do showed in the boy's wide-eyed, frightened face. "And it ain't too far away. It's just down on the Old Shephard's Highway a few miles. Tommy learned there's this doctor—don't know his name, but I think he said he's from Virginia—he travels around to places where doctors won't do no abortions and he does them. So Tommy gets in touch with the people who get him in touch with this doctor and they just set it up. Tommy figured he and Missy'd be gone just a couple of days and they'd get in trouble and all but no one'd know about her being pregnant and all. That was the big thing he said they had to deal with. He said the other stuff would be small potatoes."

"But where exactly is this going to happen, Petie?" pressed Bruener.

"There's this old farm house about fifteen miles down the Old Shephard's Highway. The owners must not live in it much anymore. I guess this doctor must have rented it or something 'cause Tommy told me that's where it was going to be done."

"Do you know the address?"

"No sir. Just what I told you. That's all I know."

"And did you tell all of this to Mr. Doyle?"

"Yes sir. He was going to kill me if I didn't. That's why I was running so hard to get here and tell my Ma. You've got to stop him Chief. He's going to blow Tommy away if someone don't stop him."

"Okay." Bruener motioned to his officers. "Harry, Duke, let's go. We've got to get to that place before Frank Doyle does, if we're not too late already."

"Chief," Jim said, "can I come with you? Perhaps I can be of some help."

"Sure Reverend, come on. You just might be able to help."

Bruener, his deputies and Jim quickly left the Nobles house and jumped into the two patrol cars parked outside. The Chief and Jim jumped into the one car and Harry and Duke into the other and they headed out to the Old Shephard's Highway, lights flashing and sirens wailing. Old Shephard's Highway was a lightly traveled two-lane road that long ago had served as a main truck route. Now it only served local traffic and those who enjoyed leisurely traveling America by the scenic routes. Once on the road the police vehicles, the Chief in the lead, gathered speed in a frantic race against the clock.

"Can we catch him?" Jim asked the Chief. "Frank must have at least a ten minute head start on us."

"True. But I don't think he'll be pushing his old pickup over this rough road at a speed anywhere near what we're doing. I think I know what house Petie is talking about down the Highway. I'm pretty sure we can catch Frank before he gets there. I'm more worried about what happens then."

They were about twelve or thirteen miles down the Highway when the Chief finally spotted Frank's pickup.

"There," he said to Jim as he pointed out the front window.

Just as the Chief said this, the old pickup picked up speed and started to bounce all over the pot-holed road. After about a minute, with the cruisers closing the gap, the old truck pulled over to the side of the road and stopped. The Chief stuck his left hand out of his open window and pointed over the roof of his car towards the side of the road. On cue, the following patrol car pulled over and slowed down as it approached Frank Doyle's truck. The Chief drove his cruiser past Doyle's truck and pulled off the side of the road about fifteen feet in front of it.

Jim turned and looked out the back window of the patrol car. He saw Frank Doyle get out of the driver's side of the truck, holding his shotgun, and go around to the passenger side. He also saw Hank and Duke take positions behind their opened car doors, firearms in hand pointing towards Doyle. He turned and looked at the Chief who was watching everything unfold through his rearview mirror. Slowly, the Chief opened his door and stepped out with his hands up and away from his own holstered gun.

"Frank," the Chief called out as he slowly walked to the back of his car. "You don't want to do this. Now put that gun down and let's talk this over."

Frank slid down the side of his truck on his haunches to where the Chief could no longer see him. Jim could still see him from his vantage point and could see that at least Duke was also in a position to see Doyle.

"Charlie," Doyle shouted, "you just back off. This is my family business. Ain't no business of yours."

"Now Frank, you know that's just not so. Anytime someone takes after someone with a shotgun it becomes my business. And it's my business to stop a shooting, not just arrest the one that's done it." Bruener took a couple of steps around the back of his patrol car. "Now Frank, just give me that shotgun before you do something you'll regret, and before we both get hurt."

Doyle stood up and pointed the shotgun in Bruener's general direction. Duke looked ready to take Doyle out. Jim wanted to jump out of the car and try to calm Doyle down, but something told him this wasn't the right moment, if there ever would be one.

"Don't take another step Charlie. I'm warning you!" Doyle's hands began to shake and the Chief stopped. He put his right hand up as if to tell Duke to hold his fire. "That boy's messed up my Missy and he's got to pay."

Now, Jim decided. He opened the passenger door of the car and stepped out. Doyle, apparently unaware that there had been someone else in the Chief's car, was startled for a moment and turned the shotgun towards Jim. At that moment Jim half expected to hear the sound of gunfire, either the explosive sound of Doyle's shotgun for that split second before the pellets made Swiss cheese of him or the pop-pop of the officers' handguns likely killing Doyle before he had the chance to pull his own trigger. Chills ran up and down his spine in anticipation of somebody's, maybe his, impending death. Instead, apparently realizing that there was no threat to him from the minister, Doyle again pointed his gun at the Chief.

Quickly collecting himself, Jim took one step towards Doyle.

"Frank," he said evenly, "the boy's going to pay. But should Missy have to lose her father in the process?"

"How's he going to pay Reverend?" Doyle said, keeping his eyes on the Chief. "By going to Hell? That ain't good enough. That ain't soon enough for me. He's knocked up my little girl and now he's taking her to some butcher to kill the baby. Hell ain't soon enough for that Reverend."

Jim took another step forward.

"Frank, I'm talking about paying now. Missy's a minor. Tommy's nineteen. He's an adult. I think if you ask the Chief he'll tell you that what Tommy has done is against the law. It's a crime. Isn't that right, Chief?"

"Sure is, Reverend," Bruener answered, picking up on Jim's lead. "Frank, as soon as we catch up to them we'll arrest Tommy Nobles for having sex with a minor if that's what you want. But right now we've got to hurry to stop Missy from getting that abortion. You need to put that gun down. Now."

Doyle kept his shotgun trained on Bruener. His eyes darted back and forth between the Chief and Jim. Jim could almost hear Doyle's thoughts alternating between accepting the logic of what had just been said to him and the fervent desire to kill the boy who had defied him and defiled his young daughter. Finally, logic won out. Doyle lowered the shotgun. Bruener walked up to him and took the weapon from his hands.

"I'm going with you to find them," Doyle insisted.

"No, no Frank, you're not," the Chief said. "You're going back to town with Harry and Duke. They'll take you home and you all wait with Clara till Reverend Jim and I get back with Missy."

Bruener put the shotgun in the back of his car and instructed his officers to take Frank home. Then he and Jim got back in the car and sped down Old Shephard's Highway in search of the illicit farmhouse.

"Chief, I thought these underground abortions were done away with when the Supreme Court made them legal everywhere?" Jim asked as they bumped along the old road.

"For the most part they was, Reverend. But you still got them opportunists and butchers out there willing to make a buck on people too embarrassed to go to a hospital, or who don't got no insurance or on youngsters like Missy Doyle who are too afraid to tell their parents or have anyone know what they're doing. I just hope we're not too late."

"I hope not too."

Within a couple of minutes Bruener and Jim saw a lone farmhouse ahead on the right with three cars parked in the driveway alongside the building.

"There," said Bruener, pointing towards the driveway. "There's Tommy Nobles' old Chevy Camaro. They're here."

The Chief slowly drove his cruiser up the driveway and turned off the engine. As he started to get out of the car, Jim gripped his right arm and gently pulled him back.

"Chief," Jim said, "why don't you let me go up first, alone."

"I don't think that's a good idea Reverend. We don't know who's in there or what's going on."

"I think we do Charlie. This isn't some sort of armed gang or hostage situation. I'm sure there isn't any danger. I just think that, for Missy's sake, it might be better if the first person they deal with on this is a minister rather than a police officer."

"It's against my better judgment, Reverend. But I'll go along with you, at least at the start. At the first sign of trouble, though, I'm coming in."

"Thank you Charlie."

Jim got out of the cruiser and walked up the stairs to the front door of the old house. The bottom half of the front screen door was torn, showing, as did the rest of the unpainted house, that little care had been taken of it in quite some time. He opened the unlocked screen door and knocked on the worn wooden front door. There was no answer. He knocked again, harder. This time, after a few seconds, the front door opened.

Before him stood a white haired man, shorter and stockier than Jim, with wire rimmed glasses and wearing a white shirt and red bow tie. He looked like some of the eccentric professors Jim remembered from college. The man looked at him and at the police cruiser sitting in the driveway which he could see over Jim's left shoulder. He looked again at Jim.

"Yes? Can I help you?" he asked Jim.

The screen door remained open, resting against Jim's back. This gave him a sense of already being one step in the house, ground he would not give up.

"Yes sir," Jim said. "My name is Reverend James Donovan. I'm a minister in Paradise, about fifteen miles up the road. I'm looking for the missing daughter of one of my parishioners—a young girl named Missy Doyle. We have reason to believe she's here."

"I'm afraid I don't know anyone by that name, Reverend."

"And what is your name sir?" Jim asked.

"I'm not sure what concern that is of yours sir."

"You're right. That really is no concern of mine. But Missy Doyle is. And whether or not you know her by name, her boyfriend's car is parked right out here and she is known to be in his company. That tells me that Missy is in this house and for some reason you are trying to conceal that fact."

Jim's tone was firm, but still respectful. He knew that this man was a physician, or at least considered himself one, and speaking condescendingly or threateningly would not be productive, at least not yet.

"Reverend," the man said, "I appreciate the fact that you have a job to do. And I'm sure that you and the girl's family are very concerned about her. But I can assure you that whoever is in this house is entirely safe and nothing bad is going to happen."

"Doctor . . . May I call you doctor?"

The older man looked at Jim guardedly.

"You may call me what you like."

Jim crossed his arms. "Okay then. Doctor, I know that Missy is pregnant. I also know that Tommy Nobles arranged for her to have an abortion and that it's to occur in this house. And it's quite obvious that you are the person who is going to perform the abortion—that is, if you haven't already done so. And now you know what I know." The doctor's face remained expressionless. Jim continued. "What you may not know is that no more than ten minutes ago, our police chief"—Jim turned and pointed towards Charlie Bruener down in the driveway—"stopped Missy's father no more than three miles from here. Mr. Doyle had his shotgun and was on his way here to kill Tommy Nobles. And probably you. He was going to kill Tommy Nobles not because he got her pregnant. That he would have beaten Tommy for. But because he was causing her to have an abortion." Jim placed his left foot on the doorstep and leaned in closer to the doctor. "You see doctor, most people around here consider abortion murder, and abortionists murderers. I daresay, if the Chief hadn't caught up to old Frank Doyle, he would have carried out his threat against Tommy. And then sir, I believe you would have been next."

"I don't take kindly to threats Reverend," the doctor said. "And it ill becomes you as a man of the cloth to issue threats of murder."

"You misunderstand me doctor. I'm not threatening you. I'm merely trying to make you understand just how strongly Mr. Doyle feels about what you are about to do to his daughter."

"How do you know the procedure hasn't already been completed?"

"When I first came to the door I didn't know. But by now, if you had completed it you would have let me know that there was no reason to be having this conversation. Your silence tells me you haven't done it yet."

The doctor put his hand on the edge of the door as if getting ready to close it.

"You're very astute Reverend. But you have no business interfering in my business or, for that matter, the young lady's. She has the right to choose what to do with her body. The sad thing is what she has to do to exercise that right. Instead of having the procedure in a clean, sterile hospital, she has to have it done in a farmhouse."

Jim unfolded his arms and prepared himself to force his way in if necessary. He knew that would spur the Chief into immediate action.

"I am always amazed, good doctor, at the lengths people like you go to sanitize the language of what you're doing. She has the 'right to choose' and she's going to have a 'procedure.' Why don't you call it what it is—the killing of a life. And the so-called right to choose you fight so hard for is the right to kill."

"And I'm always amazed, good Reverend," the doctor replied with sarcastic emphasis, "at how folks like you have so little respect for a woman's ability to make such important decisions for herself; and how it is sometimes just wrong to bring a child into a world where that child will have little or no chance of living a decent life."

Strong feelings of anger began to well up within Jim. Abortion was an abomination to him, and that this man, this so-called doctor who, if he was a real doctor, had sworn an oath to do no harm and to heal, could speak of it in terms of choice and rights rather than life, enraged him. He may not have been able to save his own child from the abortionist's scalpel, but by God he would save Missy's. He folded his hands behind his back, the screen door still leaning against him. He looked back at Bruener and gave him a look that he hoped the Chief would understand meant he wanted a couple of more minutes.

"Doctor, you and I could debate *Roe versus Wade* forever, and we'll never come close to agreement. The point now is that there's a fifteen-year-old girl in this house who you are planning to commit an abortion on."

A look of surprise came across the doctor's face.

"Fifteen? She told me she was eighteen."

"Well doctor," Jim said firmly, pointing his right index finger at the doctor's face, "she's not. She's fifteen. And she's in her fourth month."

Jim didn't really know how far along Missy was. But he knew that under South Carolina law a fifteen-year-old needed her parents' consent for an abortion and that all abortions in the second trimester had to be done in a hospital or clinic. Maybe the doctor didn't feel that Mr. Doyle was any longer a threat, but perhaps the fear of the law, personified by the scowling Chief in the driveway, might be.

"I can assure you doctor, that Chief Bruener is not going to let an illegal abortion happen. Now, he has allowed me to make an effort at resolving this without force and without him taking any official action in the matter. If we can do that, you can leave, no questions asked. If you and I can't do that, then I'll just let him know that now. Illegal abortions in South Carolina are a crime and you can go to prison, and I'm sure the Chief would be more than happy to accommodate you if that is the path you choose."

The doctor again looked over Jim's shoulder at Chief Bruener, who was out of his car leaning against the front fender. He looked back at Jim. Stepping back from the door he said with resignation, "Okay. Come on in. They're upstairs."

He led Jim up the stairs and into the bedroom on the left. It had been set up as an operating room with a portable steel operating table and all of the necessary instruments laid out on another steel table. In the room were two young women dressed in nurse's whites busy preparing for the procedure. They stopped what they were doing the moment they saw him enter the room.

Next to the operating table stood Tommy Nobles. He looked at Reverend Jim and said nothing. The fear in his eyes told the entire story. In his right hand he held the pale, delicate hand of a young woman. Jim's eyes moved to the operating table.

"Veronica?" he gasped.

He knew his eyes were deceiving him. On the table lay Veronica, in a hospital gown, looking as surprised to see him as he was to see her. He closed his eyes for several seconds. When he opened them he saw a frightened Missy Doyle lying where Veronica had just been.

"Reverend Donovan," Missy exclaimed. "What . . . what are

you doing here?" Almost as an afterthought, she said, "And who's Veronica?"

"Never mind," Jim said. "Get dressed. I'm taking you home."

"No. No Reverend. I can't go home. Daddy'll, Daddy'll . . . I don't know what Daddy'll do to me. But he'll sure enough hurt Tommy something bad, Reverend. Please, don't make me go home."

"You can't make us go," Tommy chimed in. "We got rights."

"Tommy," Jim responded sharply, grabbing Tommy's shirt sleeve to add physical authority to his religious authority, "the only right you've got right now is to figure out how to stay out of jail and how to stay out of Frank Doyle's line of fire."

"But Reverend, I can't have no baby now," Missy said through her tears, her voice trembling. "I don't know how to take care of a baby. I ain't even finished high school yet. What am I going to do with a baby?"

He could see that Missy was truly frightened at the prospect of having this baby. And the fear was enough to make her do something she believed was wrong and that he knew would come back to haunt her some day. He wondered if Veronica had any fear during her abortion, and whether it haunted her now. He hoped so. He walked over to Missy and took her hand gently in his.

"Missy," he said, "I know the thought of having this baby is scaring you to death. And I know you're scared of what your parents are going to do too. I can't promise you that things are going to be easy. But your parents are good, God fearing folks. And so are you. What I can promise you is that they'll come around and support you in having this baby and taking care of it. Now I don't know what plans the two of you may have had for the future with each other. And I don't even know if a future with each other is the right thing for you. What I do know is that you're both going to be parents to this child and that's going to tie the two of you together one way or another for a long time. Missy, that's not going to make your daddy too happy, but that's the way it is and you have to find some way to work that out with him. So, get up and get dressed. We're going home. And when we get there we're all going to sit down and figure this out. Okay?"

Missy, sniffling, looked up at Tommy and then back at Jim.

"Okay," she said softly.

"Okay," Tommy echoed.

Jim turned and looked at the doctor. "Doctor, I'd suggest that you get out of here as quickly as you can."

"I hope you know what you're doing," the doctor responded.

"I know exactly what I'm doing," Jim said. "Oh, and give them back their money."

He knew that even though he had reached them in time to prevent the abortion, they could probably still have the doctor arrested. The thought appealed to him. For a moment it seemed that that could even the score with Veronica, and the doctor who had taken his child's life. He knew that it was a desire for vengeance he was feeling. And the thought of having his vengeance felt good. He watched as the doctor handed Tommy a wad of bills and as Missy came out from behind a changing curtain, dressed now, and leaned into Tommy's waiting arm. Vengeance seemed no longer important. He had saved a life. For now, that was enough.

The Chief and Jim returned Missy home after dropping Tommy off at his house. Clara Doyle was ecstatic to see her daughter home and safe. Frank was angry, but subdued in the presence of the police chief and minister. Jim knew that it would be difficult for Frank to come to terms with Missy's pregnancy and her desire to continue a relationship with Tommy Nobles. But now that there was going to be a baby, they would have to find some way to co-exist.

Jim suggested to the Doyles that they have a meeting with him and Mrs. Nobles, as well as Tommy and Missy, at the church the next morning to discuss how they would handle the situation. As he expected, Frank was, at first, resistant to the idea. With Jim's gentle persuasion, and plenty of tears from Clara, Frank relented. They agreed to meet at nine o'clock the next morning.

Jim and Chief Bruener then drove over to Ginny Nobles' house a few blocks away. They presented Jim's offer which she readily accepted. She and Tommy too would be at the church the next morning.

As they walked out of the Nobles house Charlie Bruener heaved a sigh of relief. "Jim," he said, "I'd sure like to thank you for all you've done to help us today. I think this thing could have blowed up something serious if it wasn't for you."

"I'm sure you could have handled it just fine, Charlie. Maybe I just helped to speed things along a bit."

"Weren't you supposed to be going on some sort of trip today?" the Chief asked.

Jim looked at his watch. It was six-thirty.

"Yeah. But I guess it'll just have to wait until tomorrow."

"Can I give you a lift back to your car at the Doyle place?" the Chief offered.

"No. I think I'll walk. I could use the exercise."

"Okay Reverend. Thanks again. If I don't see you before you leave tomorrow, have a good trip and I'll see you next week."

"Thanks Charlie."

Chief Bruener got in his cruiser and drove off. Jim turned left towards the Doyles' street and began walking. Along the way he stopped at Mel's Texaco to use the pay phone. He took his wallet out of his back pocket and pulled a slip of paper out from between his driver's license and his voter's registration card. On it was written a phone number with a 252 area code and a credit card number. The credit card number was registered to Sandra Chievers. Using the credit card he placed a call to the long distance number. The phone rang.

"Hello?"

Hearing the voice on the other end immediately excited him.

"Sandra, it's me," he said, keeping his voice low in case there was anyone near enough the closed station to hear him.

"Hi baby," she said. Her expectation was clearly audible in her voice. "Where are you? I'm getting all goose-bumpy waiting for you."

"I'm sorry, Sandra. Something came up and . . ."

"You're not coming?" she shrieked, horror-stricken, into the phone.

"No. No. I'm coming. But it won't be until tomorrow. Probably not until tomorrow night."

"Oh Jimmy, I don't want to be alone another night."

It was the first time in a very long time that anyone had called him Jimmy. And suddenly, he felt like an awkward teenager again.

"I'm sorry, Sandra. There's nothing I can do about it. I've got to go now. I'll be there as soon as I can."

"Okay," she said, slipping into a temptress tone. "I guess I'll just have to be *extra* special for you to make up for lost time. Sooner you get here . . ."

"I'll be there as fast as I can. I promise."

"Till tomorrow then."

He heard a kiss over the phone. He returned it.

"See you tomorrow," he said, and hung up the phone. He walked the rest of the way to the Doyle house, retrieved his car and drove home.

Renee and the girls were happy to see him and even happier that his trip would be delayed another day. Jim was disappointed, but he didn't allow it to show. After putting the twins to bed, Renee surprised him by leading him into the bedroom and undressing. They made quiet, tender love and drifted off to sleep.

The next day's meeting with the Doyles and Nobles lasted three hours. The first hour was spent letting Frank Doyle vent his spleen and then calming him down. He finally accepted that Missy was pregnant and was going to have a child, his grandchild. Accepting Tommy Nobles' role in it or his future role as the child's father was much more difficult.

While marriage was discussed, Tommy shied away from it saying he didn't think either he or Missy was ready for it. While that was true, Jim knew that Tommy was not being altruistic. It was clear to Jim that if Tommy had his choice he would have just walked away from Missy and the whole situation, just as Frank Doyle would have expected. But, at least for now, that was not an option.

Missy, for her part, was madly in love with Tommy and wanted to marry him immediately. But Frank would have none of that. So, given Tommy's and Frank's concurring positions, for different reasons, it was agreed that the kids would not get married yet.

The final solution, facilitated by Jim's skillful mediation, was that Missy would have the baby and return to school. Clara would watch the child while Missy was in school. Tommy would pay fifty dollars a week to begin with to help support the baby and could visit with Missy and the baby any time he wanted. And when Missy graduated from high school, they would discuss marriage.

After the meeting Frank Doyle let Jim know that the only reason he accepted this arrangement was that he knew Tommy Nobles would be nowhere to be found come Missy's graduation from high school.

He even doubted that he'd see much of Tommy Nobles visiting Missy or the baby. Jim suspected as much himself. But for now, Missy's and the baby's needs would be met and there would be peace within and among the families. This, he felt, was an acceptable resolution to a situation that had almost resulted in the killings of a teenage boy, a pseudo-doctor and a pre-born child. He especially felt a strong sense of relief and self-satisfaction at having been able to prevent the abortion, something he had long ago been unable to do when it had mattered so much to him.

Having accomplished a great deal in the last two days, not to mention the last several years, to bring peace of mind and serenity to others, it was time, he thought, to do something for Jim Donovan.

Chapter 9

"I'm sorry your trip was delayed," Renee said as she kissed Jim at their front door.

"No you're not," he said between kisses.

"You're right. I'm not. Even though you were gone most of yesterday chasing Missy Doyle, I had you all to myself last night. One less night for me to be without you."

She kissed him passionately, enough so that he considered delaying his departure long enough to take her upstairs for some quick afternoon delight. But the twins had said their good-byes and were down for a quick nap and it would make leaving that much more difficult if they were awakened before he left.

"So," he said, his arms wrapped around the middle of Renee's back, "what are you going to do today."

"Take the girls shopping," she said, "if you ever get out of here."

They kissed again.

"If you're going to go, go," she said, smacking him playfully on the butt.

After one more quick kiss, he picked up his travel bag, walked out the front door, went down the steps, got into his car and, waving to Renee as she stood on their front porch, pulled out of the driveway and drove off. In about half an hour he approached the Interstate 20 interchange. The large green directional sign read "I-20 WEST, TO COLUMBIA" and "I-20 EAST, TO FLORENCE." Jim turned his LeBaron onto the interstate and headed east.

Norma Hutchins' eyes slowly opened. She was surprised to find herself sitting in her rocker in the sitting room, rather than lying in bed. Then she remembered the dream. *No, it wasn't a dream*, she thought. *A vision? A premonition?* Anyway, she realized that she must have fallen asleep in her chair for awhile.

She looked at the clock on the mantel above the fireplace. It was across the darkened room from her. Despite her eighty-two years, Norma Hutchins had uncharacteristically maintained excellent eyesight.

The clock read one thirty, precisely the time it read when she had first entered her sitting room to drink her tea.

How can that be? she thought. *Well, it must be one thirty A.M.*

She pulled herself out of her rocker and walked over to the window to the left of the fireplace. She pulled back the curtains. Daylight streamed in.

My goodness, she thought, confused.

She felt something on the back of her right leg. She turned and looked down to see Cat standing on its hind legs with its front paws on the back of her leg. It began kneading on Norma's leg as it looked up at her.

"Dear, dear Cat. What could you possibly want . . ."

Then it struck her. It must be Monday. That's why the clock reads one-thirty again. And Cat—Cat is begging for food because she hasn't had any today.

She walked slowly back to the rocker to retrieve her cane. She took it in her right hand and leaned on it slightly. She looked down at her feline companion who had followed her and was looking plaintively up at her.

"Cat," she said, "how . . . how could I have slept a whole day just sitting on that rocker?"

She walked out into the hallway and towards the kitchen. Cat pranced expectantly before her.

"I must get to Reverend Donovan, Cat, before he leaves on his trip. He mustn't go. He just mustn't go."

She moved quickly to the phone that sat on a small table just before the entrance to the kitchen. She punched the number for the church office as quickly as her arthritic fingers allowed.

"I hope we're not too late, Cat."

The phone rang four times. Then she heard Reverend Donovan's voice.

"Hello. You have reached the Paradise Community Christian Church. We're sorry we can't take your call right now . . ."

"Durn," she said, hanging up on the answering machine.

She thought for a moment. Then she picked up her small blue address book from beside the phone. Her aching fingers slid to the tab marked "D" and opened to that page. She went to the name "Donovan, Rev. James," which she had entered upon his arrival in Paradise. Under the name was a phone number.

"Maybe I can catch him at home," she said to Cat, who had laid down next to her, as she dialed Reverend Donovan's home number.

The phone rang three, four, five . . . eight times. There was no answer, and no taped greeting inviting her to leave a message. She looked down at Cat.

"It's too late, Cat. He's gone. I fear for him."

Suddenly, she realized she was very hungry. She hadn't eaten in over a day. She went into the kitchen and pulled a glass bowl half-filled with potato salad out of the refrigerator. She put some on a plate. Before sitting down to eat, she put food in Cat's empty dish and set it down in its place on the floor.

As she sat at her kitchen table, eating slowly, she tried to recapture in her mind what she had experienced, to make as much sense of it as possible. But she couldn't remember any of the details. All she knew now was what had been left with her—the feelings, the emotions, the sense of what she had experienced.

Evil, she thought. *Evil is with Reverend Donovan. Within him? Stalking him?* She didn't know. She only knew it was with him, and that it meant danger for him and for all around him.

She finished her potato salad. She put her plate in the sink. Cat was now lying on the kitchen floor against the cabinets next to the stove.

"I'll talk to the Chief," Norma said to her seemingly uninterested friend. "He's likely to know where Reverend Donovan is, or at least how to get a hold of him."

She walked back to her chair to retrieve her cane.

"I always knew there was something about that man" she said as she walked slowly towards the phone. "Couldn't put my finger on it.

Nothing he ever did. There was just this . . . this aura about him. A negative aura. Know what I mean, Cat?"

Cat meowed, not bothering to move any part of its body except its mouth. Norma took that as agreement.

She had reached the phone. Before she could lift the receiver to dial Chief Bruener's number, intense fatigue overtook her. *Must be from sitting in that durn rocker for so long,* she thought.

"I'm going to take a little nap," she called out to Cat, who still hadn't moved from its spot in the kitchen. "A little nap. Then I'll call the Chief."

She slowly worked her way up the stairs to her bedroom. She knew she should get a one-story house. But she just couldn't let go of the memories of this, her home. She walked into her bedroom and without changing her clothes or turning down the bedspread, she laid down and closed her eyes.

It wasn't long before Jim had reached I-95 and turned north. Already the drive was becoming tedious. He had always hated long drives on the interstates. Not only did it deprive you of seeing the real America, he felt, but they, along with their modern technological counterparts of fax machines, cell phones and personal computers, simply added fuel to the ever increasing speed at which individuals hurtled through their lives, giving little time or thought to the need to contemplate, to relax, to just take your time getting from one place to another, answering a call or replying to a letter or, more and more often, an email.

Besides, the monotony of driving on the interstates, each of which looked just like all the others, with their huge billboards announcing the Shoney's coming up at the next exit, or the Days Inn at the second exit, EZ Off, EZ On, and the series of blue interstate information signs which always seemed to come in threes approaching each exit informing you of some of the lodging, food and gas coming up (he always wondered how certain establishments got their places on these signs—how much did they pay for them?), was hypnotic, and required him to constantly fight off the inevitable drowsiness that would overtake him. That was unacceptable on this trip, for he had a schedule to keep, and he was already a day behind.

As he drove north on I-95, keeping up with the flow of traffic which easily exceeded the posted speed limit by at least ten miles an hour, Jim struggled to keep his eyes from fixating on the road ahead. He moved them from one side of the road to the other, reading every sign, noting every farm animal grazing; every abandoned store or garage adjacent to the interstate made obsolete by its loss of access to the traveling public; every house within earshot of the roaring trucks speeding down the highway which, at night, must be as troublesome to the inhabitants as living directly at the end of an airport runway; every building and landmark that observing or thinking about could keep his mind active so as to fend off the alluring welcome of sleep.

He crossed the Little Pee Dee River and though he was tired, he passed the tacky South of the Border exit at the South Carolina— North Carolina border without stopping. Its garish Mexican-style buildings housing cheesy looking motels, restaurants, gift shops and gas stations, had absolutely nothing to do with either of the Carolinas. And the series of infernal billboards designed to lure travelers to the outpost through the use of a figure named Pedro making very bad puns in fractured Spanglish, actually offended him. How, he wondered, could any local zoning authority have allowed it.

He continued on. As he did, his mind wandered, sometimes remembering things and people past, sometimes daydreaming, imagining things to come as he would have them be. Sometimes the memories were good. Sometimes, they weren't.

Drowsiness began to overtake him. He decided it was time to fill up with gas and get some coffee. He got off at the next exit, turned left onto the overpass over the interstate and, at the next left, turned again onto a road extending about fifty yards to a Citgo station and convenience store. Unlike many other interstate exits this one didn't have several gas stations, convenience stores and motels. This was the only station on an otherwise lonely stretch of road.

There were two pump islands, both of which were labeled Self Serve. He pulled next to the inside island, nearest the store, with the pumps between his car and the store. As he got out of his car to pump his gas, he barely noticed the two vehicles on the other side of the pumps at the outside island. One was an old, weather-beaten Chevy pickup with a Confederate flag decal on the rear window and a bumper sticker that read "They'll take my gun only from my cold, dead fingers." The other, right behind it, was a relatively recent, nondescript Ford Taurus.

Jim pumped his gas and went into the store to get his coffee and pay for his fill-up. As he left the store and headed towards his car, he heard the sounds of two men yelling and cursing at each other. It was coming from the vicinity of the outside island where the pickup and the Taurus were still located.

"Who do you think you are, you fucking old man, blowing your horn at me like that?" This sounded like the voice of a relatively young man, maybe late teens or early twenties, best Jim could tell.

"You were blocking both sets of pumps," answered the other, in a loud but obviously shaken voice. "I was just trying to get your attention for you to move up a bit so my car could reach the pumps too."

"What's your fucking hurry, old man? Don't like having to wait for some redneck to fill his old truck before y'all can fill up your nice, new car?"

Jim could see the two men now, standing at the pumps where the two vehicles came together. They were just an inch or so apart. In the passenger seat of the Taurus sat a woman, obviously frightened for her husband, who was at least forty years older than his aggressive accoster and clearly no match for him in any type of physical confrontation. The old man was trying to avoid the whole unpleasant scene, but the younger man, smaller but obviously much more powerful physically, gave no indication of allowing the matter to be resolved peacefully.

"Look," said the older man, "why don't I just move my car to the other side of the island and we can both pump our gas at the same time?" The old man was trying to use logic to extricate himself from the escalating confrontation. The younger man was having none of that.

"You goddam Yankees just come down here and figure you all can just push us around, tell us to get out of your way, and we can't do nothing about it! Well old man, you ain't pushing this fucking rebel around!"

With that, the younger man pulled out a hunting knife with what appeared to be about a nine inch blade and placed it at the older man's throat. The old man's wife screamed.

"Now what are you going to do, old man?" the younger man said in a low, guttural, threatening voice.

Jim could see the abject fear on the faces of the older man and his wife. He didn't know whether the younger man's threat was real or part of a macho game, but he decided he couldn't wait any longer to find out.

"Is there some kind of problem here?" he said as he approached the tense scene at the outer island. "Perhaps I can be of some help. I'm a minister and I'm sure there's some way . . ."

At this point he had just reached the gas pumps when the younger man whirled and, with lightning speed, placed the point of the knife at Jim's throat.

"You just stay out of this, fucking Billy Graham," the younger man sneered as he pressed the point of the knife against Jim's throat with obvious bad intentions.

Jim remained motionless and silent. He fixed his gaze into the burning eyes of his angry assailant. As he continued his silent, steady stare, the young man couldn't avert his eyes, try as he might.

Jim had always preached that within every person, no matter how badly they have acted in their lives, there is good, and that within every person there is a soul desirous and worthy of redemption. He approached every situation and every individual with that principle in mind. So had he approached this situation and this particular angry young man. But as he looked deep into the young man's eyes, as he sought to peer into his soul to draw out the good within, there was, at first, nothing—a hollowness and emptiness that Jim had never before experienced in his dealings with another person. Soon the emptiness began to fill, but not with goodness from a soul seeking redemption. Instead, with . . . at first he couldn't identify it, at least not as anything he had ever directly experienced in quite this way. Then, horror-stricken, he knew. The emptiness was filling with evil, pure evil; evil which doesn't operate subtly or surreptitiously through temptation and false prophecy which takes time to corrupt the mind and soul, but total and direct evil which, once it finds an appropriate host, is capable of immediate and immense destruction of all that it sets its sights on.

As Jim remained set on them, the young man's eyes had gone from being full of life, angry as they were, to completely vacant. Now they were filling again, not with life, but a fiery darkness. Jim was filled with deep foreboding. He was being challenged, his faith was being challenged, in a way unlike any before. In this moment he understood clearly that anything less than a full belief in himself and God, and in God's ability to provide him with whatever tools he needed to defeat this evil, would result in his defeat, his destruction and the destruction of the old man to whose aid he had come.

He called on God. He knew deep within that the only weapon he had was his faith in God, and he called upon it. His eyes remained fixed on the warring pupils before him. To look away now would mean defeat. It was no longer him against the young man, but what was within him against what was within the young man. They were now only the vessels of the mighty struggle going on. They were no longer the principals.

They were both oblivious to their surroundings. The old man and his wife remained frozen, transfixed by the spectacle of a staring match which, while silent to them, held within it a raging war more explosive and dangerous than anything the old man had experienced in two wars. If Jim could have taken a chance on diverting his gaze, even for a moment, he would have urged the elderly couple to leave, as quickly and as far away as they could. But if he did, he knew that they could never move fast or far enough.

Jim began to sense a dank, cold sensation overtaking the young man. It was as if he was trapped in an underground sewer with no way out. Jim could sense the man's humanness returning. Time seemed to stand still for the young man now and Jim could feel an immense fear and foreboding overtaking him. Jim was feeling everything he was feeling. The young man wanted to run, but his legs wouldn't move. He tried to scream, but no sound could escape his throat. His heart beat so fast that he was certain it would explode at any moment.

At just the moment that the young man was certain he was breathing his last breath, Jim's grip on him was released. What Jim saw in his eyes now was not the evil, but the fear. Was it the young man's fear of him, or evil's fear of what had faced it down? Jim didn't know. For now, it was enough that the danger had seemed to pass.

"Why don't you just get in your truck and go home now, son?" he said softly to the young man.

The young man said nothing. He returned to his truck, got in and drove away, never glancing at his previous prey or the man who had backed him down.

"Thank you," the elderly man said coming over to Jim and shaking his hand ferociously. "Thank you so much. You saved our lives. I'm sure of it."

"Thank God," the man's wife cried gratefully. "Thank the Lord for sending you to us."

"Is there anything we can do for you Reverend?" the man asked. "We owe you so much. How about a donation to your church?" The old man began to reach for his wallet.

"No. Nothing," insisted Jim. He was still shaken, and just wanted to be on his way quickly. "Just put a little extra in your church's collection plate the next time you're there. It all goes to the same God."

"Yes," said the man. "Yes it does. We'll do that. We'll sure do that."

"Good. Go with peace, and God bless."

Jim returned to his car. As he went to open the car door, he realized that he still held in his right hand the cup of hot coffee he had bought. He switched it to his left hand, opened the car door with his right, climbed in and drove off. What the old man and his wife didn't know was that the brave young minister who had just come to their rescue had experienced something much more dangerous and fearful than the mere threat of being robbed, beaten or even killed.

He managed to negotiate the balance of the I-95 portion of his trip without falling asleep at the wheel. By the time he reached the Rocky Mount, U.S. 64 exit, he was grateful for the opportunity to be off the interstate. He pulled off at the exit and headed east toward the Outer Banks.

The first fifty miles or so of U.S. 64 was much like I-95, but without the billboards, the interchange motels and convenience stops. He could tell by the newness of the construction that not long before, the entire one hundred fifty mile stretch from Rocky Mount to the coast had probably been a winding, two lane road through the small farm towns bearing names like Everetts, Jamesville, Plymouth and Pleasant Grove that reflected the roots of the British settlers who had braved the hostile elements of a new world to establish a colonial foothold in the Carolinas. Others, such as Scuppernong, were named not for people or after British towns, but to reflect the local culture—in its case a town and nearby river named after the yellowish-green grape which was first cultivated in that area of North Carolina.

There was now a bypass project which, when completed, would take most travelers more directly to the Outer Banks without going through the towns themselves. It would certainly save travel time. Just as certainly, it would take away from the charm of driving through the real America.

Jim bemoaned the loss of this charm—driving through the small villages, past the small churches, most often Baptist in this part of the country, with their adjoining cemeteries hosting only a relatively few headstones; the small stores bearing simple names like "The Country Store" with barrels of seed on the floor and corncob pipes hanging on the wall; the sudden drops in the speed limit from a highway speed of forty-five or fifty-five to twenty-five miles an hour with the ever-present threat of being caught in a small town speed trap (which had never happened to him, perhaps leading to his view that this was one of small town America's charms); the wood frame houses, rockers on the front porch, with adjoining modest fields of tobacco, corn, green beans or peanuts. Yes, Jim bemoaned the loss of this part of Americana, but he stayed on the bypass. On this day, he was in a hurry.

The next couple of hours of the drive were uneventful. As he drove, his mind kept wandering back to the confrontation at the gas station. The entire episode had been intense, but he was particularly struck by the intensity of what he felt coming from within the young man. He had identified it at the time as evil, and evil it was. But as he looked back on it he tried to identify its parts more specifically, tried to put it into terms he could understand and more easily recognize. It certainly contained all of the negative human emotions—anger, hatred, bitterness, resentment, envy, jealousy, pain, and the rest. Perhaps that is what made it unique. Perhaps the combination of all of these negative human emotions in one person at one time was what created the strength and intensity of the evil he felt and experienced in that young man.

He certainly understood their destructive qualities. Anger and bitterness had visited him and, unfortunately, had directed his life more often than he cared to acknowledge, even to himself. As he thought back on the I-95 incident, he realized that the most frightening aspect of it all was that that young man could have been him. He began to wonder, what had happened in that young man's life to make him such a ready vessel for evil? Had he too been betrayed by someone he loved and trusted? Had he too been overcome with guilt by participating in an innocent person's death? Had he been subjected to other untold horrors and abuses unlike anything Jim had experienced in his own life? And whatever that young man had experienced, wasn't there anyone in his life who could have helped him, who could have demonstrated to him that there was someone who cared for him, someone who would always be there for him, someone to show him that there is a better way? Wasn't there anyone in that young man's life who, when he needed it most, could have shown him that there is a God, and that by putting his faith in God he could overcome the pain and the anger that life had visited upon him?

He couldn't help but wonder about that young man, about how things might have been different for him had he found that one person, or how they might still be different if that one person could find him soon. He prayed for that young man. He prayed that someone would come into that young man's life before it was too late—as Renee had come into Jim's life just in time to pull him back from the edge of his own abyss.

He prayed for that young man. And he prayed for himself—that someone, or something, would come into his life soon, as Renee once had, to pull him back from the edge of his new abyss.

Chapter 10

Jim's stomach growled again. It had been growling now for over an hour. He was approaching the town of Columbia, North Carolina, on the Scuppernong River. He only had about forty or forty-five miles left to go. But his hunger had grown intense. He couldn't recall ever being this hungry before. He would just have to stop for a quick bite to eat.

He thought of finding a McDonald's or Hardee's, but even his haste didn't seem to warrant abusing his body to that extent. He would look for something small and simple, and quick. He turned off Route 64 and started driving toward what the signs indicated was the direction of the center of town. Almost immediately he saw a small diner. Home-style cooking and quick service, he hoped. He parallel parked on the street just down from the diner and went in.

The diner had a lunch counter and no more than eight tables. About half of them were occupied, all by what appeared to be local folk. He figured they probably saw more out-of-towners like him on the weekends when travel to and from the Outer Banks was greatest.

He was greeted by a large, middle-aged woman wearing a large smile and a name tag that read "Bessie."

"Howdy!" she said. "One for dinner?"

"Yes. And could you let my server know I'm in a bit of a hurry?"

"Sure honey. We'll take good care of you." As she seated him she turned towards the lunch counter, which stood in front of the open kitchen, and shouted out, "Donna! Gentleman's in a hurry. Let's help him out, okay dear?"

"Sure thing Bessie," he heard a young woman's voice answer. "Be right there."

As he looked at the menu that Bessie had handed him he began to feel a strange uneasiness. It wasn't anything physical. It was nothing he could put his finger on or describe. Something just didn't feel right.

"What'll you have?"

He looked up to see a gum chewing young waitress, no more than twenty or twenty-one, waiting pen in hand to take his order. There was something oddly familiar about her, but he was certain he had never met her before.

"What do you recommend that's good and quick?" he asked.

"That's a loaded question, honey." She smiled enticingly. Jim turned his head and buried his eyes back in the menu.

"Whatever you want is good," she went on. "Items one, two, five and the special—meat loaf and mashed potatoes—are the quickest."

"I'll have the special, thanks," he said, looking back up at her.

"Anything to drink?"

"Yeah. Iced tea please."

"Sweetened or unsweetened?"

"Sweetened."

"Okay. Be right up."

She took the menu from Jim and smiled, slyly he thought. As she walked back toward the kitchen, he noticed a certain swagger in her gait. Her tone with him had been saucy, even somewhat condescending. The feeling that he somehow knew this girl grew stronger, and uncomfortable. But he couldn't place it.

His dinner was brought to him within a matter of minutes. It was surprisingly hot and tasty considering that, being the special, it was probably pre-prepared. Donna—that's the name he remembered the hostess had called out—served him without speaking to him, all the while looking at him intently as if he was someone she knew, and didn't like. His uneasiness grew. He ate quickly and asked for his check. She tore it off her pad and laid it on the table next to him. Throughout, her demeanor remained constant.

The entire bill came to just under eight dollars. He pulled two dollars out of his wallet and laid them on the table. *Strange*, he thought as he walked up to the cash register, *I've never left a twenty-five percent tip before.*

"Everything all right?" Bessie, who was manning the cash register, asked him cheerfully.

"Yes. Yes. Everything was fine."

Jim handed her a ten dollar bill.

"Good," she said as she handed him his change. "Y'all come back now."

"Yes. I will. Thank you."

Jim turned to walk out the door. As he did he had a strong sensation that he was being watched. He turned and looked back towards the lunch counter. He saw Donna, his young waitress, one bun on a stool, one leg on the floor and the other leg dangling, swinging to and fro. She was watching him intently. He felt a slight shudder. He turned back to the door and started to walk out. But there was just something about that girl. He turned to look at her again. There was a smile on her face, but it wasn't a friendly smile. It was . . . almost a sneer. That was it, he thought. A sneer. But why? Why would this waitress he didn't know, who he had just given a twenty-five percent tip to for crying out loud, be sneering at him?

Paranoia, he thought. *Too many strange things, hurtful things—causing me to imagine, fear anything, everything. Turn your head away, Jim Donovan, now. Time to go.*

As he tried to follow his own orders, his eyes were drawn to the young girl's chest. The top three buttons of her uniform blouse were undone—something which, if they had been that way all along, he hadn't noticed. She put her right hand inside the blouse and scratched the top part of her left breast just above the now visible bra line. He knew he was staring, and he knew that she knew, but he couldn't take his eyes off of her. There didn't appear to be anyone else in the restaurant now other than the two of them. He looked at her face and the sly, sneering smile remained. His eyes moved back down to her chest. Her fingers were now slipped under her left bra cup. She slowly pulled the cup up revealing, on the inside of her lower left breast, a tattoo—a black circle with a snake's head in the center, mouth open and fangs bared, ready to strike.

Oh my God! Melanie! he cried out to himself silently. *It can't be!*

He looked at her face again. It wasn't Melanie's face. But there was something . . . something eerily familiar. Her smile was now the same wicked smile Melanie had given him the night she tried to seduce him. The same tattoo, on the same breast, and the same lack of shame in baring it. *Christ,* he thought, *she's even about the same age Melanie would be now.*

He couldn't stop staring at her, wondering, confused. Then, she winked at him, threw her head back and laughed, got off the stool in a way clearly intended to give him the beaver shot he couldn't miss, and sashayed back into the kitchen.

He stood there, transfixed on the counter stool. The picture of Melanie, naked and coming on to him, burned into his consciousness, followed by the image of her parents hacked to death a few weeks later. Other images started to flash into his head. Katie. Veronica. Africa. The young man at the service station. Every negative thing that had ever happened to him, every wrong thing he had ever done, all jumbled together in a swirl of intertwined thoughts and feelings of hopelessness, guilt and fear.

I'm really a mess, he thought. *I've got to get out of here. Maybe I should just go home.*

"Excuse me! Excuse me!"

The loud voice came from behind him. It startled him out of his semi-catatonic state. He felt the door, which he had been holding partially open, being pulled away from him.

"Mister! Are you coming in or going out?" the voice insisted.

Jim turned to see two middle-aged women trying to get into the diner through the only entrance, which he happened to be obstructing. He stepped back and held the door open for them.

"I'm very sorry ladies," he said, embarrassed.

"Well you should be," one of the ladies said with a huff as they walked through the open door.

He was tempted to look back one more time, but he didn't. There was obviously a connection of some sort between Donna and Melanie, but he wasn't going to stick around to find out what it was. He had too much going on in his life and his mind that he had to figure out to be dealing with a ghost, or ghosts, from the past. At least he hoped it was the past.

The warm summer air touched his skin as he walked toward his car.

I really should go home, he thought. *Someone's trying to tell me something.*

He got in the car, put the key in the ignition and turned it. As the engine hummed smoothly, he looked out his window in the direction of Nags Head. Thoughts of Sandra began to crowd out everything else in his mind.

She's only an hour or so away. I've come this far.

Everything else was gone now. Nothing else mattered. He shifted into drive, did a U-turn and headed back to U.S. 64. He turned east.

Chapter 11

Dusk had fallen. The sun had set behind him. Jim approached the long, narrow drawbridge that would carry him over the Alligator River. River seemed a misnomer. According to his road map, this body of water was a finger extending southward from Albermarle Sound and was much wider than what one would expect of a river.

Looking over the guardrail that he was hugging despite being barely within the centerline of the bridge, it appeared that he was no more than ten feet above the water. He passed over two men in a small fishing boat pulling in their lines. They must have had a good enough day, or a bad enough one, Jim thought, that they had lost track of time and would have to race the darkness to the shore. He was now only about forty minutes from Nags Head, and he was beginning to get anxious.

He crossed the Alligator River and entered the Alligator River Natural Wildlife Refuge. He immediately noted the signs cautioning drivers to be on the lookout for bears and red wolves. The road was two lanes. Occasionally there were side roads off to the left. On the right there was nothing but forest and a canal between the trees and the road. A greenish hue on the canal indicated an algae slick on the surface.

Darkness fell. Aside from the light from the rising moon there was no natural or artificial illumination. In fact, it dawned on him that for several minutes he had seen no oncoming headlights nor, for that matter, any approaching from the rear.

Suddenly, from his left, a shadowy form darted out from the

darkness. He instinctively went for his brakes, but it was gone so quickly that even his instincts didn't have time to complete their assigned task. His car, with a momentarily shaken but relieved driver, continued its progress without the slightest interruption.

It remained eerily quiet and isolated. He still was seeing no headlights either ahead of or behind him. Then, just as suddenly as before, but now from his right, he saw another shadowy figure darting out about two hundred feet ahead of him. This time it stopped, right in the middle of his lane. And this time his instincts brought the car to a screeching, rubber-odorous stop.

At the other end of his high beams he could make out the form of a four-legged animal. It was about two to three feet tall, with a slowly wagging, bushy tail. Its body was facing to the north with its head turned at a right angle facing in his direction. He couldn't distinguish any specific features or colors at this distance, but what he could see were two sparkling, glassy white eyes in the reflection of the car's front lamps.

For the second time in a few minutes Jim had been startled by something in the road. This time he could see that there was something there and he needed to be careful not to hit it. He eased off his brakes and allowed the car to move slowly forward in order to get a look at his roadside visitor before it overcame the hypnotic effect of his headlights.

As he got closer he began to make out specific features. At first, it looked like a German Shepherd, but it was larger, with longer legs and a wider head. It was about six feet long and looked like it weighed anywhere from a hundred to a hundred twenty pounds. He finally realized that what stood before him, continuing to maintain its position as he slowly drifted closer and closer, must be a red wolf.

Jim knew red wolves were rare. He certainly had never seen one before. He hoped he could get within a few feet of it before it spooked. The absence of any other traffic on the road seemed to be making it more possible.

Rolling slowly closer he kept his eyes fixated on his visual prey. The wolf didn't move, nor did it avert its gaze from his car. He wondered whether red wolves were as disabled as deer were by a car's headlights.

He inched forward at less than five miles an hour. He moved

within thirty feet. Still, the wolf didn't move. His eyes still fixated on the animal, he suddenly experienced the sensation that its eyes weren't entranced by the headlights. They were fixed on him, on *his* eyes.

He was within twenty feet now. He was beginning to feel strangely uncomfortable and disoriented by this staring contest between man and beast. It certainly was a magnificent looking creature, but he decided that he'd seen enough. It was time to move on. He set out to accelerate and go around the animal leaving it to its habitat. But despite his determination, his body wouldn't do as his mind directed. His eyes remained fixed on the wolf's, and his car continued to slowly inch forward, foot by foot until, quite by instinct, his foot applied the brakes and his hand put the gear in park. His car was no more than a foot or two from the wolf. Still, the animal didn't move.

He didn't know at what point it had happened, but he now noticed that the wolf's eyes, though still in the glare of the shining headlights, were no longer glassy white, and they weren't sparkling. They were now a bright, yet dull—maybe vacant was the right word—red. The color and texture seemed to defy the bright white lights shining directly into them.

Still, the wolf didn't move. It didn't bare its fangs, pant or make any sound. It stared. It just stared, directly (there was no mistaking it now), piercingly into his eyes.

Jim sensed—didn't feel, didn't remember—just sensed, a familiarity with the stare. He searched his mind quickly for information, data, to explain the sensation—silly comparisons with disapproving mother stares and schoolyard bully stares. This was nothing like those. Yet he knew the stare. He knew it from not long ago, but his mind simply couldn't call it up.

It seemed like ten minutes had passed since he stopped. Yet he knew it could have been no more than one. Still, no other cars on the road. Still, the wolf didn't move. Still, the two-legged and four-legged beings' eyes remained fixed, one on the other. It was Jim who was frozen now, trapped in the hypnotic trance of this majestic beast. Trapped. Wanting to move, wanting to escape. Totally incapable.

As he sat there, immobilized, the muscles in his neck began to tighten. He felt a pain begin just below the wing bone on the left side of his back. It radiated up through his shoulder, his neck, and into the base of his skull. Beads of perspiration began to form on his eyebrows, working their way down his eyelids into his eyes. Though the sweat in his eyes burned, his gaze remained fixed, unblinking, on the wolf's dull red eyes.

He broke out in a sweat all over. He felt feverish. It was as if a high fever had broken, but went up instead of down. He was having trouble breathing. He realized that he was in the throes of a full-blown panic attack. Yet he couldn't move. And the wolf chose not to.

Without the slightest idea of what was happening or why, Jim was convinced he was about to die. He thought of Renee and the kids. Who would take care of them? How would they manage? Why wasn't he a better husband and father? He prayed to God for their well-being, that the memory of his strength and his love for them would sustain them in his absence and in their sorrow, that Renee would find a way to provide for Carly and Jessie. He thought of how unfair it was that he would never see his girls grow, never see them in their prom dresses, never give them away at their weddings, never play with his grandchildren. Then, in what he was convinced were his last moments on earth, his thoughts turned to Nags Head and the purpose of his trip. He thought of the lost opportunity. And then he felt shame.

At just that moment, the attack dissipated, more quickly than it had struck. He no longer felt feverish. The sweating stopped. His neck muscles relaxed and the pain disappeared. He sensed that he once again had control of his car and, more importantly, himself. While his gaze had remained fixed on the wolf, he had stopped seeing it while he was in what he had believed were his death throes. As he refocused on it, the wild canine's head turned slowly to the north. In no particular hurry, it ambled across the road and disappeared into the darkness.

Jim gathered his wits. He shifted into drive and quickly accelerated to sixty-five, damn the speed limit. It was time, he thought, to get the hell out of Alligator River National Wildlife Refuge, and as fast as possible. A stiff breeze disturbed the dead calm that had languished over the scene. A car's headlights approached him from the opposite direction. As he sped away from the spot of his terrifying encounter, he thought he heard a voice whisper in the wind—

"Fuckin' Billy Graham."

Chapter 12

Traffic had returned to U.S. 64. As he continued on his way, Jim was still shaken and frightened by his encounter with the red wolf. In fact, the entire trip had been surreal. He wondered how it was that fate had stepped in in the form of the delay caused by his having to deal with Missy Doyle's near abortion the day before. But for that, he would have been on the road Sunday and wouldn't have had the threatening showdown on I-95 or the encounter with the wolf. *Probably wouldn't have eaten in that Twilight Zone of a diner either,* he thought.

He was shaken all right. All three incidents seemed connected somehow. No way it could be chalked up to coincidence or just bad luck. Something was going on. But he was tired. Too tired to analyze it, to put the pieces of the puzzle together. Too tired to figure it out. Or maybe he just didn't want to, he admitted to himself. Too tired to even figure that out, he thought as he struggled to keep his heavy eyelids open as he drove along. He longed to reach his destination, desperate for the comfort and reassurance of a gin and tonic, and a soothing voice. He prayed for a speedy and uneventful end to his journey.

Soon he was entering Manteo on Roanoke Island. As he looked at the town's welcoming sign he seemed to remember that some celebrity lived here. Andy Griffith maybe? *Doesn't matter,* he thought. *Just keep driving. Almost there.*

As he drove through the quaint town, past *The Elizabethan Gardens, The Weeping Radish Brewery, The Silver Bonsai, The Christmas Shop,* and the numerous other indigenous restaurants, inns and shops which, interspersed with the ubiquitous and ever present fast food chains, lined U.S. 64 as it passed through Manteo, he bemoaned the fact that the child-like enthusiasm with which he had begun this holiday had been all but sucked out of him by his strange encounters—just as surely, he thought, as the violent spirals of a great Midwestern twister suck the air, contents and people out of the homes unfortunate enough to intersect their random paths. *Random?* he wondered. *Do natural disasters pick their victims randomly? Is anything random?*

As he drove on his fear of the wolf receded—*proof of the power of prayer,* he thought—and was relegated to the "explainable phenomena" compartment of his mind. It had simply been the product of the coincidental confluence of otherwise unconnected elements— the dark and solitary surroundings, his fatigue from the long drive and his first experience observing this unique and unusual creature. And the redneck was just that, a redneck bully he had had to stand down. And the waitress? Just a snotty kid who happened to have the same tattoo as Melanie. Probably can get it at any tattoo parlor. *Yes, coincidence,* he thought. *And yes, there is randomness in events. Not every little thing is foreordained. Sometimes things just happen.*

This heightened level of awareness removed the fear. For this he was grateful. Yet, as he approached the Washington Baum Bridge which would take him over Roanoke Sound and into Nags Head, he cursed the series of events, and the lateness of the hour, which had soured his mood.

He entered Nags Head and drove directly to Old Oregon Inlet Road, the southern extension of the beach road. He turned south. Along this stretch of the road the only commercial activities he saw were two hotels and a fishing pier. Both sides of the road were dominated by single and multi-family vacation homes and cottages, all made of wood. He could tell there were various colors. But it was night now, and their silhouettes appeared only as various shades of gray. They were all built on stilts. Jim guessed that such construction was required to provide protection from the storm surges and flooding that surely accompanied the hurricanes, tropical storms and Nor'easters that seemed to regularly visit the Outer Banks of North Carolina.

Driving down Old Oregon Inlet, he strained to see the roadside mile markers. Sandra had warned him that the mile markers are much more significant than street names or addresses in finding one's way around the Outer Banks, and he was looking for the right one. As he passed the eighteen-mile marker his mood began to lighten once again at the thought that he was only minutes away from the house he would call home for the rest of the week.

Looking hard, he finally saw the sign he was looking for—Elysian Way. *How apropos,* he thought. He turned left. The street ended at the beach. There were several houses of varying sizes on either side of it. He turned into the driveway of the second house from the beach. It appeared to be made of a darker wood than most of the houses he had passed. It bore the address twelve hundred sixty. He pulled his car into the open garage under the house between the pilings that supported the structure on either side. He turned the engine off. He was parked behind a new Buick Regent with South Carolina plates.

The outside porch lights were on. He could see that the ground level open carport included a laundry room and outdoor shower. The front porch above the carport spanned the width of the house. There were stairs at the left of the building that went up from left to right. Once on the porch a wide set of sliding glass doors constituted the home's entrance.

From within the carport he could see stairs at the back of the house heading up towards the left. On the right side of the house was a third set of stairs that went straight up steeply alongside the house. He got out of the car and walked over to the side to see where they led. He saw a landing with a screen door on the left that seemed to go into an enclosed porch area. The stairs then continued upward leading to a high porch. A widow's walk, he figured, though he couldn't really see from where he was. Based on the height of the stairs, it was apparently at or above roof level at the back of the house.

Widow's walk. What a neat name for a balcony, he thought. He just liked the name. Always had, even before meeting the Widow Chievers. They were quite common along the eastern seacoast. In days gone by, New England seafarers in particular would often build them on their houses to give their wives a place from which to watch for their husbands' returning ships and the news as to whether they were still wives, or had become widows.

He was expected, but he had arrived later than planned. He

returned to his car, grabbed his bag and went out into the driveway towards the front stairs. Looking around, he found it curious that the houses on either side of this one were completely dark. There were no cars in the driveways or the carports. They looked unoccupied, which was hard to believe given that late summer was the busiest time of the year for tourist towns like this.

Having completed his initial survey of his new surroundings, Jim began to make his way up the front stairs. When he was halfway up, the front porch light went out. He stopped for a minute to get his bearings in the new darkness. His eyes adjusted and he continued up the stairs. When he reached the sliding glass doors he could see a dim, flickering light being cast from behind the drawn shades. He put the fingers of his left hand in the narrow slot that served as a door handle and tried the door. It was unlocked. He slid the door open and groped the drapes looking for an opening. Realizing it was one piece he reached to his left, found its end and pulled the drape aside.

Before him was a round wooden table that matched the wood of the house. In the middle of the table was a bronze candleholder with a round base. It had a stem going up one side to another smaller round section sitting over the round base, with an amber colored glass in the shape of an upside down bell set into it. In the inverted bell was a lit candle. It was the only light in the room. The flickering candle cast just enough erratically pulsating light to create an atmosphere of warmth and romance.

Behind the table and the candle was a couch. It sat in the middle of the room facing the sliding glass doors. Lying on the couch was a woman. Her head, which was to his left, was tilted slightly, resting on a large cushion. Her long auburn hair radiated out neatly in all directions. Her breasts were barely concealed and were straining to emerge from the low hung neckline of an elegant, blue silk nightgown. Her right leg was fully extended. Her left leg bent slightly upward and over the right, exposing the entire leg and thigh far enough to reveal a smattering of pubic hair. Jim Donovan knew he was in Nirvana, with the most beautiful woman in the world.

Her eyes were longingly expectant. Her thick, sensuous lips moved almost imperceptibly, inviting him, even before joining with her vocal chords to make a sound. Smiling sheepishly, in stark contrast to the anything but sheepish vision she had created for him, she purred, "Hello sweetheart."

His heartbeat accelerated. He imagined his heart pushing out from his chest like in a silly cartoon. Knowing the futility of controlling this most involuntary of muscles, he tried nonetheless. But not for long. He quickly surrendered to all of the senses, emotions and physiological effects that passion inevitably unleashes. He walked over, knelt down next to the couch, put his dry lips on her warm, moist ones, and kissed her a kiss of classic tenderness and desire. When done, he looked lovingly into her shining green eyes. All he could think to say was, "I've missed you so much."

"Mmm. I've missed you too," she said as she ran her hand through his hair. "I thought you'd be here earlier than this."

"It was a long, and strange, trip. I'll tell you about it later."

He kissed her again. He wanted her badly, and he could tell the feeling was mutual. But, despite the overwhelming urges that had overcome him upon entering her seductive lair, the long trip had taken its toll on him. He was afraid that his fatigue would prevent him from performing up to his own expectations, and from meeting hers. But Sandra Chievers showed herself to be a perceptive and sensitive lover.

"Get up," she said.

"Why?"

"Just get up."

He did as he was told. She raised herself up into a sitting position.

"Take your clothes off and lie down," she said.

As he did as he was told, her eyes followed every article of clothing off his body and lingered salaciously on the skin newly exposed. Once fully undressed, he lay down on the couch as she had instructed.

She sat on the edge, her hip nudging his, and began to softly run her fingers up and down his body.

"Sandra," he said, "you've been waiting a long time too and . . ."

"Shh."

Without speaking a word she convinced him that it would be better if she just pleasured him. Being as tired as he was, he welcomed having the pressure taken off of him, though he'd never admit it. He welcomed even more the sensory explosion she brought to his weary mind and body through nothing more than the gentle, skillful use of her hands and mouth.

Norma Hutchins' eyes opened abruptly, with stark terror. Her torso shot up, forgetting that it was 82 years old and racked with arthritis and bursitis.

"Sandra!" she screamed.

It was pitch dark. She fumbled for the light switch of the lamp on her nightstand. She finally found it and painfully switched it on. The old, small alarm clock on the nightstand read eleven forty.

She didn't need to look outside to realize that she had slept for almost another ten hours. But how long she had slept was of no concern to her. What did concern her was why. What, or who, was keeping her from doing anything to find and warn Reverend Donovan. And now, now it was much worse. Now she knew that whatever was shadowing Reverend Donovan somehow involved Sandra. She had seen nothing, heard nothing, dreamt nothing. But when she awoke so abruptly and Sandra's name expelled forcefully from her mouth, she *knew* something. She knew Sandra was in danger.

She had to do something, and do it now. She began to move her legs towards the edge of the bed. But her eyes became very heavy. Fatigue was overtaking her again. She would fight it this time. *I have to contact the Chief,* she thought. *No. Not the Chief. Mrs. Donovan. She's the key. She must know something. She . . .*

Norma Hutchins' eyes closed. She fell into a deep sleep.

Jim gently woke to the soft daylight of the late morning sun tempered by the drawn beige drapes covering the sliding glass doors. He was lying on the couch which had served as the backdrop for Sandra's live portrait, as well as the stage for her one act performance the night before. His left leg was bent up, its bareness confirming what he had sensed in that precise moment of regained consciousness a split second before opening his sleep-filled eyes—that he was naked. His right leg lay flat on the couch separated from the left just enough to create a crevice which formed a perfect fit for a woman's body the precise dimensions of Sandra's. Her head rested on his chest, turned inward toward the back of the couch.

From this position he could survey her entire prone body. His eyes began at the crown of her head, moved down to her mature, yet still youthfully fresh face; along her back to where her negligee clung to her ass so perfectly fitting her cheeks that only the fabric's color betrayed any covering on her skin. He continued slowly, savoring these voyeuristic moments to himself. He glided along her silk-covered legs with healthy thighs of just the right amount of fleshy matter to make anything held between them feel joyously lost in down-like softness and warmth. They ended at feet which were, for the relatively tall woman she was, petite yet proportional, her painted toenails color coordinated with her nightgown.

Jim knew Sandra's true age. She was forty-six, and he reveled in every year it took to create precisely what he now held in his arms. He kept looking at her, admiring her, modulating his breathing to coincide with the slow, regular pattern of hers so as not to risk disturbing the serenity of the moment by waking her. She stirred slightly and cooed softly, a uniquely feminine affectation signaling the beginning of the end of her gentle sleep. He remained still, wanting to draw every ounce of sweetness from this scene.

As he lay there coupled with Sandra, his mind drifted back to the night before. He had been so tired that even as her long, slim fingers had begun to softly finesse his genitals, and even though he achieved an immediate erection, he had trouble staying awake. As first her tongue and then her lips gently stroked him, he felt suspended in an eerily dream-like emulsion. He was half asleep and, at the same time, he was experiencing excruciating sexual arousal. His external body was paralyzed while internally his blood coursed through his veins with such rage that every subcutaneous inch felt unquenchably inflamed. He remembered thinking how much he wanted to come and how much he never wanted it to end. When it did end it was so draining that deep, sound sleep overtook him before his orgasmically arched back dropped lifelessly back to the couch. He didn't move for the rest of the night.

He recalled a dream. Returning home from an outing—what kind of outing he didn't know—he had a strange feeling that something was wrong. He called out Renee's name and got no response. Suddenly he was standing before their bedroom door. He didn't remember having climbed the stairs to get there. The door opened by itself, and before him stood Renee. She was pulling up her jeans. Then she zipped and fastened them. Lying in their bed, under the covers, was a man. Jim didn't recognize the face, but it was someone he knew. Then, again suddenly, he and Renee were in their living room. She was seated stiffly upright in her favorite bonefish white, high-backed chair. He was demanding some kind of explanation from her. Her gaze fixed straight ahead not even acknowledging his presence. She was coldly unresponsive. His frustration at trying to get some sort of response from her turned to anger and pain. Then he began to cry, pleading with her to answer him, to talk to him, to let him know why. She turned her head and looked at him, still cold, still silent. He begged her again and again to talk to him, and to forgive him.

Thinking of the dream upset him. He didn't understand it and it was an unwelcome intrusion on what had otherwise been a morning of pleasant thoughts. Sandra stirred and cooed again. He was brought back to that happier place. The ever so slight movement of her silk garment against his naked skin aroused him and took his mind completely off the dream. She gently, and with obvious intention, pressed her stomach against his erect penis.

"I assume that means you're happy to be here," she slowly murmured, her eyes still closed.

"If only you knew how much," he said as he gently ran his fingers through her long, unkempt, yet somehow perfectly laid out hair. He looked at his watch. It was eleven o'clock.

"I think I know what you want," she purred.

"You think so?"

"Um hmm. But you don't get any today."

"I don't? Why not? I came a long way just for that you know. You think I'd be here otherwise?"

"Don't know. But it doesn't matter." She lifted her head, opened her eyes, and smiled. Her index finger gently stroked his cheek. "No casual sex today, hon. I've got some special plans for tonight. And a day of abstinence will make it that much better. Then we can spend the rest of the week naked if you like."

"No," he said. "I rather enjoy the way you package yourself, and the thrill of unwrapping the gift."

She put on her most fetching face and her voice became low and sultry.

"Good, cause baby, tonight I'm going to blow your brain, not to mention . . ."

Before she could finish her thought, and with every intention of not waiting until that night to make love, Jim gave Sandra a long, deep kiss. His right hand worked its way down the back of her nightgown. But it never made it below the small of her back.

"Nice try big boy," she said as she slid out of his grasp and sat up. "Let's clean up."

They got up and showered separately. They both dressed beach casual—he in cut-off jean shorts, flip flops and a tank top which showed off his naturally athletic physique which was more a result of genetics than working out. She wore sandals, a halter-top with no bra and short shorts which exposed just a taste of her lower buns as she walked. It was clear that she relished her ability to compete with nubile waifs half her age for the puerile attention of men of all ages. She showed pride in her body right down to her still relatively firm, unsupported breasts. And he knew that she knew that with every furtive, rapacious glance she received from other men, especially younger men, his ever-salacious appetite for her intensified.

It was noon. While Sandra had stocked the refrigerator, they decided to go out for lunch. They took his car and headed north towards Nags Head proper. Just beyond milepost seventeen they came to a place called *Sam and Omie's*, a small restaurant and bar which, as they would learn from the historical menus, had been a part of the Outer Banks' culture for over sixty years. Named after father and son fishermen, it was housed in a rustic wooden shack-like building. It had the simple décor inside that its outer shell suggested—an L-shaped room with booths along the east side of the building, tables situated closely together in the interior and a bar with barstools in the far interior of the building forming an L parallel to the walls. Pictures of boats and fishermen standing next to their prize catches decorated the walls.

They hadn't beaten the lunch crowd, but they only had to wait ten minutes to be seated. How fortunate, Jim thought, to be given the last booth at the top of the L, away from the crowd. He didn't mind being around the other people in the joint. He simply wanted to get lost in the oneness of him and Sandra. Every contact with others was an unwelcome intrusion.

They each took a menu and silently read the history of the place contained on the back before opening it to the food offerings.

"So, how was your trip?" Sandra asked looking up from her menu.

"Aside from being much too long, it was . . .okay."

"Last night you said it was strange."

"Did I? I don't know why . . ."

"Can I start you with some drinks?"

Jim was thankful for the waitress's interruption. He had decided that he didn't want to tell Sandra about the incidents on the trip, partly because he didn't want to recall the unpleasantness it caused within himself and partly because he was afraid of sounding like some kind of crazed idiot.

"I'll have water," Sandra said.

"The same," Jim said. "And I think we'll just order while you're here."

"Sure thing, hon," the friendly waitress replied setting her pencil to her order pad ready to write down their selections.

Sandra ordered the tuna melt, Jim the fried oyster sandwich. With a smile and a pleasant "Got it," the waitress disappeared into the din of the crowd of lunch guests.

"So how was church Sunday? I'm sorry I missed it," she fibbed. Jim was relieved she had gone on to another subject. "I'll bet you gave a hell of . . . ah, heck of a sermon."

"It was pretty good I thought. It was on forgiveness."

"Ooh," she mused, smiling slyly. "That's one I probably should have been there for."

They both giggled. The thought struck him that they were like children playing "I'll show you mine if you show me yours," knowing they're being naughty yet determined to explore the forbidden zones; discovering that what everyone was trying to hide from them wasn't ugly or dangerous, just weirdly different; their childish laughter, caused both by the embarrassment of what they had seen and shown and the shared satisfaction of not getting caught. Each brought out the child in the other. Neither one of them had anyone else in their life who did that.

It wasn't long before their food arrived. They ate at a leisurely pace. Their talk was about small, unimportant things. Jim marveled at how even the simplest things with Sandra took on an added luster, and brought him such relaxed pleasure.

When she had finished her meal she excused herself to go to the ladies room. As she walked away, he found himself following her semi-exposed bouncing buns as if they were the bouncing ball hopping over the lyrics of a song called *Follow Me*. He glanced around the restaurant and saw at least four other men, including the young bartender, following those same bouncing buns. *What a turn on,* he thought to himself with smug pride.

While she wasn't gone long, it seemed like an eternity to him. Now that he was with her, this moment not actually in her presence was hateful to him. Not only were his urges and desires for her intensifying during this momentary absence, but they existed side by side with pangs of conscience and guilt which, at the same time, were growing stronger the longer she was away. Thoughts of Renee and the kids began pounding on the door of his compartmentalized mind—the door marked "Private, Do Not Enter" housing his "I'm Entitled to Pleasure" room. They pounded, intruding unwelcomed, with cries of "This is wrong," and "How could you do this to us?"

These plaintive cries were affecting him. He asked himself how could he, a minister, a married man, a father, do these things? What could possibly justify his affair with Sandra?

Why, Renee, of course, he responded to his anguished self-examination. *If she was fulfilling my needs, I would never have gotten involved with Sandra in the first place. There's no other explanation.*

Of course, he knew that Renee provided a home of comfort and respite for him. Over the years she had worked to help with the family finances. She also took on the lion's share of the household burden, not to mention taking care of the kids. She was the perfect minister's wife—no, the *penultimate* minister's wife—and was highly respected by the parishioners of the church, as well as the other townsfolk. Most importantly, she was totally and absolutely in love with and devoted to him, her husband. Of course, he knew these things. He had always known these things. But try as he might, he couldn't overcome an overwhelming sense of deprivation, a feeling that he was missing something with Renee. But what? The sex, yes. In that department Sandra blew her away—would probably blow anyone away. But it wasn't just the sex. He knew that. At least he believed it. He had to. In moments of clarity, as he had mulled these things over and over in his mind, he knew this was more his problem than Renee's. But in Sandra Chievers' presence, he had very few moments of clarity. She had filled a void in his life, a need he could not even describe to himself, but that he felt intensely. And he had as much trouble imagining life without her as he did imagining it without Renee.

"Are you ready baby?"

Sandra's words snapped him out of his contemplative fog.

"Yeah. Let's go."

Jim got up. He walked to the counter to pay his bill. As he did so, he could feel the eyes of every man in the room following him and his woman. When finished paying the bill he escorted that woman, more than fifteen years his senior, past the leering eyes of all of the jealous males in the joint and out into the afternoon air.

Chapter 13

It was a pleasant, balmy day with enough scattered cloud cover to provide occasional respite from the direct heat of the high summer sun—a perfect beach day. Jim and Sandra walked over the dune crossing and started down the stairs to the beach. It was crowded. Everywhere they looked they saw groups of people, family clusters, with beach-goers ranging in age from one to eighty-one. All around were assorted tools of the family tourist trade—umbrellas, chairs, beach tarps, volleyball nets, plastic buckets and shovels, boogie boards and rafts. Kids were romping in the surf, playing volleyball, Frisbee, football and hacky-sack. Grandparents and parents walked along the beach, wading in the surf, or sat on their beach chairs drinking beer and reading the most recent novels by the likes of King, Koontz and Grisham.

Unlike many seaside resorts there were no boom boxes or radios blaring. People seemed content to amuse themselves or be amused by what the shore had naturally to offer. And the beachwear was modest by the day's standards. To be sure, there were well-endowed, shapely women and girls in attractive two-piece suits that in days past may have been considered risque'. But by contemporary standards there were no over-the-edge suits, no thongs, no side-less one-piece outfits, no see-through fabrics, no men in Speedos. There must be an unwritten rule, Jim thought, that if anyone were to offend the good taste of Nags Head's summer society, they would be quickly put upon and unceremoniously expelled.

Jim and Sandra found a spot about twenty-five yards south of the Elysian dune walkover and laid out their beach towels. It was a spot with no houses behind them. Between the row of houses on the southern side of Elysian and the nearest ones further south was an expanse of undeveloped, thick scrub measuring as much as a hundred yards, perhaps more. The sea oats on the dune and the dense vegetation beyond created a natural backdrop to this stretch of beach that, though real, was no more than an illusion of nature preserved in the midst of this heavily built-out portion of the barrier island.

Nonetheless, many of nature's lesser creatures seemed to have adapted to the human invasion of their habitat and went about their business of daily survival. Some, such as the sand fleas, mosquitoes and horseflies served no apparent purpose but to antagonize the two-legged sun worshippers, but not enough to keep them away. Others provided those same interlopers with entertainment. There were the sandpipers which, looking for food in the sand, would follow the tide as it rushed out to sea only to abruptly turn and scurry away from the incoming waves. Somehow, they were always able to stay no more than an inch or two ahead of the oncoming ocean, eschewing a winged escape, yet never getting caught by the swiftly moving water. Then, when the tide reached its apogee, they would turn again to chase it back to the sea. The dolphins too, swimming and playing near enough to shore to allow the more adventurous swimmers to get within five or ten feet of them, but teasingly no closer. There were the sand crabs that, by staying mostly in their burrows during the day and coming out freely and scampering across the sands at night, made peace with the gigantic humans by avoiding them. On the other hand, the flocks of white seagulls with their black-tipped wings played the role of collaborators, comfortably settling in and interacting with the beach's occupiers in return for a constant diet of bread, lunchmeat, potato chips and Cheetos.

All in all, Jim found the non-human activity on the beach amusing and infinitely more interesting than the human—that is, of course, except for the goddess beside him. Propped on one elbow, he looked down at her admiringly. She wore an attractive, deep blue, two-piece swimsuit. It was significantly revealing yet within the limits of Nags Head's unwritten codes. She lay on her back sunning herself. Her eyes were shut, hidden behind color-coordinated blue tinted sunglasses.

"What are you looking at?" she said.

"I thought your eyes were closed."

"They were. I could feel you looking at me." She reached up and rubbed the bicep of his arm. "Ooh."

Jim laughed.

"You're really something. You know that?" he said.

"Um-hm."

He gently stroked her stomach with the knuckles of his index and middle fingers.

"Tell me something," he said.

"Sure."

"Why Paradise?"

"What do you mean?"

"I understand why you would want to move to a small town after what happened with you and your husband. But why Paradise? I'm not even sure it's on the map."

He had always wanted to ask her this, but the time never seemed right. For some reason, it did now.

Sandra didn't move. He could tell even through the sunglasses that her eyes were directed up to the sky, not at him.

"Sandra?"

"That's personal Jim," she said.

He lifted himself up off his arm and sat up, wrapping his arms around his knees.

"Personal? We've exchanged bodily fluids. How could it be any more personal than that?"

For the first time since he first made love with her, he found himself feeling peeved at her. Not a crisis, he knew. But an unpleasant feeling nonetheless.

"Well, maybe personal isn't the right word," she said. "It's private. Some things are meant to be private."

"Sandra, I can't imagine what could be so awful that you can't tell me about it. And if you're concerned about your privacy . . . well, you've got to know that whatever you tell me will stay just between us. My God, aren't we both keeping a pretty big secret right now?"

Sandra sat up. She looked straight out at the ocean. She didn't say anything for a minute or so. She looked at Jim and then looked out at the sea again.

"Norma Hutchins is my aunt," she said finally.

That sucker punch to his solar plexus was totally unexpected. He remained silent while trying to catch his breath.

Sandra turned and looked at him again.

"How's that grab you, Mr. Magoo?"

Jim felt like Magoo, that loveable, blind cartoon character, without his glasses. He even squinted his eyes as he looked at her.

"How are you . . . how long have you . . ."

He could do nothing but stammer. It wasn't the fact that there was a surprise about Sandra's background. Everyone had secrets from their past. But Norma Hutchins? Of all the people in Paradise, why did it have to be Norma Hutchins?

"I didn't know Norma was my aunt until I came to Paradise." Sandra looked out at the sea again. "It seems that Aunt Norma had a sister who was several years younger than her. She wasn't real pretty. And apparently she was . . . I guess you'd say a bit slow. She wasn't married. As far as anyone knew, she most likely had never had sex, or even kissed a guy."

Sandra reached over to the sand at the edge of her towel away from Jim and scooped up a handful. She let it run through her fingers. She turned her face and looked at him.

"Her name was Ellie. Ellie liked to spend her time at the library. Since she read slowly, she'd spend a lot of time there because it took her so long. She liked the library because no one would bother her there.

"One night, while she was walking home, she was raped. Some guy—they never caught him—he dragged her into the bushes, raped her and threatened to kill her if she told anyone."

"But she did tell," said Jim.

"Not right away. She was scared. Only when her parents discovered that she was pregnant did she tell what happened to her."

Sandra turned and looked out at the sea again.

"In those days," she continued, "people were ashamed of their daughters if they got pregnant outside marriage, even if they were raped. So it was all hushed up. Ellie was sent to stay with an aunt in Fayetteville until she had the baby. Of course, the plan was to give the child up for adoption. All of the arrangements had been made before the birth.

"It was a difficult birth. Ellie died three days later. I was adopted by an insurance salesman and his wife—Karl and Sheila Kuhl."

There was a brief silence, as if to give this news time to sink in. The manner of Sandra's birth and adoption was not particularly shocking to him. On the other hand, the connection with Norma Hutchins did take some getting accustomed to.

"How did Mrs. Hutchins learn . . ."

"Oh, Aunt Norma always knew where I was," Sandra interrupted. She turned and looked at Jim. "She didn't interfere, or even have contact with me or my parents. But she kept tabs on me, wherever I went and whatever I did."

"Why am I not surprised?" Jim said sarcastically.

Sandra chuckled.

"Anyway, my parents died in a plane crash when I was twenty-three. When Ray and I split up I didn't really have anywhere to turn. I had no brothers or sisters and my parents' families weren't particularly close. I was still running my boutique in Atlanta. But I was miserable. My whole life was there. And everyone I knew, knew what had happened. I was embarrassed, and ashamed."

She was close to tears. Jim took her hand in his.

"One day, this elderly woman came into my shop. She said she was a seamstress in a small town in South Carolina and was looking to retire. She wanted to sell her shop, but not to just anyone. It had to be someone who was a great seamstress. She said she had heard that I was very good and wanted to know if I was interested.

"Now this was very weird. I *am* a very good seamstress. My mother had been too and had taught me from a very young age. But very few people knew that. I sold brand names in my shop. As for making or mending clothes, I never wanted to do that commercially. I did it for my own pleasure, and only for a few friends. Besides, how would some old lady from South Carolina know anyway?"

"Maybe one of your friends came across her somewhere and told her."

"No. Aunt Norma never talked to any of my friends. When I asked her how she knew about me, she said she 'just knew.' Anyway, at first I said no."

"Then she told you she was your aunt?" Jim guessed.

"No. She didn't. Not then. She just sort of convinced me to come to Paradise. I still, to this day, don't know how. She seemed to know I was looking for something, for a way out. And she convinced me it was in Paradise."

"So when did you learn she was your aunt?"

"The day we closed on the shop. We went from the lawyer's office to the shop. She gave me the keys, turned over some cash that was still in the till and invited me to dinner. At dinner, she told me—told me everything."

"Nobody in town knows?"

"No. That wouldn't do. When Ellie left, everyone was told that she had been sent to Atlanta to see doctors, specialists, to treat a serious illness. When she died, she died of that illness."

"Another 'Paradise secret.'"

"There are a lot of them in a small town."

"And your relationship with Mrs. Hutchins—how is it?" Jim asked.

"It's good. She loves me very much. As I do her."

"Is she . . . do you think she has any suspicions . . ."

"About us?"

"Yeah."

"I don't know. She's very perceptive you know."

"Yes. Yes I do."

"For some reason she didn't seem too happy about me joining the bazaar committee," Sandra said.

"I thought I saw some animated discussion in the hall at your first committee meeting," Jim said.

"Yes. She was warning me, about being too visible, too 'out there;' was warning me that I'm much too attractive as a widow . . ."

"Does she know the truth about that?"

"Yes. But she agrees widow is better than divorcee. Anyway, she says I'm too tempting for the yokels in a small town like that; even, and especially, the married ones."

Jim smiled.

"Sounds like Aunt Norma knows what she's talking about," he said.

Sandra laughed. He seemed to have removed the glumness from her face, and hopefully her heart. She leaned over and kissed him. Apparently he had.

"And now my big hunk," she said, "I'm going to get some sun."

She turned over and lay on her stomach. Jim laid on his back and softly stroked her shoulder.

"Thank you for telling me," he said.

"You're welcome" she mumbled into her towel.

Chapter 14

Norma Hutchins checked with Chief Bruener first thing Tuesday morning, as soon as she awakened from what seemed like a twenty-year sleep. As she feared, the Chief knew nothing about Reverend Donovan's whereabouts.

Now that Sandra might be involved, Norma's attitude regarding Reverend Donovan had begun to harden again. It didn't much matter to her whether the evil she was sensing was within Reverend Donovan or pursuing him. If it was within him, he had to be stopped. If it was pursuing him, as a man of God he should have the strength, the will and the faith to defeat it. She feared the latter as much as the former because she wasn't convinced that Reverend Donovan had what it took to resist the devil's wiles. And if she was right—pray to the Lord she wasn't—and if Sandra was involved, her niece, her only blood descendant, was in grave danger.

The other dilemma, of course, was Mrs. Donovan and those lovely girls. Whatever Reverend Donovan's failings, his innocent family didn't deserve to suffer. Did Mrs. Donovan know what was going on? If not, what could, what should, she do about it?

She had come to the conclusion that her only hope of finding Reverend Donovan, and probably Sandra, was through Renee Donovan, however awkward that might be. She decided to go see her and find out what she could learn, not only about Reverend Donovan's whereabouts, but also about what, if anything, Renee knew about her husband's connections—relationship?—with Sandra. She wouldn't ask directly, though. If there was something going on between the

Reverend and her niece, it wouldn't be said that Norma Hutchins told the aggrieved wife about any such thing. On the other hand, if the aggrieved wife figured it out for herself . . .

Renee heard the knock on her front door. As she went to answer it she could see the elderly, former seamstress, Norma Hutchins, peering curiously through the screen door into the house.

"Good afternoon Mrs. Donovan," Norma said not waiting for Renee to get all the way to the door.

"Good afternoon Mrs. Hutchins," Renee said. "Is there something I can do for you?"

Renee stood at the door, but didn't open it or ask Mrs. Hutchins if she wanted to come in. This was uncharacteristically impolite of Renee and she knew it. But for some reason she didn't understand, it seemed appropriate at that moment. Mrs. Hutchins didn't ask to enter nor did she seem offended that Renee didn't invite her in.

"By any chance is the Reverend Donovan at home?" Mrs. Hutchins asked. Unlike most of the congregation, Norma Hutchins always referred to the minister only by his last name.

"Why no, Mrs. Hutchins. The Reverend's gone for the week and won't be back until late Saturday night," Renee responded with corresponding formality. "If it's an emergency, Reverend Blair from First Baptist offered to make himself available in Reverend Donovan's absence."

"Oh dear, no. That won't be necessary. It can wait until Reverend Donovan returns. I trust there's been no family emergency that calls him away?" Norma Hutchins asked this nosily in the sly manner she had perfected which seemed to demand no answer beyond a simple "no" yet required one just the same.

"No, thank God," Renee answered. "He's simply taking some time off to relax. He's been working very hard lately and just needed some time to himself."

Renee seemed to be feeling defensive in responding to Mrs. Hutchins' inquiry. While she had always treated Renee warmly, this was one time she was looking to make her feel uncomfortable.

"Yes, yes. Of course, my dear. I think it's absolutely necessary for one whose life is to minister to the needs of others to take care of his own needs. Else how could he be expected to do his job very well?"

Mrs. Hutchins fully intended a double meaning by her comment. Renee gave no sign of reading anything into it.

"Well, my dear, perhaps you *can* help me," Mrs. Hutchins continued. "As you know, I'm once again in charge of this year's church bazaar. I spoke with Reverend Donovan last week regarding setting the final dates for it. Seems that our first choice conflicts with this year's high school homecoming. I swear," she said, pounding her cane on the floor of the wooden porch, "I'd like to know who would select a weekend in October without first checking the Fighting Tigers' schedule! Just the same, we must begin lining up all of the out of town vendors, but we still can't tell them the exact dates. The Widow Chievers is this year's thrift sale committee chairman and I must speak with her about the matter."

Mrs. Hutchins stopped and looked at Renee. For a moment she lost her train of thought.

"And?" Renee asked.

"And?" Mrs. Hutchins echoed.

"What about the Widow Chievers?"

"Oh, yes. Well, Saturday I went to her shop. I so love to return to the shop whenever I can—such warm memories. Well, I went to the shop and there was a sign on the door saying that the shop was closed and wouldn't re-open until two weeks from yesterday."

This last comment held within itself its own incredibility, and Mrs. Hutchins knew it. Nothing in Paradise escaped her notice as long as she was suggesting the Widow Chievers' absence from town had. And she knew that Renee knew that as well as anybody.

"So, as you can see," she continued, "with both Reverend Donovan and the Widow Chievers out of town this week"—she hesitated for a brief moment—"and she being the last committee member I haven't spoken to about this yet, well, I just wonder if maybe you know something."

Norma Hutchins carefully scrutinized Renee's expression, looking for any sign that her double entendres had struck a chord. While she had no proof, her well-honed instincts, not to mention her disturbing vision of the Sunday before, told her something was wrong, terribly wrong, and she was more convinced than ever that it involved both the Reverend Donovan and Sandra Chievers. She looked for confirmation in some sign of recognition or knowledge on the part of the minister's wife. There was none. If Renee knew or suspected anything, she hid it well. More likely, concluded the old woman, the young wife was oblivious.

"I'm sorry Mrs. Hutchins, but the Reverend has said nothing to me about it," Renee said.

Well of course not, the town's seer snidely thought to herself.

"I'll be happy to have him call you, or the Widow Chievers if necessary, as soon as he returns, to help you solve your problem. I'm certain it will all work out and that it will be a splendid bazaar, as always."

"I'd be a might grateful," Norma Hutchins intoned in a slow, measured drawl. "And should the Reverend Donovan phone you during the week, don't consider it necessary to bother him with these matters. Just give him my regards." She considered it highly unlikely he'd call.

"I certainly will," Renee said with a nod of her head and a smile. "And have a good afternoon, Mrs. Hutchins."

"Good day to you, Mrs. Donovan," the old woman answered as she turned to walk away.

Norma Hutchins could feel Renee's eyes watching as the frail, elderly woman, her thinning white hair slightly mussed by the light summer breeze, slowly descended the front porch steps, carefully coordinating the efforts of two unsteady legs and two arthritis-weakened hands, one holding the stair rail and the other manipulating her wooden cane. The conversation they had just had, though common and mundane, had been intended to leave the minister's wife with a feeling of unease and discomfort, even foreboding. Mrs. Hutchins sensed that it had done that, but could not tell whether it was enough to spur the lovely young woman into action. If not, the old woman knew, there would be immense pain to be suffered for a long, long time.

Renee continued to watch Mrs. Hutchins as the unsteady octogenarian slowly ambled up the walk towards her home, some two blocks away. What Renee couldn't see were the two solitary tears, one falling from each of the tough old lady's eyes. Renee had been her last hope of getting to Reverend Donovan and Sandra in time. Now she feared that the drama would play out in full. And all she could do was wait and hope for the best.

Chapter 15

"**W**atch that ear, Ned! Wouldn't do to have a mayor who couldn't listen to the wishes of his constituents, now would it?"

Mayor Lowe laughed at his own joke. He would repeat it every time he got a haircut at Ned's Barber Shop, and would laugh each time as if it was the first time he had told it.

The mayor was the only customer in the shop. Their barber shop chatter had been non-stop since he had sat down in the old, worn chair that he preferred over the newer model that Ned had purchased only months earlier for his two-chair shop (though Ned was the only barber). The conversation this day had ranged from who was going to win the Super Bowl — Ned favored the Redskins, the mayor assured him it would be the Panthers — to the latest rumor around town that Paradise High's football coach, Ross Browning, had supplied star quarterback Wade Connors with steroids over the summer.

"Ain't no way Ross would do that," the mayor protested.

"No?" said Ned. "Then how do you explain that spindly kid's sudden growth into an incredible hulk over just one summer?"

Ned Ferguson was the only person in town who could match Mayor Lowe word for word in non-stop conversation, a talent well placed for each of their chosen professions.

As the two old friends talked, a stranger stared intently at them through the shop window. A tall, middle-aged man of medium build, he was dressed in black with a white collar encircling his neck. His hands, cupped on both sides of his head, were pressed against the window. If anyone could help him, he figured, the town barber should be able to. He stepped back from the window and walked into the shop.

"Afternoon," Ned greeted the stranger. "Have a seat. I'll be with you in just a couple of minutes."

"Thank you," said the stranger. "But I'm not here for a haircut. I'm looking for someone and I hoped you might be able to help me."

"Well, if whoever you're looking for is in this town, I reckon between me and the mayor here, we ought to be able to help you."

Ned stepped out from behind the barber chair and extended his hand to the stranger who grasped it in a firm handshake.

"My name's Ned Ferguson and this here is Mayor Andy Lowe."

The stranger stepped over to the barber chair and shook the mayor's hand.

"Thank you. Thank you," the stranger said. "My name is Father Ray Chievers. I'm from Philadelphia."

"Mississippi?" Ned asked. "I've got a cousin . . ."

"No," the priest interrupted. "Pennsylvania. Philadelphia, Pennsylvania. I'm looking for Sandra Chievers. I understand she lives somewhere around here."

"The Widow Chievers? Why she sure does," Ned said enthusiastically, beating the mayor to the punch largely due to having suddenly jerked Andy Lowe's head to the left ostensibly to trim his left sideburn. "Are you her brother or something?"

"No, I'm . . ." The priest could barely hide his surprise. "Did you say the *Widow* Chievers?"

"Yep," the mayor jumped in. "Lost her husband a few years back apparently. Before she came to Paradise. Don't know how. She don't talk about it. But you being a relative and all I would have expected you'd have known about that."

"Well, it's been a long time since Sandra and I have spoken to each other," Father Chievers answered slowly, measuring each word carefully. "Do you know where I might find her?"

"She owns the seamstress shop right across the square there," Ned said, pointing out the shop window. "Right next to Harold's. But she ain't there. She's out of town and won't be back till Sunday or Monday a week, as I understand it."

"Do you know where she went? It's very important that I find her."

Ned and the mayor looked at each other, shrugged their shoulders and shook their heads.

"Nope," they chimed in unison.

"Would anyone know?" Father Chievers recognized that his anxiety must have been obvious to the two men, but he didn't have time to worry about what others were thinking.

"Don't know for sure," Ned said. "Even my wife, Belle, who knows just about everything about everyone in this town, don't know where she went. I reckon the only other person who might know would be Mrs. Hutchins. She sold the shop to the Widow Chievers and sort of keeps an eye on her when she can."

"Where does Mrs. Hutchins live?"

"She lives on Jackson. Go out the door, turn right, three blocks, then a right on Lee. Jackson's the next left and she's the second house on the right."

"Thank you. Thank you very much."

Father Chievers wasted no time. He hurried out the door and turned right.

"Well now," said Mayor Lowe. "That was kind of strange."

"It was a might peculiar," agreed Ned. "Did that fella ever say how he was related to the Widow?"

"Not that I recall. Nope, not that I recall at all."

Ned turned the mayor's chair so it faced the mirror on the back wall.

"Looks good," Andy Lowe said, running his hand over his newly cut hair. "Looks real good."

Father Chievers had no difficulty finding Mrs. Hutchins' house. It was a large, two-story, ante-bellum wooden house with a porch that went from the front and wrapped around both sides. There was a porch swing on either side of the front door and matching tables and chairs on each side porch. The house and its external furnishings were in perfect symmetry.

Father Chievers climbed the front porch stairs and approached the front door. The main door was open. Only a screen door stood between him and the interior of the house. He could see that the home was cooled with fans, as was the porch. It gave the feeling that Mrs.

Hutchins was of that rare stock, even in the South, who eschewed the use of air conditioning.

He knocked on the screen door. Almost immediately he heard an elderly voice shout from what appeared to be a parlor on the right.

"Just one minute! I'm an old lady, you know. I'm coming as fast as I can."

As he peered through the screen he saw the old woman walk slowly out of the parlor, cane clutched in her right hand, and down the short stretch of hallway to the front door. Though the sight of a tall, strange priest at her front door was certainly out of the ordinary, Mrs. Hutchins looked almost as if she was expecting him.

"Yes?" she said.

"Good afternoon. I'm looking for a Mrs. Hutchins. Might you be her?"

"You found her, young man. Now what do you want with her?"

She was curt, but not impolite, indicating one who likes to get right down to business.

"My name is Father . . . Raymond," he said. In light of the conversation at the barber shop he decided it was best to avoid his last name for the moment. "I've come to Paradise to see Sandra Chievers. It's a surprise visit, actually. I've been told she's out of town. It's really rather important that I get in touch with her. The barber, Mr. Ferguson I think it is, and the mayor suggested that you might have some information about where she's gone. I'd be very grateful for any help."

There was a long pause as Norma Hutchins appeared to take his measure. He understood that it was important that she recognize him as a good man who was looking for Sandra Chievers for a proper purpose if he expected any cooperation from her.

"And what might your business be with the Widow Chievers, Father?"

"Well, it's rather personal."

"Is she in some kind of trouble?" she persisted, rather perceptively he thought.

"I'm not sure." He was being skillfully drawn into a much more detailed conversation than he cared to have with this inquisitive woman. "Possibly. That is why it's urgent that I contact her immediately. Can you help me?"

Mrs. Hutchins paused again.

How, he wondered, could he persuade her to help him without disclosing more information than he wanted to?

"I'm sorry Father . . . Raymond did you say?"

"Yes."

"Father Raymond. I don't know where she's gone off to. Been gone over a week. Didn't tell me where she was headed. Don't know if she told anyone."

He couldn't hide the disappointment on his face. There was urgency in his words and his mission—which was nothing less than to save Sandra—that he made no effort to hide. By now, it also did not matter much to him that the old lady may have realized that there was a bond between him and Sandra that went beyond that of priest and penitent.

"Perhaps Mrs. Donovan could help you," Mrs. Hutchins went on. "She's the Reverend Donovan's wife. Maybe she knows where Sandra's gone to, being the minister's wife and all. Reverend Donovan's out of town himself." She paused, as if looking for some kind of reaction. Father Raymond showed none. "But perhaps she knows something."

"Where would I find Mrs. Donovan?" he asked.

Mrs. Hutchins gave him the brief directions to the Donovan house. He thanked her for her help. As he bade her farewell and headed down the front steps, the old woman called out to him.

"I hope you find what you're looking for, Father. And I hope you're in time."

Her tone was foreboding. He also hoped he would be in time.

As he approached the well-tended home it was apparent by the two tricycles in the front walkway that this was a home with small children and occupants who took pride in their appearance and surroundings. He walked up to the front screen door and knocked. Within seconds he was greeted by an attractive, well-groomed woman.

"Hello. May I help you?"

"I hope so. My name is Father Raymond Chievers."

"Please, come in," she said as she opened the screen door.

"Thank you, but I don't want to impose, with your children and all."

"Don't worry. They're napping."

He stepped into the house.

"Let's go into the kitchen," she continued. "I was just about to have some iced tea. Would you like some?"

"That would be very kind," he said.

He followed her to the kitchen at the back of the house. He sat down at the kitchen table as she prepared their drinks. She placed a tall glass of sweetened iced tea before him and sat opposite him with a glass of her own.

"Thank you, Mrs. Donovan."

"Please, Father, call me Renee. People around here are so formal with me I don't often get to hear my first name."

"Certainly. Renee."

"Where are you from, Father?"

"I'm the associate pastor at a parish outside of Philadelphia. I'm originally from Atlanta. I came to the priesthood rather late in life and this is my first parish."

He took a long sip of the refreshingly cold tea. He wasn't quite sure why he went into the explanation of how late he came to the priesthood. Just nervous, he guessed.

"You said your last name is Chievers?" she asked, breaking an awkward silence.

"Yes, it is."

"Our town's seamstress is Sandra Chievers. Are you any relation?"

"Actually, it is Sandra who I've come to see," he answered, avoiding a direct answer to her question. "I understand that she's out of town and no one seems to know where she's gone to. I was hoping you might have some idea."

"No I don't, Father. But what led you to think I might know where she is?"

"Well, I understand your husband is Sandra's pastor. I thought maybe she might have said something to him of her plans. I'm told he's out of town as well . . . but perhaps he said something to you. Or when he calls home, maybe you could ask him if he knows where Sandra is. It is rather urgent that I speak with her."

"He didn't say anything before he left. And I don't really know whether he will call for the next few days. But I'd still like to know who told you I might know where Sandra is." The minister's wife appeared genuinely bewildered that this religious stranger with the same last name as the Widow Chievers somehow expected her to know where Sandra was.

"I was speaking with an elderly woman named Mrs. Hutchins. She indicated you might be able to help me."

"So *that's* what Mrs. Hutchins was getting at," Renee said, a look of anger spreading over her face.

"Excuse me?" Father Ray said, somewhat bewildered.

"Well, I can't help you," Renee said brusquely, barely restraining her voice and hardly concealing her agitation. "Mrs. Hutchins is just an old busybody who likes to make trouble. I have no idea why she would have sent you here."

She stood up from her chair. Father Ray thought that she was going to ask him to leave. Instead, she picked up his now empty glass and, in a softer, more pleasant voice, asked him if he would like more tea.

"Yes, please," he said. "And please, forgive me. I meant no offense. I'm simply trying to find Sandra."

Renee placed a full glass of tea before him and sat down again. She appeared very troubled. His asking questions about Sandra, and the fact that Mrs. Hutchins had directed him to her, seemed to have caused a great deal of distress. There also appeared to be some underlying tension involving Sandra and the minister being gone at the same time. Father Ray realized that he was getting into the middle of something and that he was treading on some very sensitive, and maybe dangerous, ground. But he had no choice but to push on.

"No, *I'm* sorry, Father," Renee said. "I had no right to talk to you that way. I don't know what came over me." She took a long sip of her tea. "Perhaps," she went on, "you've been led here so that we can help each other."

"I do believe that God has a purpose in everything we do, Mrs. . . . Renee. But I don't know how I can be of help to you, though if I can please let me know how."

"Well, to begin with," Renee said, smiling and taking advantage of the opening, "you could tell me a little bit about the mysterious Widow Chievers, starting with your relation to her."

Father Ray hesitated. He knew that he had already fueled the gossip that is a regular and refined pastime in a small town like Paradise simply by giving his last name. It was something he had done without thinking of the consequences at the time. He certainly didn't want his and Sandra's past life to be laid out for the entire town to see, especially for Sandra's sake. Obviously she had made a new life for herself, and by calling herself the Widow Chievers she had made abundantly clear her desire to keep the facts of her past to herself.

Yet it hadn't taken long for Father Ray to realize that Renee Donovan was not one who would find joy in being a rumormonger, despite her emotional outburst about Mrs. Hutchins, and perhaps because of it; that she was a good, decent, Christian woman; that she could be trusted. He came to the conclusion that maybe they could help each other. And to do so they would both need to be open about who they were and what they needed. He decided that it might as well start with him.

"I'm Sandra Chievers' former husband."

Renee looked stunned and disbelieving.

"But how . . . how . . ."

"How can I be a Catholic priest?" he finished her sentence.

She nodded.

"We had the marriage annulled in the Church. That is, I had it annulled. As far as the Church is concerned, I've never been married. The Catholic Church's little white lie—calling a divorce an annulment—allowed me to become a priest."

"But why would she tell everyone she's a widow?"

"I suppose it's her way of forgetting a painful past, and not having to recount it. Can you imagine explaining how it is that you're divorced from a priest?"

"I guess that would be difficult." She paused. "So, how is it that she's divorced from a Catholic priest?" she asked, resting her cheek in her hand and smiling disarmingly.

Father Ray freely described his life and relationship with Sandra—their courtship and marriage, their successful and influential lives among Atlanta's elite, their inability to bear children, Sandra being born again, his rediscovery of his Catholic faith, and the ultimate break-up of their marriage. If Ray's telling of the tale were to be compared to Sandra's, he supposed they probably wouldn't have been much different, including the pain and resentment that he caused Sandra by what he agreed was his abandonment of her for the Church. They hadn't seen each other since the final hearing on their civil divorce years ago and hadn't spoken to each other since Ray had asked her to help with the annulment, which she had angrily refused to do.

Since his separation from Sandra, Ray had never talked about her to anyone else in such detail. He was surprised at how easily and freely he was willing to discuss these things with Renee. Doing so brought him a feeling of great relief—the relief that inevitably came from releasing painful memories and feelings withheld from others in the foolish belief that by suppressing the pain and keeping it to himself he would somehow avoid the pain.

A tear fell from his eye as he struggled to retain his composure. Renee placed her right hand on his left and squeezed gently. She smiled reassuringly. Without saying a word she was telling him that she understood, and that everything would be fine. Comforted by her empathy and gentleness, he returned a grateful smile.

"So," Renee said, breaking the tender silence, "why is it so important that you find Sandra now?"

"I'm afraid she may be in danger."

"What kind of danger?"

"I don't know."

"Well, what makes you think she's in danger?"

"My guilty conscience."

"*That* you'll have to explain, Father. You've lost me now."

"Of course. It does take some explaining." He took a long sip of his tea. "I've been counseling a man for several months. His name is Rick. Rick has been suffering from severe depression. He's had professional therapy, prescriptions for drugs—Paxil, Prozac, who knows what else. Still, he's depressed. He's not a particularly religious man, but a friend of his is a member of my church and suggested that perhaps spiritual counseling might help."

He looked down at his glass. He picked it up and rotated it making the ice cubes swirl around.

"At first Rick was reluctant to talk much. But after a while I gained his trust and he opened up. He told me that he believed he knew the cause of his depression. He insisted it wasn't a matter of digging deep into his past or his subconscious. He was experiencing such a deep sense of shame and guilt that he felt no amount of therapy or medication would help. I suggested that maybe what he really needed then was forgiveness, not only from God, but from himself. And that's what we began working on."

Father Ray put his glass back down. He looked directly into Renee's eyes as he continued.

"Rick and his high school sweetheart—Ashley—got married right out of school. They were from a small town in West Virginia. Their parents disapproved of their relationship, so they eloped. Ashley wanted to stay in West Virginia and try to heal the rift in the families caused by their marriage. But Rick insisted on leaving to get away from the arguing and fighting. It was just overall an unpleasant scene and he wanted out.

"Rick also had always wanted to live near the ocean. And he thought a big city would be exciting. So they moved to Miami. It didn't take long for Ashley to become unhappy. She was far from her home and family. She never felt that she and Rick fit in with the unique culture of Miami. They didn't speak Spanish. Their West Virginia accents made even their English sound funny to some. She felt that they were two West Virginia hicks who had plopped themselves down in an environment entirely alien to them. Neither of them could find a really good paying job. Before long, they began to argue, constantly, and over everything."

The story was a long one. But Father Ray noticed that Renee appeared to be listening to every word intently, and with sincere concern. He continued.

"Rick became unhappy at home. He began looking for happiness elsewhere. He started drinking a lot, hanging out at bars and pool halls until all hours of the night, leaving Ashley alone. He also began fooling around with other women, women he would meet in the bars. Sometimes prostitutes.

"One night, Rick got drunk at a bar and got into a fight with another fellow. Neither of them was seriously injured, but Rick got arrested. By the time he could make bail he had missed two days of work. He got fired. He couldn't find another job that paid as well. So, naturally, they started having more money problems. The less money they had the more they argued. The more they argued, the more Rick went out drinking and leaving Ashley alone. It became a horrible cycle of misery for both of them.

"Finally, Ashley had had enough. She left him. She stayed in

Miami long enough to divorce him. And then she moved back to West Virginia, or so Rick thought. Actually, she was too embarrassed to go back home, too afraid of facing her parents day in and day out. Instead, she moved to New York. She figured that in such a large city even a girl from West Virginia with just a high school education should be able to find a good job and make a life for herself. She didn't hide from her family. She kept in touch. But she never returned home, not even to visit."

Father Ray had finished his tea and had chewed all of the unmelted ice. He stood up and took the empty glass over to the sink. After placing it down, he turned and stayed standing, leaning against the kitchen counter. Renee shifted her chair slightly so she was still facing him.

"Rick moved too, to Philadelphia. He wanted to be closer to home. But he had sworn he'd never go back to West Virginia, at least not to live. Being in Philly, it was only about a seven hour drive home. He got a decent job. Began to make a life for himself too. Many times he thought of calling Ashley, thinking that time might have cooled her anger enough to allow him back into her life, at least as a friend. He still loved her. And he had come to blame himself for the failure of their marriage. But something held him back. Each time he thought of calling her, he put it off for another week. Weeks turned into months, months into years.

"Then, one day, he saw a story in the *Inquirer* about the brutal murder of a prostitute in Central Park in New York. Rick looked at the photograph of the beautiful victim as she stared at him from the page. It's a stare that's haunted him ever since. It was Ashley."

Father Ray saw a knot form in Renee's throat as if his telling of Ashley's fate brought back some painful memory of her own.

"Since that day," he continued, "Rick has found it difficult to live with himself. He holds himself responsible for her death."

"But why?" Renee said, quickly re-focusing on Rick's story re-burying whatever story of her own it may have called up. "He may have things to feel guilty about, but not her murder."

"Oh, but he feels he does. He feels that if he had called her, if he had kept in touch, he would've known what was happening in her life. He thinks he would have . . . you know, been able to do something about it. She was in danger, and he didn't know, because he made no effort to know. It's how he feels, and nothing he's done since then has changed that."

"That's a sad story, Father. But what does that have to do with you and Sandra?"

"Renee, do you believe that everything that happens is, in some way, a message from God?"

"Or a temptation from Satan," she countered.

"Yes, that too. But even Satan's temptations are, like . . . in the opportunity they give us to see through his deceptions, resist him and prove our faith . . . even they're messages from God, to those whose hearts are open to Him."

He returned to his chair across the kitchen table from Renee.

"I believe that Rick was sent to me by God, to let me know that my failure to keep in touch with Sandra has kept me from knowing that she is in some kind of danger. I felt this so strongly during my last session with Rick two months ago. I knew then that I had to find Sandra right away, to protect her, or at least to warn her. It's taken me so long to find her, though. She certainly did find an out-of-the-way place to disappear into-—no offense."

"None taken," Renee responded with a slight giggle.

"Thank God she has kept in touch with at least one of our old mutual friends. Even so, it took quite a bit of cajoling and pleading on my part to get her to tell me where Sandra was. I'm afraid, though, that I may be too late."

"I think, Father, that this isn't just about a guilty conscience. It sounds to me like you still love her."

"Of course I do. I never stopped loving her. I . . .I just had to love her in a different way, a way she couldn't understand, or couldn't accept."

"Mommy! Mommy! Can we get up now?"

Carly came bounding into the kitchen in her nightshirt and underpants having just awakened from her nap.

"Of course, sweetheart," Renee said as she gave her daughter a hug. "Go upstairs and put some clothes on. And tell Jessie to get dressed too."

"Okay Mommy."

Carly looked curiously at Father Ray. Then she quickly turned on her heels and headed back up the stairs.

"She's a beautiful child," he said.

"Yes, she is. Thank you."

"So, I've told you what I need. And even though it appears you can't help me, it's your turn to tell me what you need."

His last few words were spoken in his best priestly manner.

Renee looked straight into his eyes. She responded firmly, with a slight quiver in her voice.

"Father, I need to know if my husband is having an affair with your ex-wife."

Chapter 16

The sun had begun to sink into the late afternoon sky. Every once in awhile it would disappear briefly behind one of the scattered clouds that sprinkled the western sky. Jim wasn't ready to leave the beach just yet. The continuous lapping of the waves onto the beach was hypnotically soothing. It had been a long time since he felt so relaxed. Even so, it had taken awhile to get there. As Sandra slept next to him, his mind had been troubled by the growing fear that there was some kind of connection between his rendezvous with her and the surreal events of his trip. He had certainly had other strange and even frightening things happen in his life. But he had managed to suppress them or brush them off as over-exaggerated products of a slightly paranoid mind. But now, as if he was connecting the dots in a puzzle, they all seemed to be related somehow. The picture wasn't complete yet. The thought of what it would be when finished and recognizable increasingly alarmed him. But the waves had washed those thoughts away for now drawing him into the deep meditative state where no thoughts exist.

"Hey!"

A very distant voice intruded on his blank solitude.

"Hey you!"

This time not only were the words much louder, they were accompanied by the touch of a hand on his shoulder and the shaking of his body. The vacuum of his mind was shattered and he opened his eyes. Sandra was looking down at him, her face no more than two inches from his.

"What?" he half mumbled and half groaned.

"Thirsty?"

He thought for a moment as he gained his bearings back in the physical world.

"I could go for a beer," he said. "You want something?"

"Yeah. I could use a beer too," she said as she stood up. "I'll go get them. I have to tinkle. Be right back."

Before he could say anything else she had turned and headed towards the dune crossover.

Jim propped himself up on his elbows and looked down at the water. A few kids remained in the ocean trying to body surf on totally inadequate waves. He got up and walked down to the water's edge. He stood looking out over the expanse of the ocean. Two middle-aged women walked by, occasionally stopping and stooping over as if to determine whether any of the shells lying in the surf were worthy of their collections. A family of dolphins was taking its regular evening swim heading home from whatever labors and pleasures their day had consisted of. He became entranced by them, and the idyllic life he imagined they lived—just swimming, playing and eating all day.

"Hello Jim."

Another meditative state rudely interrupted by a familiar voice coming from behind him. He turned and was surprised, and shocked, to see Dr. Westin.

"Dr. Westin! What are you . . . what a wonderful surprise," Jim lied. "Is Mrs. Westin with you?"

He knew that there must have been, at least for an instant, hand-in-the-cookie-jar guilt written all over his face. He hoped he had collected himself quickly enough for Dr. Westin, as perceptive a man as he was, to be at least uncertain enough of Jim's reaction to give his still-to-be-created plausible explanation of what he was doing there the benefit of the doubt.

"Maribel's here," Dr. Westin said. "She's taking her afternoon nap. I was just taking a stroll and saw you standing here. What a coincidence, huh? Where are Renee and the kids?"

Jim had barely heard what Dr. Westin was saying. His mind was distracted by the need to prepare an answer to the question, which he had known was coming before it was asked. He sensed a somewhat prosecutorial tone in Westin's voice. He hoped it was nothing more than his guilt-ridden imagination.

"They're at home," he said, his gaze fixed, searching Dr. Westin's countenance for any signs of doubt or disbelief. He could read nothing. "Renee's getting the kids ready for the start of school and this seemed like a good time for me to get away and recharge my batteries."

"You're alone then. Well, why don't you join Maribel and me for dinner tonight. We've ordered crabs from *Dirty Dick's*. What a shameful name for a restaurant, don't you think? But they sure have good crabs. Anyway, I'm sure we'll have enough for three. Maribel would love to see you."

While the words were innocent enough, Jim heard in his former teacher's voice and saw in the lack of symmetry in the older man's wrinkled face, a trap being set. Had he seen Jim and Sandra? Had he detected Jim's dissembling? Or were Jim's own evasiveness and guilt causing him to suspect a nefariousness in Dr. Westin's words that just wasn't there? Whatever the case, he needed to quickly develop a believable excuse for not joining them, as well as a way to cut the discussion short without seeming rude. This wouldn't be a simple task. After all, this was his mentor, a man to whom he owed a great deal. He wasn't someone who could be dismissed lightly or summarily.

"I would love to join you, Dr. Westin. But I'm afraid I can't tonight. I promised to have dinner in Kill Devil Hills with a family from my church who are here on their summer vacation. In fact," he said as he looked at his watch, "I need to go call them now to confirm the time and get directions. How about tomorrow night?"

"Tomorrow night would be fine."

"Great," Jim said. "Let's meet here about four o'clock tomorrow afternoon and we can figure out the details then."

Now he could relax a bit. He had presented Dr. Westin a reasonable explanation for not joining them for dinner that night as well as an excuse for making this conversation between old friends brief. Sandra would understand if she had to spend one dinner and maybe even one evening without him in order to keep their cover. They would have to avoid going out together in public, of course. But the thought of spending the next four days alone with Sandra at the beach house wasn't exactly a depressing one.

Dr. Westin placed his hand on Jim's shoulder. As he did, Jim caught a glimpse of Sandra walking down the steps of the dune crossover, beers in hand. He knew she would be circumspect enough not to approach him if she saw him talking to someone. But he still didn't know if Dr. Westin had seen him with her earlier. If he had, seeing her now he would realize that one of those beers was for Jim, and what was going on.

"Of course Jim. That would be fine," Dr. Westin said.

"Good," said Jim.

As hard as he tried, he couldn't keep his eyes from flickering briefly over Dr. Westin's left shoulder. As if alerted by a loud bullhorn, Dr. Westin turned in the direction of Jim's glance. Sandra was walking, a beer in each hand, toward the towels which lay directly between her and the two men. Suddenly, she made a ninety-degree turn towards no one in particular.

Westin turned back to Jim. He said nothing for several seconds. They seemed like an eternity to Jim. When Westin did speak, he spoke with the sound and the look of a sorely disappointed father.

"But if I were you Jim, I'd go home. Right now."

Jim said nothing. He was caught. He knew there was nothing he could say to make things right.

"Go home," Westin repeated sternly. With that, he turned, and without looking at Sandra, walked away.

Jim was shaken. He watched as the one man who had taught him the most about religion, about what it took to be a good clergyman, about life, slowly crossed the sands and disappeared over the dune. In less than fifteen words he had supremely chastised his protégé and had conveyed profound disappointment. The knife had cut deep. At the same time, he had also reminded Jim that he had a choice. And he had provided him with a simple road map—a road map to redemption and a return to grace.

Go home.

Dr. Westin's powerful words stayed in his mind. They weren't really repeating themselves. It was more like they remained implanted as one continuous, unending statement. They beckoned him to a safer, truer place. *Home.* Where his wife and children were. *Home.* Where his mission was. *Home.* The foundation of his values, his faith, his life.

During the six months since he first slept with Sandra nothing had hit him as powerfully as these words. Not prayer. Not Renee's looks of longing as he slowly distanced himself from her. Not the guilt which would briefly engulf him after sermonizing to his followers about evil and sin, knowing what he had done and that he would be coupling with Sandra again as soon as he could arrange it. Nothing since that first day in Sandra's living room had so starkly confronted him with the choice he had been making, eyes closed, every minute he spent with her.

Dr. Westin had forced his eyes open. The full import of his choices and their consequences were suddenly very clear to him. With that clarity began a raging battle for his emotion-wracked soul. His fear, his guilt and the goodness within him argued strongly and persuasively for ending his relationship with Sandra then and there; for returning to the life and people he had committed himself to; for seeking forgiveness. But his passion, his need for Sandra and what she provided him, remained unrelenting, overwhelming. Images not only of the physical ecstasy she brought him, but of her compassion and understanding of his needs, flooded his brain and dominated his thoughts. He searched in vain for love and faith to interject themselves into this titanic struggle within, to provide the footing he needed to make the right choice, to save his soul. Were they hidden deep beneath layers of deceit and denial? Or were they no longer even there?

This last thought particularly frightened him. Had he lost the capacity for real love? Was he losing his faith? He now knew how lost he had been, how lost he was. He now realized how much work he had to do to redeem himself, and how hard it would be. Dr. Westin had been a messenger. And the other strange occurrences on this trip? They too must have been messages. Evil, the devil himself, had been stalking him. And he was making it too easy. He had heard the message. He knew what he must do.

"Who was that?" Sandra asked as she reached out to hand him his beer.

He turned and looked at her. She had a quizzical expression. It appeared to be a look of concern for him. Her hair blew sensuously in the ocean breeze as if she was posing for a glamour magazine. Her sun-bronzed body glistened in the late afternoon rays of the sun. Every cell in his body cried out for her.

"My theology professor," he answered. "We'll have to be careful about going out."

"Did he see us together?"

"I don't know."

Jim knew that Dr. Westin had seen them, or at least knew what was going on, but he didn't want to get into a discussion about it right then.

"But whether he did or didn't, he . . . I . . . I just want to be careful."

"Of course hon," Sandra said. "Why don't we just go back to the house?"

He doubted that he was doing a very good job of hiding the fact that he was seriously disturbed by this meeting with his mentor. Her solicitousness seemed to confirm it.

"Yeah. That's a good idea," he said.

They picked up their towels and headed back to the house, keeping a respectable distance between themselves. Jim knew what he must do. At the same time, his hormones had gone into overdrive.

I'll do it after this week, he promised himself.

Sandra cooked a simple dinner of linguini with white clam sauce, salad and rolls. They ate quietly. Sandra seemed to understand that Jim was troubled and she left him to his thoughts.

The chance encounter with Dr. Westin (*Or was it chance?*) forced many troublesome thoughts on him. *Why here? Why now? Will Dr. Westin say something to Renee? What would Renee do?* Questions, and more questions, with no answers, or answers he didn't want to contemplate. Frightening questions that led to more unpleasant and fearful thoughts. Thoughts which began to morph into a collage of images from his past, both distant and recent—from scenes from his childhood to his encounters and confrontations with a force, or forces, he could not explain. It was as if he was watching a slide show of his life running at warp speed; a slide show in his mind that over time was repeating itself more and more.

"Are you done?" Sandra asked.

His mental projector turned off. He looked down at his plate. He hadn't even eaten half of what she had served him.

"Yeah. It was really good. I'm just not very . . ."

"That's okay," she interrupted. "I understand."

She got up from her seat and began to clear the table. They hadn't bothered to change out of their beachwear. Watching Sandra go back and forth from the kitchen table to the sink in her bathing suit made the rest of the world go away. He was ready again to be with her.

"Would you like to take a sunset walk on the beach?" he said.

"The sun sets in the west dear, not on the ocean," she teased.

"Well, it's still going to set." That was one thing he still felt somewhat certain of. "And if we're walking on the beach when it does, it's still a sunset walk."

Sandra walked behind Jim's chair and began to massage his neck and shoulders.

"Of course. I'd love to," she said. "But what about your theology professor? You wanted to be careful about going out."

"They're having a crab feast tonight." He rolled his neck around as she dug her fingers into his shoulders and shoulder blades. "By the time they're done it'll be pretty dark even if they do come down to the beach. I think it'll be fine."

As she skillfully manipulated her fingers on and around the muscle knots that pervaded his back and shoulders, Jim began to feel that everything would be okay. He would enjoy every touch, every kiss, every sensual pleasure, every second of this week with Sandra. Then, somehow, some way, he would gather the willpower and strength to end the affair and begin to rebuild his marriage. He would return to the life he was meant to live. Sandra would understand. During their time together everything she had done seemed designed to please him and meet his needs. She would surely accept that this is what he needed to do if he told her he must. He would explain that not only was it his will that they separate, but that it was God's. He was certain she would understand. But he wouldn't tell her now. It would be a great week. Then he would tell her.

The sun had dropped below the horizon as they walked south, hand in hand, along the water's edge. The gentle tide occasionally came far enough ashore to coolly wash over their bare feet. They paid little attention to the others on the beach. For now, the beach was theirs, and theirs alone.

They were in a quiet moment, just looking into each other's eyes as they walked along, saying nothing. Out of the corner of his eye, in the southeastern sky, Jim caught an unusual light display. It was enough to draw his attention away from Sandra's hypnotic emerald eyes. Starting at the horizon and emanating from a single point were six bands of multicolored light spreading to the northwest like a peacock's tail, or like six rainbows that had been pulled from both ends to straighten them out.

"Look at that," he said to Sandra, pointing to the display.

By now others had seen the phenomenon and stopped walking, gathering in groups to discuss what might be causing this unusual display. One man suggested it looked like the aurora borealis. Another instructed that they were too far south for even unusual sunspot activity to allow the Northern Lights to be seen here.

Jim and Sandra listened to all of the amateur astronomers and their pseudo-scientific discourse. They added nothing to it. They just watched. As it grew darker the aurora's lights grew brighter. The blue went from a sky blue to a deep ocean blue. The yellow went from pale to rich. And the pinkish-orange band went to a fiery red. It was as if Disney had built a magic theme park in the middle of the ocean and was entertaining the Outer Banks with an evening-ending laser light show.

It wasn't Disney, though. It was nature, the real thing. Jim stood in awe of its beauty and its power—its power over those below who didn't know what it was or where it came from, but stood looking at it, transfixed and powerless to avert their eyes. He marveled at how God could wield and reveal His power in such simple ways. Then, in an instant, it was gone. The lights had gone out as if the celestial hands that had straightened the six rainbows simply turned the light switch off. And, as quickly as the lights went out, a deep darkness fell over the beach.

The darkness, in its own way, was as spectacular as the aurora. Despite the artificial lighting of the homes running along the beach at the dune line, the beach remained dark enough to allow a view of the sky so littered with stars and planets that it could honestly be said that the color of the night sky was white with black. The Milky Way was clearly visible running from the southwest sky to the northeast. It was a sky rarely seen anymore by city dwellers and fast being lost to light pollution in even more rural areas of the country. It was a sky unlike any Jim had seen since his days in Africa.

The darkness of night also created a new and different world on the ground. The sand crabs were now out in force, scurrying to and fro, playing their nightly game of risk, seeing how close they could get to walking human feet without getting crushed. The crabs almost always won, getting a bonus when an unsuspecting two-legged creature — usually female, but not always — would scream out at having been startled by the quick sand warriors darting across her path. Jim hadn't realized that a moonlight walk on the beach could involve so much activity, or be so humorous.

The pitch darkness of the post-aurora night began to give way to the softening nightlight of the rising moon in the low sky over the almost still sea. As the moon rose, the sea whispered back to it with the reflection of its own light—a whisper so soft and alluring as to make friends of strangers and lovers of friends. Closer to shore the waves of the calm sea continued to roll slowly in, the separated white-foamed breakers joining together like earth-borne shooting stars colliding and forming as one, then disappearing as quickly and mysteriously as their heavenly cousins.

It was as perfect a night as two lovers could ask for. Jim and Sandra drank in the perfection, walking hand in hand, arm in arm, stopping occasionally to look into each other's eyes, kiss softly and avow their love for one another. They talked about nothing in particular and consciously drank in every moment in an effort to slow time down enough to make the night last just a few hours short of forever.

As it approached ten-thirty, Jim could no longer restrain his growing passion. And there was no question that Sandra's hormones were raging just as wildly.

"If we don't get back to the house soon," he joked, "people walking on the beach are going to have something other than sand crabs to watch as entertainment."

She laughed and softly caressed his left buttock. They weren't far from their dune crossover. They left the wet sand of the water's edge and walked up the dry sandy beach. As they walked past the undeveloped scrub just south of their dune crossover, Sandra suddenly lurched against Jim and let out a short, sharp shriek. They stopped. Looking to his left and immediately beyond her, he saw a small, furry, four-legged animal darting onto the beach through the sea oats just behind the dune. It ran towards three similar animals that had already come out of the scrub. The four animals then passed by the couple, all the while appearing to be scouring the beach for food. They moved slowly, and in a pattern that never took them more than a few yards away from Jim and Sandra.

"What should we do?" Sandra asked Jim in a trembling voice.

"Just stand still for a minute," he said. "They're not interested in us. They're looking for food. Just don't startle them. They're wild and they could be rabid."

He was reassuring, but she seemed little comforted.

"What are they?" she asked, gripping his arm with both of hers.

"They look like foxes."

"At the beach?"

"They probably live in the scrub."

It was a guess. Jim knew nothing about foxes.

"When can we move?" Her grip on his arm was so strong now that his circulation was being cut off. "I'm scared just standing here."

"Well, they seem to be preoccupied," he said. "Let's go. Just hold my arm, a little more gently thank you"—he pried her vice-like fingers a little looser—"and walk very slowly."

They moved cautiously toward the crossover that was still about a hundred feet away. The foxes stopped their digging in the sand and turned to watch the loving couple walk slowly away from them. His back now to the animals, Jim felt a sharpness in four different spots on his back. It was as if each pair of fox eyes had staked out its claim on him. Then, in a blink of one of those eyes, the animals sprinted northward. Three of them planted themselves on either side of the couple while the fourth planted itself directly in front of them.

Jim and Sandra stopped. She was close to hysterical.

"What do we do Jim?" she pleaded. She was trembling hard and her fingers locked themselves back onto his arm, her nails digging painfully into his flesh.

He looked at the fox directly in front of them. His mind immediately shot back to the incident the day before with the red wolf. But this small animal was nowhere near as menacing. Nor was he paralyzed as he had been with the wolf. *On the other hand,* he thought, *yesterday I was in a car. There's nothing here between it and us.*

148

"Stay still," he soothingly whispered to Sandra. Again he pried her fingers loose. He kissed her softly on the cheek.

He looked around for a rock or piece of wood he could use as a weapon. There was nothing within easy reach. The animals maintained their positions. They made no sounds. They weren't baring their teeth. They just stood and watched. The stand-off continued for a couple of minutes. To the distraught couple it seemed much longer. Then, from the landing of the crossover came a loud voice.

"Look! Foxes!" a young boy cried out.

On the landing Jim could make out three people. It appeared to be a boy and his parents now looking and pointing in his direction. All of a sudden the young boy, who couldn't have been more than eight, sprinted down the steps and ran towards them.

"No! Bobby! Come back here!" the boy's father cried out.

It was too late. The foxes turned towards the boy. Bobby, now appearing to have recognized the danger, stopped. But before he could turn to run back to the crossover, the animals raced towards him and attacked.

Bobby's screams pierced the still night air. He fell to the ground, his hands and arms trying to cover his head and face, as the foxes' sharp teeth snapped and grabbed at him. His father ran up to the pack and tried scaring them away by kicking and throwing sand at them. He was able to drive the animals back a foot or two, but then they immediately set upon the boy again. Then, in an act of paternal self-sacrifice, the father dove into the pack and threw himself onto his son, covering and protecting the boy with his larger body. The boy continued to cry out.

"Daddy! Daddy! Get them off! Get them off!"

The foxes couldn't reach the boy now. Instead, they attacked the father with the greater ferocity his larger size demanded. As they tore at him with increasing fury, the mother stood on the crossover wailing.

"Help them! Somebody please help them!"

"What do we do?" Sandra cried out. "We've got to do *something* Jim!"

It had all happened in the wink of an eye. The horror of the scene unfolding before them had frozen Jim. Sandra's cries unfroze him. He looked around. Near the dune he saw what appeared to be a large piece of wood that could be used as a club. He ran over, picked it up and headed towards the attacking pack. When he reached them he swung at the nearest fox. He struck it square on its right hindquarters knocking it shrieking several feet from the pile. The other three immediately stopped their attack on the father and son. They turned towards Jim.

He stood facing the three angry animals holding the club in a baseball batter's stance. He wanted to keep all three of them within his sight. Despite being freed for the moment from their vicious attackers, the man and his son didn't move. Jim couldn't tell whether it was from fright or the extent of their injuries, but he was too busy concentrating on the hunters whose prey he had now become to focus on the others.

The three animals moved slowly and warily towards him. As they did so they created more space between themselves. It was as if they had a plan, a plan developed by intelligence, not merely instinct, to spread their ranks and make it impossible for him to hold off all three at once. The fox he had previously identified in his own mind as the leader, the one that had stood directly in front of him and Sandra, was in the middle and walked a few paces ahead of the other two. Jim's eyes darted quickly from left to right to follow all three of them, as he slowly retreated leading the animals further from the wounded pair they had abandoned for the time being.

Suddenly, the fourth fox, having recovered from the shock of Jim's blow, its pain having turned into ferocious, bestial anger, raced through the gap between the leader and the fox on Jim's far left, and lunged at him, leaving its feet and aiming directly at his throat. Just before its teeth would have sunk into his flesh and likely severed the carotid artery, he instinctively raised his left arm and hit the animal directly under its jaw, repelling it onto its back and momentarily stunning it once more.

At that, the fox on the left made its move. It stayed low to the ground and streaked swiftly towards him. He swung the club low, missing the animal but causing it to veer off to the left. He immediately turned his head back to check on the other two and saw the attack from the right just in time to swing the club back again. He missed but caused the fox on the right to cut short its attack.

The leader seemed content for the time being to watch the action like a general directing his troops from behind the lines. Jim swung back around to his left and saw a mass hurtling through the dim moonlight at him. He swung the club hard and this time made contact, hitting the animal square on the side of its head. It hit the sand with a dull thud. He didn't have time to make sure it was down for good. The first injured fox and the fox on his right had both resumed their attacks. He swung the club wildly, back and forth, to keep their snarling, snapping jaws from tasting the flesh of his exposed legs. The two animals advanced just far enough to avoid the blow their colleague had taken and then moved back. Forward again, then back. Several times. As they did so they also moved sideways, one to the left and one to the right, requiring an ever broader range to Jim's swings until they had gone so far that they were actually once again both within his field of vision. But to keep them within his sight, he had been turned completely around so that his back was now to the leader who had still not jumped into the fray.

Jim was totally preoccupied with keeping the two attack foxes at bay. Without his knowledge, the leader took aim at his back. It sprang into the air and hit him between the shoulder blades with enough force to knock him face first into the sand. The sudden shock of the blow threw the club from his hand. Dazed, he knew he was now defenseless against the rabid pack of animals. He instinctively put his hands over his head and curled his body into a ball. He figured he needed just a few seconds to clear his head. Then he could try to get up and defend himself. And he knew that a few seconds, at best, was all he had.

"Get out of here! Go! Git!"

It was a loud, thunderous voice. He wasn't sure where it was coming from, except that it was from up above him

If that's you God, he thought half-joking as he lay there, *it's a great time to finally hear your actual voice.*

The foxes backed away. Jim raised his head just a bit to see what was going on. He saw the lead fox look back towards the crossover from where the voice had apparently come. Without making a sound, all four of the animals turned and ran back towards the scrub. As they reached the dune, the lead fox stopped briefly. It looked back at Jim, showed its teeth in what looked eerily like a grin, and quickly joined the others over the dune and into the scrub.

Jim slowly picked himself up and started back to where the man and his boy had been attacked. He was out of breath and his whole body ached from the battle. But he had come out of it uninjured. Sandra ran to him, her face wet with tears and filled with horror. She threw herself into his arms.

"Oh Jim!" she cried. "It was so horrible. I thought you were going to die."

He hugged her hard.

"It's all right sweetheart. They're gone. They can't hurt us now. They're gone."

He held her for a moment, then gently pushed her away.

"Let's go see how the others are," he said.

When they reached the boy and his parents, Bobby and his father were being attended to by a man Jim hadn't seen before. If this was the man who scared the foxes away, he thought, he wasn't nearly as large as his booming voice would have led one to believe. In fact, he was a slight, bespectacled, almost timid looking man.

"Here, let me look at you," the man said to the still frightened boy. "I won't hurt you. My name's Perry. What's your name?"

"Bobby," the boy said, still sobbing.

"Okay Bobby, let's look at those scratches."

"Is there anything I can do to help?" Jim asked.

"Not really," replied Perry. "I called 9-1-1 on my cell phone. The paramedics should be here any minute. Are you all right?"

"Just a little shaken up. I'll be fine. How do you think the boy and his father are?"

"Some pretty nasty bites here."

Jim could see that both father and son had received numerous gashes and were bleeding from various parts of their bodies. The boy's mother went over to Perry and her son and took Bobby into her arms and cradled her child as he continued to cry.

"You and your son will have to be treated for rabies," Perry said to the father. "But everything will be all right."

"We're so grateful to you, to both of you," the father, still somewhat stunned, told Jim and Perry as he sat next to his wife and son. The cuts on his body continued to bleed. But he ignored them. "We could be dead if it wasn't for you. How can we ever repay you?"

"No need for that," Perry jumped in. "Here come the paramedics. Now just relax and let them take care of you."

"Thank you. Thank you so much," the mother said again, her eyes still filled with the tears shed for her child.

The red lights of the ambulance that had pulled up on the road at the foot of the crossover steps flickered in the night. The paramedics rushed up and down the crossover with their equipment and a hand-held stretcher. As they tended to Bobby and his father, cleansing their wounds and preparing to take them to the hospital, Jim, Sandra and Perry climbed the steps of the crossover and stopped on the landing. They looked out at the beach where the attack occurred. Jim put his arm around Sandra to comfort her. She laid her head on his shoulder still softly crying.

"I've never heard of foxes attacking people like that," Jim said to Perry.

"No, it is very unusual," the stranger confirmed, "except when they're rabid. Then they might. But these foxes didn't seem to be acting rabies-mad. They almost seemed to have a purpose, don't you think?"

"I . . . I don't know. I . . . I'm sorry. My name is Jim Donovan. And this is my . . . this is Sandra."

Jim held out his hand, wondering about what the stranger had just said but deciding that he should at least learn who this man was who had just rescued him.

"Pleasure," the stranger replied. He took Jim's hand and shook it. It was not a firm handshake; not what he would have expected given his first impression of this man. "My name is Perry Lachaise."

"Tell me Mr. Lachaise . . ."

"Please. Perry."

"Okay. Perry. Tell me, how is it you could make those foxes run off just by yelling at them?"

"Don't know," Perry answered. He moved his wire-rimmed glasses up the bridge of his nose with the middle finger of his left hand. "Guess I've just always had a way with animals. And you Mr. Donovan—may I call you Jim?"

"Of course."

"You, Jim, are a very brave man for what you did to save that little boy and his father."

"Not really. I just reacted."

"Very brave reactions. If I might ask, what is it that you do, Jim? For a living, that is."

"I'm . . . I'm a teacher."

Jim considered this at least a technically honest answer.

"Ahh. A teacher," Perry said. "Yes, a brave profession as well."

Jim looked back down onto the beach where the attacks occurred.

"I'm still baffled by those foxes even being here," he said. "Isn't it strange for them to be so near the beach?"

The stranger's prying into his personal life had been disquieting. Jim looked to steer the conversation back to what had just happened.

"Apparently not. I understand this family of red foxes . . ."

"They weren't red," Jim corrected. "They were gray, or silver."

"Doesn't matter," Perry said. "They're the same thing. Silver foxes belong to the red fox family. Anyway, I understand there used to be hundreds of feral cats around here. The foxes came and cleansed them out. Now they've made this area their home. They live off discarded human food, sand crabs, anything they can find. Guess they like oceanfront living, just like we do."

"What do you suppose would cause foxes to attack people like that, Mr. Lachaise?" Sandra asked, assuming their new acquaintance had a level of expertise much greater than their own regarding the animals.

"I expect something or someone provoked them, ma'am."

"No. No one did anything," she protested.

"Perhaps."

The stranger looked at her and grinned. There was an oddness about him that Jim couldn't identify. He had a strange feeling of *déjà vu*, that somehow he knew him. But he couldn't imagine where they would have ever met. *Even the name sounds familiar,* he thought. His thoughts were interrupted by the orders being barked out by the paramedic in charge directing the placement of Bobby and his father into the ambulance for transport to the hospital. The three of them turned and watched as the ambulance pulled away.

"What do you do for a living, Mr. Lachaise?"

Sandra too seemed to be curious about this unusual man. Her curiosity appeared to trump her distress, at least for the time being.

"I'm a freelance writer, ma'am."

"What do you write?"

"Stories. Stories about people, life, death. I find writing lets me be very creative. I can make things up completely, or I can take real experiences and put them in my stories."

The more Perry Lachaise talked, the more familiar he seemed to Jim, and the more uneasy Jim felt about him.

"In fact," Lachaise went on, "I think what happened tonight might fit right into a story I'm writing. I especially like the power of being able to make the story end any way I want. It's almost . . . almost God-like. Wouldn't you agree, Sandra?"

"I . . . I wouldn't know, Mr. Lachaise. I'm not very creative myself."

"Nonsense. We're all creative in one way or another. Every day each one of us creates a new chapter in our own book of life. Some are just better at telling the story than others." He looked at her and grinned again. "Well, I guess I should be going. Good evening Jim. Good evening Sandra."

"Good night Mr. La . . . Perry," Jim answered.

Perry, he thought. *Dr. Pe're? Is that what's familiar about this guy? Just the coincidence of that name? Yes. And no. There is that, but not just that. What about Lachaise? I've heard, or seen, that name before too. But where? When? This guy looks nothing like Dr. Pe're. Yet . . . yet . . .*

Jim took Perry's limp hand and gave him a firm handshake nonetheless.

"And thank you," Jim said. "Thank you again."

"I'm just glad I was here to help," Perry Lachaise responded. "Kismet, I suppose. Good night."

Lachaise turned, walked up Elysian Way, and disappeared into the night.

Sandra looked at Jim.

"Let's go home," she said plaintively.

"Amen to that," he said as he kissed her on the forehead.

As they turned to go down the stairs to the street, Jim looked up in the sky and saw a brilliant, flaming meteorite. It was much larger and lasted many seconds longer than the average shooting star. *Nothing about this trip has been normal,* he thought. He didn't bother to point out or mention the meteorite to Sandra.

Chapter 17

"Mommy! Mommy! Look! A shooting star. A really *big* one!" Jessica's cries pierced the still summer night as she pointed to the star-filled sky. Unlike most shooting stars, this brilliant, flaming red and yellow streak across the sky remained visible long enough after Jessica's excited outcry for Carly, Renee and Father Ray to see it before it dissolved into a fine meteoric dust and scattered into the atmosphere never having the opportunity to call the earth its home. When it disappeared Jessica and Carly began jumping up and down.

"I get to make a wish! I get to make a wish!" they both shouted.

"Huh uh!" Jessica yelled at Carly. "I saw it first. It's my wish."

"I saw it too!" Carly shot back. "I get to make the wish!"

"Girls, no fighting," Renee scolded them mildly.

She motioned for them to come over to her at the patio table where she and Father Ray sat. The girls walked slowly to her, each of them wearing a pout. She put one arm around each of them, one on either side of her.

"You know," she said, looking from one to the other, "when you both see the same shooting star, if you get together and agree on a wish, it has twice as good a chance of coming true. Do you think if you talk about it you could come up with a wish for both of you?"

"Sure Mommy." Big sister (by five minutes) Carly took over. "Let's go on the swings, Jessie, and figure out a wish."

The girls ran over to the swing set in the far corner of the Donovan backyard to begin their negotiations. Renee and Father Ray were left alone on the backyard patio.

"You're really wonderful with those kids," Ray said. His finger absent-mindedly traced the rim of his coffee cup as he talked. "Some people are just born to be great parents."

"Yeah, I wish." Renee chuckled. "However good I may or may not be as a parent right now comes from a lot of trial and error. Mostly error."

"Thank you again for having me for dinner. And for recommending the Magnolia House. You guessed right. They were booked. But the manager—Jane was it?"

"Yes. Jane McCorkle."

"Jane said that the extra room kept for the innkeeper's mother could be used in special circumstances. I guess a referral from you is considered a special circumstance."

Father Ray stopped fiddling with his cup and drank the last of the coffee in it.

"It's the least I could do, Father. Especially after being so rude to you this afternoon."

"No Renee. You weren't rude at all. You were honest with your feelings. I don't know if anything's going on between Sandra and your husband. But if there is, we have to find out. And find a way to stop it. Whatever is going on with Sandra, I feel she's in danger. And if she's with your husband, then I fear he may be in danger too."

Carly and Jessica ran up to their mother with enthusiasm.

"Mommy, me and Jessie have a wish to make on the star together," Carly announced proudly.

"Wonderful." Renee beamed at her children. "What is it?"

Carly turned to her sister with her hand outstretched as if to introduce her.

"We wish that Daddy will come home tomorrow!" Jessica shouted. "Is that a good wish Mommy?"

Renee and Father Ray looked at each other. Renee turned back to the girls and took each one by the hand.

"That's a wonderful wish," she said with a comforting Mommy smile. "That's my wish too. And you know the great thing about your Daddy? Even when he isn't here, he's always with us in spirit. Tomorrow I'm sure he'll be with us in spirit even more than today, just because of your wish."

The twins looked at each other gleefully and shook their little fists triumphantly at their success in developing such a great and powerful wish. Getting up from her seat, Renee took them both by the hand.

"It's time for bed girls. I've let you stay up way past your bedtime tonight. Say goodnight to Father Ray."

"Good night Father Ray," they said in unison.

"Can you come back tomorrow?" Carly asked him.

"I don't know. Maybe."

"Then if me and Jessie's wish comes true, you can meet my Daddy!"

"Yes, I would like that. I would like that very much."

"I'll just be a couple of minutes," Renee said as she started to walk the girls into the house.

"Renee," Father Ray said as he rose from his chair. "Thank you again for dinner and a wonderful evening. I need to get up early tomorrow. There's not much time left to find . . ."

"I understand," Renee said. "Thank you for your company, and your counsel."

He started around the house to let himself out through the side gate. Before he had quite disappeared around the corner Renee called out to him.

"Father! One favor?"

He stopped and looked back. The picture of the lovely young mother, children in tow, created a precious image.

"Certainly Renee. What is it?"

"Could you say a special prayer tonight?"

"Of course. With pleasure. And hope."

She smiled. The girls pulled on her hands and dragged her into the house.

He had left his prayer book back in his room, but he didn't need it. The appropriate prayer came to him right away. He turned and faced the Donovan house. He folded his hands together and closed his eyes, and prayed.

"Visit, we beseech you, O Lord, this house and family, and drive far from it all the snares of the enemy; let your holy angels dwell therein, who will keep us in peace, and let your blessing be always upon us; through our Lord Jesus Christ. Amen."

He crossed himself and walked the few short blocks to the Magnolia House Bed and Breakfast.

The children were asleep the moment their heads hit their pillows. Renee returned to the backyard. She had kept most of the house lights off so they could see as many stars as possible. It was Tuesday night. On Tuesday night she liked to listen to a radio program that played music from Broadway hits. She loved musicals and the show would often brighten her mood when she most needed it. *And I certainly need it now,* she thought to herself.

She placed her radio on the patio table and turned it on. She lay back in the recliner chair to look up at the stars and listen. Wafting from the radio's speaker came the eerie introduction to *The Music of the Night* from Andrew Lloyd Webber's *The Phantom of the Opera*.

Nighttime sharpens, heightens each sensation;
Darkness stirs and wakes imagination.

How true, she thought. The image of Jim and Sandra Chievers together was bad enough when she first allowed it into her head that afternoon. But at night, especially now that she was alone, the image was so much sharper, so much more real. This song, she knew, would certainly not elevate her mood. But she couldn't turn the radio off. She couldn't resist listening to the haunting words of this darkly beautiful song; its call to *surrender to your darkest dreams,* to *let your fantasies unwind in this darkness which you know you cannot fight,* to *let your mind start a journey through a strange new world.* She knew this song was being sung to her. But why? To seduce her? To invite her into a new world, a world of mystery and darkness? Or to warn her? But of what? Her future? Jim's? Jim and Sandra? Her and . . .?

As she listened to the final refrain, she didn't know whether to be angry, or afraid.

> *Floating, falling, sweet intoxication.*
> *Touch me, trust me, savour each sensation.*
> *Let the dream begin, let your darker side give in*
> *to the power of the music that I write,*
> *the power of the music of the night.*
> *You alone can make my song take flight,*
> *help me make the music of the night.*

Chapter 18

Hot pellets of water shot out from the showerhead. Jim had completed washing himself and was enjoying the total relaxation several moments of immersion in the hot stream provided. It had been a tiring day. More so than he would ever have anticipated. When they had returned to the house, Sandra, herself still shaken, had noticed his fatigue.

"Why don't you take a long, hot shower," she had suggested.

"Yeah, I think I will," he had agreed. But he couldn't hide the deeply worried, even sad, look on his face.

"Wipe that clown's frown off your face," she had said with pursed, pouting lips while she stroked his cheek. "That won't do for what I have planned for tonight."

He had tried to force a smile as he turned to go undress.

"And hon," she had said as he walked towards their bedroom, "don't wear anything but your briefs, and meet me on the widow's walk."

The hot shower was working. As he stood there motionless, he felt all of the tension in his usually tight neck and shoulders melting away. Just a few moments earlier Sandra's words alone had been unable to do the trick. But now, as if in meditation, he found all of his troubling and bothersome thoughts escaping his mind and being carried away in the steam. Visions of Sandra now entered his emptied mind—smiling, beckoning, promising pleasure unparalleled. The rest of his mind was blank, forming a black background against which the image of her naked body stood out in stark relief. Every muscle in his body and mind reached a level of complete relaxation, except his member that had fully hardened at the mind's sight of this female perfection. Sandra was waiting. It was time to turn fantasy into reality.

He got out of the shower, dried himself off and put on a pair of black bikini briefs. It was at times like this, he thought as he admired himself in the floor length mirror on the bathroom door, that he particularly appreciated the good genes his parents had passed on to him.

He walked out of the bathroom. The living room was dark. All of the lights in the house were turned off. It took his eyes a few seconds to adjust. When they did, he walked to the back door and out onto the back porch. The night was totally dark. The moon, which had hung low on the horizon earlier that night, had disappeared. The houses on either side of theirs were also dark. How curious, he thought again, that those houses appeared empty at this time of the year.

The houses across the undeveloped scrub were lit, but they were far enough away that their lights had little effect on the darkness around him other than to further accentuate it. The only other light came from the Mariners' sky, ancient stars whose resplendent light, having traveled over miles and time incomprehensible to the human mind, was reduced to little more than sparkles and specks scattered on the vast black canvas of space. All in all, it was a perfect night for outdoor romance.

He turned to his right to the enclosed portion of the porch immediately under and supporting the widow's walk. He entered the enclosure and walked to the door on the other side which led to a platform on the stairs upward. He went out the door, turned to his left and climbed the stairs. There was a light cool breeze. *Just enough,* he thought, *to keep our bodies from getting too sweaty.*

At the top of the stairs he turned to enter the elevated balcony. To his left, against the railing nearest the house and overlooking the main roof, were a table and two chairs that had been moved to the far edge of the porch. On the table were a boom box, two wine glasses, a bottle of *Chateau Mouton Rothschild 1971* and a dozen raw oysters on the half shell. Between the table and chairs and the wooden railing furthest from the house on the right lay a fully inflated, queen size air mattress.

On the mattress sat Sandra, upright, her legs tucked and extending back on her right side. It was dark, but not too dark for Jim to see that she was dressed in a crimson, two-piece lace negligee. The top was untied, each side held loosely in place against the side of its respective breast. Both breasts were fully visible through the flimsy fabric. The matching bottom was obviously not designed to conceal the ultimate goal. All it did was create the illusion of an obstacle that must be overcome to reach it.

From the boom box came the romantic crooning of Frank Sinatra. Sandra looked at Jim with a child-like expectation in contrast to the very grown-up scene before him. The contradiction was a powerful aphrodisiac.

She smiled.

"Do you like?" she asked, almost bashfully.

"Do I like? What's not to like?" He sat on the air mattress facing her. "The night is perfect. You're perfect. This place is perfect. Or so it seems. What about the neighbors?"

"Don't worry about that," she said. "I've rented both houses next door for the week. No one will be bothering us."

"It sounds like you've thought of everything," he said admiring this beautiful woman with brains to match.

"Since this is the first time we've been able to spend this much time together," she said, "I just want everything to be perfect."

Her voice softly sounded the desire that her eyes screamed out. She took the already opened bottle of wine and filled each glass. She raised her glass. He followed.

"To us," she said as they clinked glasses.

"To us."

"Forever," she added as she raised her glass to her lips.

"Forever," he agreed, remembering what he had promised himself earlier that day, but putting it aside for now.

They drank the rich, red wine. They fed each other the oysters straight from the shells. They talked lovers' small talk and laughed at each other's silly jokes throughout Sinatra's anthology. During the sweet love songs they kissed tenderly and held hands. Without any verbal agreement they refrained from petting or doing anything more that could lead to full lovemaking before that unspoken, agreed-upon time when they would both know it was right. They sang along with

Old Blue Eyes as he ripped through *My Way* and *That's Life* as if these were anthems he was singing just for them.

Just as they finished off the wine, the tape ended. Jim's sexual desire was at its peak. He could see that Sandra was there too. The wine was coursing through their systems stimulating their bodies and their minds. The oysters were working their mythical magic. They looked at each other in the stillness of the night. The sides of her top had long before fallen away fully exposing her breasts. They both knew it. The time was now. Jim leaned over, put his hand on her breast and started to kiss her.

She pulled away.

"Wait," she interrupted. "We've got to have music. We can't do it without music."

The wine had made her giddy. He watched with amusement as she fumbled through a handful of tapes on the table trying to see their covers in the dark. Finally, she found what she wanted.

"Here. This is the one," she said as she clumsily replaced the Sinatra tape. "A real golden oldie—*The Doors' Greatest Hits*." She put her arms around Jim's neck. "There's nothing," she cooed in her most siren-like manner, "like screwing to The Doors."

As the first cut started to play, Sandra removed her top, put her arms back around his neck, swayed her hips from side to side, and playfully sang along to the words of *Hello, I Love You.*

Only two lines into the song, she sang no more. In one coordinated movement, Jim swung her legs around, gently pushed her onto her back, placed his lips on hers, inserted his tongue deep into her mouth, placed his right hand on her left breast playfully fingering her nipple and began what he was certain would be the most passionate night of his life.

Jim could almost feel the burning needles of passion jumping from her softly caressed breast deep into her loins. She wrapped her left leg up and over his hip and pressed her pelvis against his while returning the thrust of his French kiss. They were already well on their way to an unrestrained, unthinking sexual plunder when the tape moved on to the delightfully decadent wailing of Jim Morrison singing *Light My Fire.*

It was almost too much for Jim to bear. Whatever shred of human conscience and awareness had remained was torn away in the explosion of primitive lovemaking caused by the addition of Morrison's unstable fuel to the highly combustible body heat they had increasingly generated over the course of the past six months, each session hotter than the last, magnified exponentially the longer they were apart.

The night was on fire. He pulled at her panties so hard he tore them right off her body. She barely got his briefs to his knees before she grabbed his penis and put it between her legs.

"Put it in. All the way," she groaned. "Into my belly, baby! All the way into my belly!"

Nothing else existed. No one else existed. Aside from the words of the song and their own animalistic cries, human thought and language no longer existed. Even the words of the song became lost to his mind. Like the music itself, they were simply felt, experienced. There was no knowledge. There was no cognition. Pure instinct had taken over.

That pure instinct, with the help of Sandra's insistent hand, led Jim's penis to her vaginal lips and beyond, thrusting forcefully through the warm moisture deep into her surprisingly snug canal— snugness enhanced by an erection the likes of which he had never experienced. With each thrust the damp and tender friction it created sensitized it to such a pitch that there was nothing else for the joyful burning of expectant ejaculation to do but to radiate throughout his body. Within him there grew the image and sensation of his entire body coming, semen flowing not only from the tip of his penile head, but from all of his orifices, all of his appendages, all of his pores. The image itself further excited him causing a never ending circle of alternately enhancing sexual sensations. He was in the throes of an unearthly rapture and all he could do was thrust harder and faster and cry out words and sounds he himself could neither hear nor understand.

They were one. So much so that he now felt her feelings and thoughts as if they were his. For a moment they even supplanted his own. He felt—he *knew* she had never been penetrated by something so large. With each thrust now came the feeling that the head of his penis was about to burst through her navel. Each time he expected her to feel pain, but there was none—only a fullness and a rush of millions of pin-prick sensations from head to toe so intense and addictive that every time he withdrew, her hands, planted firmly on his ass, pushed him back into her with as much force as the two of them, working together, could deliver.

He might have been concerned about the effect her shrieks of joy were having on anyone within half a mile of their air mattress if, at that moment, he had been at all capable of existing outside the impenetrable fortress of ecstasy their mad copulation had created for them. But no one else was on his mind or in his heart. As they writhed, thrusted, shrieked and groaned in each other's arms and bodies, nothing existed but the pleasure of the moment, and the expectation of the overwhelming thrill they were about to enjoy together.

Enjoy it they did. As Morrison sang the last refrains of *Light My Fire* Jim grasped the cheeks of Sandra's buttocks. He lifted her pelvis towards him as he rammed himself into her as far as he could. Then, letting out a long, wailing groan, he expelled an enormous stream of warm semen. Sandra, seeming to have recognized that his moment was at hand, and about to come herself, dug her nails into his firm buns. As the warm flow of his seed entered her, her body tensed and then trembled violently as her exploding orgasm matched his. Her repeated cries of "Oh God!" and "Oh shit!" continued well after his groans had turned to panting.

They remained in the missionary position holding each other tight, his still erect penis refusing to come out. Without speaking, he knew, and was sure she did too, that they had both just experienced the fuck of a lifetime. As he lay there, his head resting on the mattress next to hers, his eyes closed. He thought how ironic it was that this most intense of sexual experiences occurred in the most normal manner. There were no exotic oils, no sexual toys, not even unusual positions. Just the standards—good wine, romance, the stars, Sinatra and . . . well, The Doors were something of a twist.

Another image formed in his mind—the image of a gleeful, loving Renee inviting him into her arms and her bed. Her look was seductive, yet pure and full of unmistakable love for him. It was a pleasing and pleasurable image, one of joy and longings fulfilled. For a brief moment it was Renee he was in; Renee who was holding him; Renee who had pleased him with such reckless abandon, loss of inhibition and lack of modesty; Renee who had loved him so fully and totally; Renee who deserved his true and absolute love in return.

"Mmmm," Sandra purred with blissful delight, instantly bringing him back to the moment, back to her.

He lifted his head. Being careful not to slip out of her, he raised himself up and looked down at her face. Her eyes were closed but her face, anchored by the satisfied grin of her lips, was the epitome of contentment. It was not Renee, but Sandra, who was the source of this night's nuclear eroticism. It was Renee he loved, but it was Sandra he had to have.

"Was it as good for you as it was for me?" he asked mockingly.

"It's never as good for the woman as it is for the man," she answered, feigning indifference. She giggled and quickly kissed him. "God, that was the greatest I've ever been fucked. Where did you get that enormous cock? Did you have a transplant or something?"

"I don't know."

He truly was equally amazed.

"But I'm not complaining," he said. "I just hope I can keep it because now you're spoiled."

"Well, so far you're keeping it just fine," she said as she tightened the muscles of her vagina around it. "Does that mean you're ready for more?"

Before he could answer, The Doors launched into *Love Me Two Times*. They looked at each other and broke out in laughter.

"Does that answer your question?"

"Mmm hmm. It sure does," she said.

She pulled his head to hers and kissed him passionately. Jim's hips and pelvis began to slowly move up and down, guiding his still oversized member in and out of Sandra's private portal of love.

Don't let it ever end, he thought. *Don't let it ever end.*

Chapter 19

"Renee! Renee!" Jim's voice, distant and agitated, pierced the screen of Renee's open bedroom window.

"Renee!"

She got out of bed. Dressed only in her full-length cotton nightgown, Renee ran outside into the still night.

She called out to him.

"Jim!"

"Renee!" returned Jim's voice. It came from the direction of the church.

She ran towards the church, her bare feet quickly becoming sore from pounding on the cement sidewalks and asphalt roads between their home and the church.

"Jim!" she shouted as she turned on Dixie and the church came into view. There was no answer this time. When she got to the church she tried the front doors. They shouldn't have been unlocked, but they were. She went in. The church was empty, except for Jim. He was standing behind his lectern. He was smiling strangely, yet with a pained look on his face.

"Jim!" she cried out to him. Then, he was gone. Panic-stricken, she ran out of the church.

"Jim!" she called out again.

"Renee!"

His voice, still distant, now came from the woods beyond the edge of town leading down to the river. She followed it, running into the woods, scratching her feet on stones and twigs, falling once, finding herself moving ever more slowly on weighted legs. She called out again into the darkness.

"Jim!"

No answer.

"Jim!" she called out again. Still, no answer.

When she got to where the river should have been, there was no river. Instead, there was a large stone building built in the classical style. She saw a long flight of steps leading up to a portico containing several Corinthian columns and large wooden doors. By the size and looks of them she thought they must be very heavy doors. She ran up the stairs. When she got to the top the doors, on their own, opened wide.

She darted in, fearful that the doors would close before she could find Jim. She didn't know how or why, but she was certain that he was in this building. She found herself in a rotunda of what appeared to be a museum. Classical sculptures ringed the outer edges of the circular room. She was aware of paintings on the walls, but paid no attention to them. Her attention was drawn to a hallway directly across from her on the other side of the rotunda.

She walked towards the hallway. The floor was bare and cold on her feet sending a chill throughout her body, which was naked but for the nightgown. When she got to the hallway she could see entrances to other rooms off each side of the hallway. There were no lights or candles that she could see, but everything was dimly lit from some unknown source. She squinted trying to see what was at the end of the hallway, but it disappeared into the dimness.

She slowly walked down the hallway. At the first room on her left she stopped and looked in. It was totally dark.

"Jim!" she called into the blackness. Her voice echoed through the fabricless chamber. There was no answer.

She turned around to the room on her right. It too was totally dark. She called out Jim's name again. Again there was no answer.

Room by room she looked into the darkness and called out Jim's name, and received no response. Fear and doom began to overtake her. She couldn't breathe. She so wanted to wake up from this nightmare. Then, from down the endless hallway on her left, she heard it.

"Renee."

It was spoken softly and evenly this time.

"Renee," he repeated.

She followed the sound of Jim's voice to a room several paces ahead on her left. Unlike all of the other rooms, this one was lit. While her heart raced at the thought of seeing Jim, she entered slowly, cautiously. Something told her that this was a room to be wary of, a room that could destroy both her and Jim.

She could see immediately that it was a room of wealth and beauty. It was a gallery. On the walls were masters' paintings of all types and from all periods—modern, abstract, Impressionist, Cubist, Baroque, Renaissance—giving the impression of having been arranged by a wealthy collector with no knowledge of art or interior decorating.

But the far wall was unlike the others. It had only one large painting. It was wall to wall and almost floor to ceiling. It was simple and uncluttered in its beauty—a peaceful meadow with waist high golden grass, and a hazy orange, setting sun illuminating the near horizon's spotted clouds in hues of orange, yellow, purple and red in an otherwise blue sky. It was an awe-inspiring scene, its size adding to its magnificence and allowing it to dominate this room of masterpieces.

Renee, at first almost blinded by the room's lights and exquisite contents, hadn't immediately seen him standing before the large painting.

"Jim!" she cried.

She moved towards him to hold him and be held by him. Something—she didn't know what—stopped her.

"Renee," he said softly. He smiled at her. He then moved back towards the painting and placed the right side of his body into the canvas. Or at least it looked like he did. He moved his right arm back and forth. As he did so Renee could see the grass in the painting move with it.

He's, he's in the painting, she thought. *That can't be.* But there he was, before her eyes. Or was he? He looked back at her. Still smiling, with an almost childlike joy, he said to her, "See?"

"Jim, no. Please come home with me," she pleaded. She didn't know where this was going, but she knew that if he left her now, he would be gone forever. She tried again to go to him, but she still couldn't move.

Jim looked back into the painting. Then he looked back at her again.

"Renee. See?"

"Jim, no!" she sobbed.

He turned his face away and began to turn his body towards the painting.

Renee folded her hands and bowed her head. "Oh God, don't let him go in," she prayed frantically. "Please stop him. Please."

Jim took another step into the painting. Suddenly, his left hand was being held and pulled on, keeping him half in and half out. Renee looked up. She saw a man dressed in the white vestments and miter of the Pope holding Jim's hand firmly. The look on Jim's face was neither happy nor sad, joyful nor angry. It was just curious.

The Pope turned and looked at Renee. She looked at his face. It wasn't John Paul II. It was Father Ray. As they just looked at each other, she heard footsteps on the marble floor coming from her right. Moving ever so slowly towards the painting was her father.

The scene before her was surreal. But she didn't have time to try to figure it out. The only thing on her mind was to save Jim.

"Please! Father Ray! Pull him out! Bring him back!" she pleaded. "Please Daddy! Please help!"

"I do what I can," Father Ray said as he strained against the pull of the magnificent meadow. "I do what I can."

"We do what we can," her father echoed.

Renee shot up in her bed. She was in a cold sweat and her eyes were filled with tears. The image of Ray and her father looking sorrowfully at her remained seared in her mind.

"Please," she whispered. "Please."

Chapter 20

This round of their lovemaking was neither as forceful nor as furious as the first. Jim was maintaining a steady, rhythmic pace, confident of his ability to hold it for a long period of time now that he had come once. He interspersed his in and out action with circular, probing movements while deep inside Sandra. This seemed to bring her great pleasure, at least as much as he could tell from the increased pitch of her moans of joy.

The Doors, having finished shouting the last lines of *Love Me Two Times*, slipped into the darkly melodic *Riders on the Storm*. The song's effects of rain hitting the earth and far away thunder, along with its gloomy melody, enhanced the night's ambience drawing the lovers further away into a world where no one existed but them and nothing existed but the raw sexual energy enveloping them.

They were oblivious to anything but the sounds of their pleasure and the music, the feel of their bodies intertwined and interconnected, and the unequaled sensations attainable only through their mutual, selfless sexual stimulation. They were oblivious to their histories. They were oblivious to those who loved or had ever loved them. They were oblivious to their morals and their beliefs. They were also oblivious to the clouds which had begun to roll in, seemingly from every direction at once with a speed which, had they noticed, would have appeared to be the result of time lapse photography.

The oblivious couple continued in the pursuit of their second perfect coming. Their bodies now flowed in perfect synchronization. They had reached a higher level of sexual being, their bodies seeming to hover weightlessly above the air mattress. They moved so effortlessly in, out and around each other that it was clear to Jim that this was where they were meant to be, that this level of mutual sensual perfection could be attained only by soul mates, only through the hand of God.

Riders on the Storm was ending. All that could be heard now were the rain and the thunder at the end of the song. Jim was nearing another explosive orgasm, and he was sure Sandra was too, as he felt raindrops fall softly on their bodies, adding yet another sensory element to their already volatile sexual mixture.

Something, he didn't know what, caused him to stop for a few seconds. *What's that?* he thought. *In the distance. I . . . I . . . Forget about it fool. It's nothing.*

"You tease. Don't stop, even for a second," Sandra said as she began to quiver with ever greater excitement.

There it is again. He thought he *felt* it this time. It was something his mind couldn't articulate in words or images, a sense of hope and despair co-existing simultaneously, with equal force, pulling in opposite directions. He stopped again, lifted his head and looked around, not knowing what he was looking for. The rain was coming down harder now. He felt it now as rain instead of another ingredient in the sexual elixir he had been sharing with Sandra.

Something from deep within told him to stop. It was still not in words or images, but a feeling, a sense that it had to end now, this moment, or it would be too late. He looked down at Sandra's face, twisted in contortions of rapture. Wanting nothing more than to transform it into one of screaming joy, he nevertheless began to pull himself out of her.

As his penis slowly withdrew, she tried to stop it by flexing her vaginal muscles.

"No no no, baby," she said as she tried to coax it back. But it was too late. By the time she had started maneuvering he was almost fully withdrawn.

Sandra opened her eyes and looked directly into his. As he looked back, he felt confusion and even fear. He knew he wasn't hiding it very well and couldn't have even if he had wanted to.

"I don't know what's wrong," she grunted. "And I don't give a shit. You're not stopping until I fucking come again, Goddammit."

She placed her left hand behind his head, pulled it down to hers and snaked her tongue into his mouth as she planted her full lips on his. At the same time, she placed her right hand on his buttocks and pushed as hard as she could while thrusting her pelvis up, forcing his penis all the way back into her.

The dual sensation of Sandra's tongue plunged into his mouth and his penis pulled back into her vagina was electric, and overwhelming. Jim made one last feeble attempt to protest, grunting "uh uh" through her dancing tongue. It was to no avail. Any thought of stopping was gone forever. Once again he succumbed to the charms of this delicious woman and found himself lost in the sinful forest of their lust. Just over the horizon was an orgasmic sea and he was powerless to stop their inexorable slide into it.

But this time, through the grunts and groans, the clawing and flailing, the exchanges of bodily fluids and stimulation of sexual organs, and the transporting of each other from their ponderous realities to a world of no boundaries and no limits—this time, one small ember of another person, another life, began to flicker. As his tongue danced with Sandra's and as he renewed his rhythmic pumping, he silently prayed.

Forgive me Lord. Forgive me Renee.

Chapter 21

The intensity of the rain had grown stronger. The distant thunder of *Riders on the Storm* had been seamlessly replaced with the real thing. The lovers didn't notice. Their naked bodies, soaked by sweat and rain, slid madly through each other as they approached another simultaneous climax. Jim marched silently towards the orgasmic moment. Sandra cried out, "Do it! Do it baby!"

Suddenly there occurred the deafening, crackling sound of lightning striking nearby. The startled lovers stopped and looked wide-eyed at each other, rain dripping from their faces. Sandra put her hand to her mouth stifling a laugh.

"Jesus!" she said, giggling. "I knew you were good, but not *that* good!"

They resumed their manic screwing. They were about to come when they were again startled by the loud crash of a lightning bolt. This one caused the widow's walk to shake violently. There was the smell of burning wood.

Jim instinctively pulled out of Sandra. He looked up and saw the east railing of their love nest cracked and smoldering. Before he could say or do anything, there was another loud crackle, and then another. The first struck in the scrub just a few feet from the house. The second hit behind the house to their left.

He looked up into the sky. Clouds were swirling as if they were being stirred in a witch's cauldron. The thunder was no longer distant. It was all around and above them. Clapping, grumbling, roaring continuously. It was as if every type of thunder he had ever heard had been gathered together for one combined atmospheric symphony. The sky and air were filled with constant lightning. In most of the sky's great dome it was atmospheric lightning. It flashed seemingly in rhythm with the thunder. Around the edges were the lightning bolts, some traveling straight down striking the earth with triumphant glows, others traveling horizontally before striking targets miles away, still others seeming to streak skyward as if trying to strike the heavens themselves.

"Let's get inside," Sandra said. Her voice betrayed her fear. Jim didn't move. He remained sitting on the air mattress staring into the sky.

"Jim. Did you hear me? We have to go inside. It's getting dangerous out here!"

She got up and retrieved her lingerie from the back of the chair it had been thrown on. She turned and looked down at him. Jim looked at her standing over him, fear writ all over her face, her exquisitely nude body trembling and jerking with each thunderclap. As his eyes made their way from her head downward, they stopped at the sight of semen running down her inner left thigh. His eyes opened wide and an almost sadistic grin creased his face. Just then, a loud bolt of lightning which seemed to stop in mid-air above her, knocked Sandra down onto the air mattress next to him.

She was flat on her back. Jim looked down at her. As she looked up at him, her face showing both fear and bewilderment, he began to feel her feelings and hear her thoughts. It was as if the lightning had created some sort of melding or fusion that let him slip into her mind and her body, seeing what she saw, feeling what she felt, hearing what she heard.

Neat, he thought. *Don't know why or how, but hope it lasts.*

He continued to look at her. And he knew what she was thinking and feeling—that whatever he was seeing, wasn't her.

The rain was coming in tropical storm strength now. The cacophony of the thunder and lightning was truly frightening her. Jim was unfazed. As she lay on the mattress, shivering and beginning to cry, he was drawn by . . . *by what,* he wondered . . . *by something,* to stand up. He stepped over to the southern banister and looked out over the scrub. At that moment a bolt struck immediately in front of him, shaking the foundation of the house and causing Sandra to scream. Jim didn't move.

"Jim! Please! Let's go!" she cried out.

He didn't respond. He slowly lifted his eyes to the swirling sky. In a few seconds he nodded. He had heard nothing, but he knew what he was to do next. He turned and looked down at Sandra. His face showed no emotion. It was a physical and emotional blank slate.

"Get downstairs," he instructed her in a lifeless monotone.

"You're coming with me, aren't you?" she said. She was sobbing now, frightened as much by the thought of what was happening to Jim as by the storm.

"Get downstairs. NOW!" he yelled.

The sudden change from unemotional monotone to bellowing anger frightened her out of her wits. He watched as she ran down the stairs to the platform, opened the screen door to the enclosed portion of the porch, and threw herself on the wooden floor.

Interesting, he thought. *I can see her through the floorboards.*

She was crying uncontrollably now. She was lying against the outer wall of the small enclosure under an open screened window. Together, the wind, lightning and thunder cut through the room like the obnoxiously loud music and maddening, never-ending flashing of strobe lights she imagined one would find in those nightclubs where rages were held and drug-ravaged kids threw themselves into mosh pits, foolishly placing their trust and safety in the hands of the drug-addled minds of other kids who didn't know who they were catching, and didn't care if they did.

The rain lashed against the house and sprayed through the screens, coating Sandra and her empty room with a fine film of water. She tried to collect herself, tried to clear her mind so she could make sense of what was going on, could understand the intensity of the storm and, more importantly, Jim's reaction to it and why he wouldn't come inside. He watched her, and listened to her thoughts, with an almost childlike curiosity and mirth at his secretive eavesdropping.

Sandra struggled to control her near hysteria. She managed to reduce her sobbing to a whimper. She had to get back to him, to hold him and convince him to come inside away from the danger, which she was beginning to fear involved more than a dangerous thunderstorm. No sooner had she stood up to return to him than the earth beneath her trembled, shaking the house violently. She was thrown hard against the inner wall of the room. She felt a sharp jolt of pain shoot from her right shoulder up her neck and into her skull. It seemed to shoot all the way through and out the top of her head. Her left hand instinctively grabbed her right shoulder as she screamed in pain. Then, not sure in her own mind, clouded as it was with fear and pain, whether she was crying for help or to help him, she cried out frantically: "Jim! Jim, please! I'm hurt! Please help me! Please come down here and help me!"

For a moment she heard nothing other than the sounds of the monster storm. Then, from above, on the widow's walk, she heard a long, piercing, blood-curdling scream. It was Jim. It was a sound like no other she had ever heard, a sound evincing a level of pain that the most vivid and macabre imagination couldn't conjure.

The pain was more than he had ever experienced or believed possible. It was preceded by a thunder roar that had sounded almost like a low, guttural laugh. When he turned to look up at the sky, a bolt of lightening struck him square in the chest. Searing, burning pain. He looked down and could actually see the current still flowing from the sky above and through his chest. His scream even frightened him. It was made doubly frightening by his feeling Sandra's reaction to it. Yet, amazingly, it hadn't killed him, or even knocked him off his feet.

How can that be? he wondered. Then, he heard a voice talking to him. With each spoken word the current of electricity was twisted within and through his wound.

"You will kill her."

The voice was commanding, powerful and demonic.

"You will dismember her, NOW!" it demanded.

The long, wordless scream, which had caused Sandra's skin to ache and her heart to stop, was followed by a loud, wailing plea.

"What?! What?!" A brief silence followed. Then: "Pleeease! Nooo! Pleeease! Pleeease!"

The wind grew stronger and the rolling, clapping thunder became intermittent bursts of ever louder explosions, almost as if in response to his pleas. With each burst the floor and walls of the house vibrated, heightening Sandra's already uncontrollable trembling. Suddenly she was blinded by a flash of light coming from the window screen. It was accompanied by the loud crack of a striking lightning bolt that had hit very close to the house.

She rubbed her eyes hard and opened them slowly. She looked towards the window and saw a reddish-yellow glow coming from outside. Frightened to look, yet more frightened not to, she dragged herself across the floor of the small room. When she got to the window, she slowly lifted herself up and looked out. A large part of the scrub was on fire, burning within a few feet of the house. She watched for several minutes. Despite the heavy rain the flames burned bright and fiercely. They seemed to be fueled by the rain rather than doused by it. The wind, still strong and frequently changing direction, blew the flames around. They were so close and so unruly that she feared for the safety of the wooden house. It was a miracle they hadn't reached the house so far. One small miracle that held out at least the hope for more.

She stood there, transfixed by the hypnotic beauty of the fire. The wind, rain, thunder and lightning continued, but for the time being they formed only a backdrop for the brilliant blaze. It was as if it was the fire's turn to play a solo. It was a virtuoso performance, so much so that Sandra forgot her fear and her pain and became totally oblivious to the roiling storm still raging around her.

Her trance-like state was shattered by the bellowing of another long, shrieking cry. It was so eerie and horrifying that she dropped to her knees and covered her ears with her hands trying to block the sounds out. But she couldn't. The sound and feeling of the cry ran through her entire being. When it finally ended she heard directly above her pounding and banging on the floor of the widow's walk. It sounded as if two men were fighting or wrestling. Then, a loud thud, followed by another long, loud scream. It was Jim. Or at least she thought it was Jim, though the sound of his voice was now much lower, more resonant. This time, instead of sending chills through her, she was overcome by a feeling of hollowness, as if every organ and fluid had been removed from her body. She tried to swallow, but couldn't. It was as if her body was rejecting her own self.

She began to panic. She was certain that she was losing her mind, that something had snapped throwing her into a false world of madness and nightmarish illusion. *I'm probably in some mental ward,* she thought, *being treated for paranoid schizophrenia or some such disease. What else can it be?*

"Please dear God!" she pleaded. "Deliver me from this living Hell! Jim, help me! Jim, please!"

Another howl pierced the troubled night. This time the pitch and intensity modulated, turning the scream into a groaning cry. The hair on the back of her neck raised again, chilling her body and drawing her out of her illusion of paranoia and into her more frightening reality. The wind howled back, as if answering her.

She heard sounds from above again. Only this time it was Jim's full, rich voice, not screaming, but talking. He was speaking loudly as if trying to be heard over the din of the still raging storm. She stood again slowly and put her ear to the window screen straining to hear what he was saying. She could hear him clearly now, but she couldn't understand him. He wasn't speaking English.

> Kyrie o Theos tis sotyrias mou, imeras
> Ekekraxa ke en nykti anantion sou.
> Eiseltheto enopion sou I prosefchi mou,
> Klinon to ous sou tin thesin mou, Kyrie.
> Oti eplisthi kakon I psichi mou, ke
> I zoi mou to athi ingise . . .

She neither spoke it nor understood it, but it sounded like Greek to her. Its fluid, poetic cadence, which she had heard often at ethnic festivals and during the one European vacation she and Ray had taken during their marriage, was hard to forget.

I didn't know Jim spoke Greek, she thought. *Why is he speaking it now? What's he saying? And, and who is he talking to?*

She listened closely as Jim continued to speak. Whoever he was talking to, it sounded as if he was beseeching him, pleading or praying for something. Jim kept talking. Sandra kept listening. Unaccountably, mysteriously, she began to understand what he was saying.

> Thou hast laid me in the lowest pit, in
> Darkness, in the deeps.
> Thy wrath lieth hard upon me, and thou
> hast afflicted me with all thy waves.

Selah.
Thou has put away mine acquaintance far
from me; thou hast made me an abomination
unto them: I am shut up, and I cannot come forth.
Mine eye mourneth by reason of affliction:
LORD, I have called daily upon thee, I have
stretched out my hands unto thee.
Wilt thou shew wonders to the dead? Shall
the dead arise and praise thee?
Selah.
Shall thy loving kindness be declared in the grave?
Or thy faithfulness in destruction?
Shall thy wonders be known in the dark? And thy
Righteousness in the land of forgetfulness?
But unto thee have I cried, O LORD; and in the
morning shall my prayer prevent thee.
LORD, why castest thou off my soul?
Why hidest thou thy face from me?
I am afflicted and ready to die from my youth up:
while I suffer thy terrors I am distracted.
Thy fierce wrath goeth over me; thy terrors
have cut me off.
They came round about me daily like water;
they compassed me about together.
Lover and friend hast thou put far from me,
and mine acquaintance into darkness.

Sandra recognized it. It was Psalms 88, the psalm of the darkness of death. A silence fell over the house at 1260 Elysian Way. There was no more wind or thunder. The rain had stopped pattering on the wood over her head. The lightning had stopped as well, casting Sandra's little room into total darkness.

Jim's words and the darkness haunted her. She sat down under the window and pulled her legs up to her chest in an effort to hide her nakedness. But from what? Or who?

There was silence. It brought some respite, but no sense of safety or security. She was too afraid and too exhausted to move. She sat there in the total darkness. She no longer tried to figure out what was happening. She just wanted to get through this night with her sanity intact and her body in one piece. She feared for Jim's safety too and wanted to go back upstairs to check on him, but she dared not. She didn't know how long it would take for her to feel safe enough to move, but it wasn't now.

Over and over bolts of lightening had pierced Jim's chest, twisting and turning within him like a corkscrew before receding into the angry clouds. Each one was stronger and more excruciatingly painful than the last. His own cries of pain were as eerie and frightful to him as he knew they were to Sandra below. And how could it be that he wasn't dead? Or was he? At this point he knew as little about what was happening as she did.

Suddenly, he was knocked to the floor of the deck. By what, he didn't know, but it felt as if there were several arms groping and grabbing him. He couldn't see anything but he could feel the invisible appendages wrapping themselves around him. They squeezed, tighter and tighter. Breathing became difficult. Soon, he realized, he wouldn't be able to breathe at all.

He at least knew he was still alive, for the time being anyway. He grabbed at what had hold of him and rolled around, trying to free himself of his unseen predator.

"Please Lord," he whispered as he clawed away at his own body. "Give me strength."

He could feel the force of whatever had hold of him, but he couldn't feel anything physical, anything of substance. He continued to claw at his body, especially his chest, where he felt the pressure points.

"Please Lord," he gasped again as he rolled on the deck.

Without warning, without his knowing how, the pressure disappeared in an instant. He could breathe again. He struggled to his feet and staggered over to the southern banister. He looked into the fierce and still brutal sky.

He understood now. *This is my final battle,* he thought. *The final battle for my soul—my own Armageddon. The final test of my faith, and the final judgment of the value of my life.* He wondered how and why Sandra was a part of this. For whatever reason, he knew that somehow her survival would depend on him. He wished he could communicate with her, to somehow ease her fear.

Another bolt of lightening crashed through him. He howled and groaned until the electric arrow receded. He gripped the banister firmly and cast his eyes upward, to where he knew his fate would ultimately be decided. As the storm raged on, he found himself reciting the eighty-eighth Psalm. Strangely, he was reciting it in Greek, a language he had never studied.

A sense of calm came over him. His white-knuckled hands relaxed their grip on the banister. But before he could completely relax, a nasal voice, seeming to come from every direction around, above and below him, spoke.

"It is good that you and your little plaything are beginning to realize that your so-called Lord has cast off your souls."

Jim looked all around trying to find the source of the voice.

Who is that? he thought.

"Who am I?" the voice said.

How . . . how did you know what I was thinking?

"How did I know what you were thinking?" the voice parroted. "I've *always* known what you were thinking. In fact, my foolish little man, I've often *given* you your thoughts."

Jim felt a discomforting sense of familiarity with—with what? The voice? No. The presence.

"Who . . . who are you?" he asked.

"Who ...what am I?" the voice sneered. "Let's just say I've been your life-long companion."

"My companion? When? Where?"

"When? Where? Always, and everywhere, my foolish little man."

"I would have known if someone . . ."

" . . . was always with you?"

"Yes."

"And haven't you?"

The voice laughed. It echoed all around Jim. It was eerie, and evil. Then, silence.

Jim stood at the banister looking into the storm-ridden sky.

"Who are you?" he cried, wanting to know, but afraid of the answer.

Still, silence.

His thoughts returned to Sandra. Whatever was happening to him, why was she caught up in it too? He would know soon enough. He decided he should go down below to see how she was, and comfort her as much as he could. He tried to turn toward the stairs. Try as he might, he couldn't move. Something had a hold of him freezing him at the banister. At that moment, Sandra's being—her feelings, thoughts, experiences—became a part of him again.

Sandra began to shiver. The air was warm and humid, but she was feeling extremely cold, and progressively so. There had been situations in her life when her nakedness had made her feel emotionally vulnerable, but she had never before felt physically threatened simply by being nude. She desperately needed a blanket or some clothes. She decided that, as strange as it seemed, she was in danger of overexposure and freezing to death in the North Carolina late summer night. The only choice was to make a move indoors. She figured that it had been about half an hour since the storm had subsided and that it was as good a time as any to make her way into the house.

As she got to her feet, the crystalline stillness of the night was shattered by a clap of thunder, the crackling of lightning and another outburst from Jim. She couldn't know that Jim had just been pierced again by a bolt of lightning, as he had several times before. Excruciating, torturous pain again, enough to cause him to wish for death, which unaccountably eluded him.

Another loud bang of thunder echoed over and around the house. The wind quickly began to howl once again and lightning lit up the sky with the brilliance of a Fourth of July fireworks display. Sandra heard the house's wood again being assaulted from the sky, but it sounded louder this time. She could almost make out each individual collision. She looked out the window and saw that the rain had returned, this time accompanied by hail the size of golf balls.

She was even more afraid now, but she was still freezing. She knew she couldn't survive long unless she got warm soon. She decided she had no choice but to get inside the house. Slowly and carefully she took the three to four steps to the screen door leading onto the main back porch. She pushed it open, stepped out into the storm and headed directly towards the kitchen door which was about twelve feet ahead of her and to her left.

She covered her head with her arms to ward off the falling hail. But after only a few steps she found the wind blowing so hard that she couldn't make any further headway towards the door. She leaned into the wind and threw the full force of her body forward, but to no avail. The wind blew so strongly that her breasts began to ache from being blown around. *It must be a freakish and cartoonish sight,* she thought in an instant of masochistic humor.

The hail stopped, but the rain came harder and fiercer. It wasn't falling downward in droplets. It was being driven by the wind in all directions into a steady stream of razor-like strands. Sandra felt as if she was being sliced by the sharp knives of a demonic, atmospheric Jack the Ripper.

She was making no progress in her effort to get to the kitchen door. She decided that she had no choice but to return to the porch room, catch her breath and then try again. Even turning in the fierce wind was difficult, but she was finally able to. She kept her head down to protect her face from the bladed rain. As she looked at the wooden planks of the porch's floor, she saw what appeared to be blood being washed away by the rainwater.

Panic began to overtake her. She tried to make her way to the screen door of the small room, but even facing in this direction the swirling gale kept her from moving. She was trapped in an eddy of wind and rain that seemed to be purposefully imprisoning and torturing her. She covered her face, both to protect it from the rain and in the natural gesture accompanying her fearful sobbing. She stood in her incomprehensible prison, naked, confused, stripped of all protection and dignity, with no conception of what was happening, or why.

Without thinking, she dropped to her knees and, between sobs, pleaded as loud as she could: "Dear God! Please! Please forgive me! Please have mercy on me!"

A loud thunderclap startled her and caused her head to jerk upward. The razor rain slashed her face, but she couldn't take her eyes off of what she was seeing. Above her, on the widow's walk, she saw Jim standing. She squinted her eyes to see better and when she did, she saw that he wasn't standing. He was actually hovering, motionless at the southern railing. His hands were outstretched to the sky reaching, as if he was preparing to catch or receive something.

For several seconds she remained motionless herself, transfixed by what she saw. Then she again felt the pain of the slashing rain. She tried to move but the wind still wouldn't release her. Desperately she cried out to the transcendental figure above her.

"Jim! Please! Jim! Help me! Please honey, help me!" she pleaded, her voice trailing off into the wind.

There was no reaction from Jim. She was convinced she would die where she stood, her naked body sliced and diced not by a madman with a carving knife, but by driving, deadly liquid lasers unleashed by a vengeful God or a gleeful Satan. Either way, she couldn't imagine a more grotesque or eternally damning ending to her life.

About to give in to her inevitable demise, she saw Jim's head begin to turn slowly in her direction. He lowered his hands and placed them on the banister as if to steady himself, though he hadn't seemed unsteady in his elevated pose to the heavens. As his face came into her view, it appeared pale and strained. His pupils had shrunk so much as to be nearly invisible against the whites of his eyes, creating an evil-looking countenance that would have frozen her in place if she wasn't already.

Jim's white eyes seemed to lock in on her. She suddenly felt even colder. She looked for some sign of recognition, some feeling of love, caring or even sympathy from him. She saw and felt none. His gaunt face with the hollow eyes, windblown hair standing virtually on end, and naked body, now turned facing her, seemingly devoid of genitalia, created a grotesque and frightening image of a man, or being, unrecognizable to her. The sight confirmed the hopelessness of her situation and created within her an end-of-life anguish and regret over Jim's equally disastrous fate, for which she felt responsible. It was time, she decided, to quit struggling and to give herself up to whatever was to be.

Jim was frightened. He and Sandra were being pummeled by a sinister force –the devil, evil, whatever one chose to call it—and one far more powerful than anything they would be able to overcome. Yet, he knew he wasn't alone. It would have been all over by now. He was the centerpiece, the prize of the battle, to be sure. He could readily see and hear and feel the wrath and pain inflicted by the one side. He could see and hear nothing from the other. But he had to keep believing it was there. He had to believe that his continued survival so far, in whatever form it was taking, was proof that there was another side fighting for him. He had to keep believing so that he wouldn't give up. Because he was sure that, to one end or the other, he was going to die. His mind wandered, to his last sermon just three days ago, chuckling to himself how he was telling his parishioners how to run *their* lives.

His thoughts were shattered by the loud and all-encompassing laughter of the voice—a sound he knew only he could hear. He tried to say something, but his lips wouldn't move. He used his thoughts.

Why? Why are you doing this to me?

"Why?" the voice responded. "It's time to collect on my investment."

Your investment?

"Yes, my foolish little man. For being your life-long companion, and tutor of sorts."

I don't understand.

"No? Then let's look, together."

Jim felt a vice-like grip on his neck. It jerked his head upward so that he was looking into the swirling clouds of the storm. Time and place were gone to him now. His eyes remained fixated as the clouds reassembled themselves into the face of seventeen-year-old Rachel Feinberg.

"Yes," the voice said again. "Let's watch together."

Jim wanted to turn his face away, but he was powerless to do so. He could see a darkened wood come into focus; then, a teenage Jimmy Donovan walking naked through it.

"Remember this?" the voice asked.

Yes. Rachel's cruel practical joke.

"Well, I wouldn't give Rachel *all* the credit."

As Jim watched himself walking through the woods he began to see and feel the uncontrollable trembling and fear he had felt that night. And then he saw the eyes, the two points of light in the darkness that had so frightened him then.

You, he thought.

"Watch," the voice said.

Something started to come into focus. He felt as if he was being asked to watch someone's home movies, but he knew that this home movie was about him. He could see now. High school. Young Jimmy Donovan being ridiculed and hazed by his classmates. The scene changed quickly. The death of his father. Now there he was in the funeral home talking to one of the funeral home employees. The name tag read "P. Lachaise." It was so familiar to him. It was . . . the voice.

Mr. Lachaise. That was you!

The story continued. He was with Katie now. But the good parts were blurred. Only the betrayals were clear and immediate. Then, there stood Katie, naked, Professor Roderick standing next to her. Jim was beginning to understand.

Professor Roderick. That was you too.

"Ah yes, I certainly provoked your anger there, didn't I," the voice said with a chuckle as Jim observed himself laying his overhand right on Professor Roderick's jaw.

Pictures of Veronica followed — their lovemaking, their argument over the abortion and his car accident. And then, Dr. Pe´re. Every single session with Dr. Pe´re. As he watched he could see how Dr. Pe´re was manipulating him, leading him to an attitude of using and exploiting people for his own pleasure and purposes, and how he was so easily led.

Dr. Pe´re was . . .

"At your service. I always love great opportunities like that falling into my lap." Another sinister chuckle. "And I rarely let them pass."

Jim's life went on. Whatever positive there was in it went by in a blur as if the tape was fast-forwarded. There was Richardson Leigh, and Melanie.

"We certainly had a stimulating debate there, didn't we?" the voice said.

Did Melanie . . .

" . . . kill her parents? Of course. They were in the way."

Then Africa. He saw the giant watching over him fornicating with Lanie. He didn't need to ask whether the voice and the giant were one and the same.

Did . . . did she have a baby?

" A beautiful child. He will be of tremendous value to me."

Jim's heart sank at the thought.

Things fast-forwarded through Paradise. It was almost all a blur, but every few seconds Norma Hutchins' disapproving scowl would come ever so briefly into focus. When it did, pain would envelop his body and she would disappear again into the fog of Paradise.

The trip to Nags Head was very clear though. First, the waitress with Melanie's tattoo. Then the encounter, that frightening encounter with the red wolf.

Yours? he asked, already knowing the answer.

"Ah, two of my favorite children. And they particularly enjoyed being with you."

Of course, Jim thought, trying to turn his mind away from what he was being told and shown. The eyes in the woods. And that *was* Melanie. And who knew where else and in what other form he had encountered them. But what about the young man at the gas station? For some reason he didn't seem to be a part of the show. He was evil. Or was he? Maybe he was a warning. A warning to turn back. To avoid *this*. A warning he ignored, just like he ignored Dr. Westin and Father McTighe.

It dawned on him that he was having these thoughts with no response or reaction from his tormentor. Was it possible these thoughts couldn't be read? It must be. However it might seem, he *wasn't* alone. There were still two sides to this battle. He . . .

Suddenly the vice on his neck tightened, jerking his focus back onto the sky.

"Watch!" the voice demanded.

There before him now, the battle with the foxes on the beach. And then, Perry Lachaise intervened. Perry Lachaise. P. Lachaise. Dr. Pe´re. The common thread became clear to him. But what did it mean?

"What does it mean?" the voice asked. "Why Perry? Why Lachaise? Call it one of my little jokes."

I don't understand.

"Do you know what Pe´re Lachaise is?"

No.

"Watch."

Jim's eyes watched the clouds form into the scene of him and Sandra making love on the widow's walk. The sound of the music of The Doors became louder and louder until Jim thought that his ears and head would explode.

I, I still don't understand, he shouted in his thoughts.

The music stopped and the vision disappeared. Then another

vision slowly came into focus. It was a cemetery. It came closer and closer. Soon, only one grave marker could be seen. It belonged to Jim Morrison.

"Welcome to the cemetery *Pe're Lachaise*."

But why . . .

" . . . use a play on that name. Let's just say as a memorial to my good friend."

Your good friend? He was one of yours?

"Oh, undoubtedly my foolish little man. Just like Rachel, and Katie, and Veronica, and Melanie and . . ." The voice paused for a moment. " . . . and Sandra."

The inclusion of Sandra's name on this list was particularly painful. All of the others were in the past. There was nothing he could do about them now. But Sandra, Sandra was now. It might make no difference to the outcome of this struggle, but for some unknown reason, it was important for him to know whether she was friend or foe.

What do you mean? he directed his thoughts up into the sky.

"They are *all* my instrumentalities—the tools of the trade, if you will. You see, *Reverend* Donovan, I have many tools I can use to get what I want, because there are so many human weaknesses to exploit. Greed, avarice, hate, anger, pleasure, power, lust. I use everyone and everything to draw you close to me. Morrison was a *great* help to me in his day. Ahh, the drugs, alcohol, sex, music—the *great* music. I was able to do *so* much with it."

Are you saying the music was evil?

"You are so foolish, dear Reverend. Don't you understand yet? It doesn't take what you call evil to create or attract me. I'm already there, in your heart, in your soul. I just have to create the right environment for you to let me thrive, help me come out. You know, nudge you in the right direction for me to be there always, just as I have been for you."

There it was. The point was finally driven home for him. This *was* Satan, the devil himself. It *was* Jim's soul he was after. And he was confident enough to say so.

And with me?

"What's my hook with you? Believe me Reverend, like any man, you've had plenty of faults, much for me to work with. But you all have at least one big one, the one that lets me do 'my thing' as they say. With you? Ah, that sweet insecurity of yours, that need for the warm, intimate love of a woman, of a mother. Just mix that together with an eye for beauty, especially the beauty of the female form, and *voila*! And no matter how much of it you did get, it was never enough, was it? Wonderful! Exquisite! So very perfect!"

That's it? That was the evil? Evil enough for me to go through this? For me to be . . . to be damned?

"Didn't need to be *that* evil, as you put it, my foolish little man. That's that free will crap you've believed and that you've spouted all these years. Don't get me wrong. I love to hear it. Plays right into my hands. No, I just needed it to be enough for me to use you when I needed to, and to ultimately get you here, to *my* widow's walk. Enough to put you within my reach. You see my little friend, it's all about . . . geography!" A loud, eerie and gruesome laughter followed. "And now, my friend, it is time to reel you in."

Jim was exhausted. The storm and the lightning bolts coursing through him had worn him down physically. The voice had done the same psychologically and emotionally. Could it possibly be that the whole struggle between good and evil, that one's eternal fate, had nothing to do with how one believed, or lived his life? That we are all pawns in some sort of celestial war determined as much on battlefield tactics and taking and holding property as any human war? It couldn't be. It was a trick. He wouldn't, couldn't believe it. He began to feel life draining out of him.

Please God, he pleaded in his thoughts, his lips still unable to move, *please talk to me. Please tell me you're there. Please tell me there is more to it than that, more for us to fight for.*

There was no response, no soothing words to give him strength in his own battle for survival. He felt his hope fading fast. But he would hold on, he decided. As long as he could. He would fight hard not to give in to the voice's trickery.

If this is it, God, he thought, *I accept it. Please forgive me. And please, please, let no harm come to others because of me.*

Weakness was overcoming him. He could feel his body levitating. A cold chill enveloped him. Then, a particularly loud thunderclap boomed. It was as loud as many before, but it had a different sound to it. How it was different, he didn't know. It was just different.

Suddenly, the chill left. His body felt as if it had more substance to it. He felt his strength returning. His lips quivered and he found he could open his mouth.

"Thank you," he whispered out loud.

He heard the crackling of lightning and a bolt pierced his chest again. He tried to scream out in pain, but this time no sound came out. Again, he could feel the life draining out of him.

The sky grew more agitated. Thunderclap followed thunderclap, lightning bolt followed lightning bolt. Soon, it was all occurring at once, thunder and lightning filling the sky non-stop. As the super storm raged Jim could feel his life alternately escaping his body and then returning, as if the same water, or blood, was being constantly poured back and forth between one cup and another. In the midst of all this he remembered Sandra, buffeted by the storm and driven into submission on the porch below him. He turned his attention to his forlorn lover. As he looked down at the pathetic figure kneeling before him, the battle of which he was the focal point raged on, with no indication of when or how it would end. The forces on either side of his mind and soul seemed equally powerful, each capable at various times of drawing sustenance from within him to gain a temporary advantage.

He looked intently at her. In Sandra he saw the unwitting instrument of evil, and of his own damnation. At the same time, he knew that he would be the instrument of either her destruction or her salvation. At that moment, though, he didn't know which it would be. He wanted so much to tell her what he now knew. But all he could do was listen to her and feel her, as much a spectator as the key participant in this macabre drama.

Sandra had kept her eyes fixed on Jim figuring that no matter how eerie he appeared, she preferred that his image be the last thing she saw before she died. For several minutes his pallid expression didn't change. She felt herself getting weaker from the constant pounding she was taking from the storm and the loss of blood from the whipping and slicing of the razor rain. She knew she was about to lose consciousness and when she did, she would never wake again. Then something in Jim's face changed. Color was returning, his pupils enlarged, and there developed a softness in his demeanor. His gaze no longer seemed cold and unfeeling. She sensed a true warmth, even love, in how he now looked at her.

Jim's transformation buoyed her spirits and gave her renewed hope. For the first time since the storm began, her tears were tears of happiness.

"Jim!" she cried out joyously. "Oh, Jim!"

Suddenly, as quickly as the color had returned to his face, it drained away. The ghost-like figure reappeared, the look of love replaced again with emptiness, even hate. The devastation of hope lost pierced her heart, but she still couldn't turn her eyes from him. As she watched, she could see that he was struggling mightily—about what, and to what end, she didn't know. His fists were clenched. All of the muscles of his body were taut. He had bitten his lower lip until it bled.

Then, again, color began to fill his face. His "human eyes" returned. They looked softly upon her with both sadness and charity. The storm continued to rage around her but she no longer noticed it.

Jim didn't know how or why, but he knew that the battle was coming to its climax. And when it did, anyone still in its path was in mortal, and immortal, danger. He had to disconnect their minds and emotions, and get her out of harm's way. He tried to call out to her, but he could barely move his lips. All he could do was think his words as urgently as he could and hope and pray that somehow she would hear him.

"Go inside now," she heard. It was Jim's voice, but hearing it confused her because she didn't see his lips move.

"Sandra, go inside now," his voice repeated as his left hand pointed to the covered porch directly beneath him.

"But Jim . . ." she began to protest. She needed so much to know more about what was happening and what was to become of him, and her.

"Sandra," he interrupted, "you must go in now." His voice was firm, but gentle. "There's not much time left."

The urgency in his voice was unmistakable and the wisdom in the instruction was clear. She stood up, looked gratefully and lovingly at him and took a step towards the screen door. The wind was still blowing mightily, but it no longer stopped her. She was able to take the few steps to the screen door, open it and step into what had become her sanctuary.

Within seconds she saw the bright flash of lightning. There was another enormous boom of thunder and then a long, painful wail from Jim. She didn't experience fear at hearing the cry this time. Instead, she felt an intense pain born of sorrow. She knew he had saved her. She didn't know whether he would be saved.

Physically exhausted and emotionally drained, she sank down to the floor. A few seconds later she heard another loud cry. This time it ended with a frightened plea.

"Please God!"

Tears rolled down her cheeks. She passed out.

"Please God," Jim said, in a whisper this time. Mercifully, Sandra would see and hear no more, he knew. He could only hope to be so lucky.

Finally, the voice had revealed itself. Jim had now seen the face of evil, a face so sinister and grotesque, containing within it every evil act, thought and feeling ever experienced by every human who had ever walked the earth, that merely looking at it had been more painful to him than all of the lightning strikes and all of the pain he had ever experienced in his life, put together.

He looked for the other side's face, for the face of God. He prayed again.

"Please God."

He saw nothing more. The storm was subsiding. There was no more lightning, no more thunder. There were no more pictures in the clouds, and no more voice. He felt something pushing him to the back end of the widow's walk. He was pushed into one of the deck chairs. He sat there, eyes staring straight ahead, waiting and wondering. He couldn't move.

Chapter 22

He had sat in the chair all night, unable to move, unable to even blink his eyes. The storm had lifted and a bright starlit night had reappeared. He had never experienced such total stillness and quiet. Nor such solitude. Was this Heaven? Was it Hell? Nothing, not even how he felt, gave him a clue.

As the sun rose, he saw people at the house far across the scrub looking in his direction and pointing towards him.

"Look," he could hear one young man say. "Up on that porch. A guy's just sitting there stark naked!" Laughter followed as three other young people looked over at him.

"He's not moving," another, a young woman, said. "Maybe he's hurt. Or dead."

"Or maybe he's just an exhibitionist," the young man countered.

They were quite a distance away, much too far for him to be able to hear them. But he could. He also knew, just knew, that one of the group had just gone to call the police.

He tried to move, but he couldn't. His eyes wouldn't move either. But somehow he could see everything around him—people walking on the early morning beach, running on the footpath along Old Oregon Inlet Road, Sandra unconscious down below, even the street sign at the entrance of their road. Strange, he thought. It read Tidal Lane, not Elysian Way.

What is this power? he wondered. *Does it mean I'm cursed, or that I'm blessed?*

He could see a police car and a fire-rescue ambulance pull up to the house. Uniformed men and women jumped out and rushed up the stairs. Not only could he see them and hear them, he could hear their thoughts and feel their emotions, just as he had been able to read Sandra the night before. He sat there motionless as they discovered him and checked to see if he was alive.

"All of his vital signs are normal," a paramedic said.

A uniformed police officer stepped up to him, leaned over and put his face within an inch or two of Jim's.

"Then what's wrong with him?" the cop asked.

"Beats me," the paramedic answered.

"Hey! Down here! There's another one! A woman!"

Up on the widow's walk, a female fire-rescue official who seemed to be the one in charge, turned to walk down the stairs.

"Sounds like the rookie found something," she said to the paramedics and police tending to Jim and investigating the scene.

The young paramedic, who was no more than twenty, bent over the naked, middle-aged woman and placed his fingers on her neck feeling for a pulse. Sandra's hair, her body and the room were soaking wet, just like the rest of the house and the naked male upstairs on the widow's walk. Sandra's face, blackened by her running mascara, had a ghoulish, Halloween-like look that made her appear haggard and older than her years. Despite his best efforts to maintain a strict professionalism, the rookie couldn't help but admire the body of this hapless woman old enough to be his mother.

Quit gawking at her! Jim screamed silently to himself.

"Is she alive?" the supervisor asked as she walked from the landing into the small room below the widow's walk.

"Yeah," the rookie said. "She's got a strong pulse. But her body feels awful cold."

"Go get a blanket or something to cover her with," the supervisor ordered. "And bring the equipment."

When the rookie left, the female paramedic knelt down next to Sandra who was lying on her side in a fetal position. She began to stroke Sandra's head.

"What the hell happened here?" she asked no one in particular.

The rookie returned with a blanket from the rescue rig and an off-white terry cloth robe he had retrieved from the house.

"In case she wakes up," he said.

The supervisor took the blanket and the robe.

"And the medical equipment?" she said.

"Oh yeah," he said as he turned and left to fetch the equipment, embarrassed at the thought that his supervisor may have thought he was staring at the naked woman, which he was.

The paramedic spread the blanket over Sandra's chilled body. She began to rub her arms and legs in an effort to warm Sandra up. As she did so, Sandra groaned softly.

"A good sign," the paramedic said softly to herself.

Thank God, Jim thought as he watched and listened from above.

Sandra's eyes opened. She experienced those few seconds of disorientation and confusion when waking up in a new or strange place. She reflexively drew back when she saw the paramedic kneeling over her.

"It's all right. Everything's going to be all right," the paramedic gently reassured her.

"Who are you? Where am I? What happened?" Sandra spit out her questions in quick succession.

"My name is Kristen. I'm a paramedic. We're not sure what happened, but you seem to have taken a bad fall. We're here to help you. Do you hurt anywhere?"

Sandra looked around and out the screen door. She could see the morning daylight. Just then, the events of the previous night flooded her mind. She quickly sat up and grabbed the startled paramedic by the arm. Wide-eyed, she frantically pleaded, "Jim! Where's Jim? Is Jim all right?"

The experienced paramedic softly placed her hands on her frightened patient's shoulders.

"Take it easy. Settle down. First tell me your name. What's your name?"

"Sandra. San . . . Sandra Chievers. But I have to know if Jim's okay."

"Is Jim the man upstairs? Is that the name of the man upstairs on the widow's walk?"

"Yes! Yes! Please tell me if he's all right. Is he alive?" Sandra cried, tears streaming down her cheeks through the already smeared mascara.

"Yes," the paramedic said calmly. "He's alive."

"Oh, thank God! Thank God!" Sandra sobbed as she fell into the paramedic's arms. At that moment the rookie returned with the equipment to examine her.

"Please, let me see him," Sandra pleaded. "I've got to see him."

The supervisor took the equipment from the rookie and motioned with her eyes for him to come around to the other side of Sandra.

"We've got to check you out first Sandra," the supervisor said. "And then we need to take you to the hospital."

"No! Please! I have to see him! I feel fine! I *have* to see him!"

Sandra was becoming overly excited which, given her condition, was of concern to the paramedics.

"Okay," said the supervisor. "Okay. Let us check you out first and then we'll decide if you're in any condition to see him. Fair enough?"

Sandra paused and looked at the two paramedics with a child-like air of resignation.

"All right," she said.

Except for her body temperature being somewhat below normal, but not dangerously so, all of her vital signs were within acceptable limits. When told this, she again asked to see Jim right away. Just then, a uniformed female police officer and a male plain clothes detective entered the tiny porch enclosure and asked her if she could tell them what happened. She told them she would talk to them, but only after she saw Jim.

Jim smiled, not that anyone could see it.

The female paramedic nodded to the officers. They left the room. She looked back at Sandra.

"I'll take you to see Jim now," she said. "But you need to be prepared for what you're going to see."

As the paramedic helped Sandra up and put the robe on her, she described the scene upstairs, and what Sandra could expect to see.

As they got to the top of the stairs Sandra saw the two police officers who wanted to question her. They were looking over the shoulders of three other paramedics who surrounded the chair at the far end of the elevated deck. The detective looked at Kristen.

"There's not much more that can be done for him here," he

informed her. "They're readying the stretcher to transport him to the hospital."

"Please," Sandra quietly pleaded. "Please let me see him."

"This is Sandra Chievers," Kristen told the detective. "She's the man's . . . friend."

The paramedics stood up at the sound of their supervisor talking and backed away from the chair. One of them reached for a blanket that lay on the wooden table. Before he could drape it over Jim's still naked body, Sandra saw the strange sight of him sitting rigid in the chair, in a pose pervertedly reminiscent of the Lincoln Memorial. His eyes were wide open, unblinking, staring blankly ahead. His body was as firm and athletic as ever, without a bruise or a mark on it.

The paramedic with the blanket spread it over Jim. Sandra ran through the collected officials and knelt down in front of her lover.

"Jim. It's me. Sandra."

She rubbed his motionless hands.

"Talk to me honey. Please, talk to me.."

There was no response. He so much wanted to talk to her, to reassure her, reach out and touch her hair. But he couldn't. And he expected he never would be able to again.

The stretcher arrived. Kristen slowly lifted Sandra up and away from Jim. Sandra didn't resist. She just stared helplessly at the bizarre form in front of her. The paramedics placed Jim on the stretcher and carefully maneuvered it down the long, steep stairs to the driveway. They placed him into a fire-rescue ambulance and sped away, sirens sounding and emergency lights flashing.

Sandra watched from atop the widow's walk. She couldn't comprehend what had happened to him anymore than she could understand what had happened to her. She only knew that whatever had gone on the night before, somehow Jim had saved her. But at what price, she wondered.

I wish I could tell you, Jim responded to his unhearing lover.

As the sound of the ambulance faded into the distance, the detective placed his hand softly on Sandra's right shoulder.

"Ma'am, my name is Dave Hall," he said. "I'm a police detective. How do you feel? Are you up to answering a few questions?"

She turned and looked at Kristen, who together with the rookie paramedic had retreated to the far corner of the deck.

"If you feel up to it, just a few right now," Kristen told her. "You can talk more at the hospital. You're still going to need a full evaluation."

Sandra sat on one of the deck chairs. The detective pulled the other one around so he was facing her and sat down. The uniformed officers and the paramedics remained standing at the railing.

As he rode to the hospital in the ambulance, Jim continued to see the entire scene back at the widow's walk. He was still connected to Sandra. He expected he always would be.

"What happened here, Ms. Chievers?"

The detective's tone was neither accusatory nor sympathetic, just professional.

"It was the storm," she replied quietly.

"The storm? What storm?"

"The thunderstorm. The vicious thunderstorm we had last night."

All of the officials on the deck looked at her and then at each other. Their faces wore expressions of pitying disbelief.

"Ms. Chievers, there was no thunderstorm last night anywhere in Dare County," Detective Hall said, "or anywhere in the Outer Banks for that matter."

The detective tried to speak carefully, obviously concerned for the fragile woman's mental state and not wanting to send her over the edge. But there was no easy way to tell her that what she had experienced never happened.

"What do you mean there was no thunderstorm?" Sandra said, her eyes darting back and forth among everyone. "Of course there was a thunderstorm. I was in it."

"Ms. Chievers," the detective responded evenly, "we've been having a bit of a dry spell. If there had been a thunderstorm, I'm sure we would have known."

She looked at their doubting and pitying faces. She rolled up the sleeves of her robe to show them the scars from the cutting rain, but there were none. She felt her face and felt no scars there either. She looked around frantically for some sign or evidence she could show them to prove there was a storm, to prove she wasn't crazy. Then she saw it. The whole house.

"Detective," she said triumphantly. "Look around you. This whole house is soaking wet. How do you explain that?"

"Now that, Ms. Chievers, is a good question. And it is a mystery. Because if it was due to a thunderstorm, even an isolated and local one, the other houses on this street would be wet too. But they're not. They're bone dry. And so is the ground around them. I was hoping you would be able to explain it."

Sandra slowly sank back into her chair. The enormity of it all suddenly hit her. She finally understood, but the irony of her understanding was that the more she told the truth of what had happened, of the awe and the majesty she had now come to know, the less she would be believed, and the less sane she would be believed to be.

Sandra looked beseechingly at the female paramedic.

"I'm very tired," she said. "Could we go to the hospital now?"

"Of course," the paramedic answered sympathetically. It was clear that in a short period of time she had come to care for this obviously bewildered, and bewildering, woman.

"I'll need a fuller statement later," the detective said.

"Yes, of course," Sandra said. "When I'm feeling stronger. We'll talk again."

Chapter 23

Renee Donovan looked through the glass portal of the door to the intensive care unit at the deathly still figure of her bedridden husband. He was hooked up to the various monitors, IVs and breathing apparatus that kept him alive and notified the doctors and nurses of his condition on a second by second basis.

It had been three days since she arrived in North Carolina. The call she had received from the Nags Head police letting her know that Jim was in the hospital had been somewhat cryptic and not very informative. She had felt it not only strange but cruel and heartless for the police to tell her that her husband was paralyzed over his entire body while not telling her what had happened, despite her to-be-expected hysterical reaction. But after she calmed down and read the police report which had been faxed to Chief Bruener as a courtesy, she understood why the young officer who had been assigned the task of calling her had had so much difficulty explaining.

She hadn't told the children yet. They hadn't expected their father home until Saturday anyway. Renee had her mother come down from Wheaton to stay with the twins while she stayed in North Carolina hoping against hope that Jim would recover quickly. Jim's mother had arrived shortly after Renee had. There had been so little contact between them since the wedding that Renee hardly recognized Mrs. Donovan. She had thought that the birth of the children, her mother-in-law's only grandchildren, would soften Mrs. Donovan's attitude about her. But it hadn't. It seemed that grandchildren being raised as non-Catholics didn't warm Mrs. Donovan's heart any.

The first sight of her son lying in a hospital bed like a vegetable did trigger an emotional response from her. It shocked her so much that she turned and staggered out of the ICU and threw up on the hallway floor before she could reach the ladies room. It caused a severe reaction in Jim as well. Even before she entered the ICU, Jim knew she was coming. He could hear her thoughts, and he could sense her presence as she walked down the hallway towards the door. It was before Mrs. Donovan entered the ICU that the nurses tracking Jim's monitoring equipment noticed a definite spike in both his brain waves and heart rate. When she entered the room the rates began to race wildly. By the time she had staggered out of the ICU, Jim's heart had gone into severe fibrillation, and then it stopped. It took the medical team almost five minutes of feverish resuscitation efforts to get it beating and get Jim stabilized. When he opened his eyes again she was gone, and so was the sense of her presence. From that point on, at the request of the doctors, and by her own desire, Mrs. Donovan stayed in the waiting room and looked for Renee to give her reports on Jim's condition.

"Any change?" Father Ray asked as he walked up the hallway approaching Renee. He had accompanied her on the trip from Paradise. He had decided to stay to help her through the early stages of what promised to be a very difficult time for her. He also hoped to find that Sandra was still in the area.

"No," Renee said, "Nothing. Any word on Sandra?"

My God, Jim thought, *that's Sandra's husband! Father Ray—Ray Chievers!*

"No," Father Ray said. "She walked out of the hospital right after the police took her full statement. No one has seen or heard from her since."

"I'm sorry, Father," Renee said.

"No. *I'm* sorry. If I had gotten here sooner maybe none of this would have happened."

"I don't think so," Renee replied in a comforting way. "I believe that for some reason we'll probably never understand, this is what had to happen. I only wish I knew why . . . and what's going to happen from here on."

"Hello Mrs. Donovan, Father Chievers."

Renee turned to see Dr. Kendrick Fleming, a highly regarded

neurosurgeon who was leading the team of doctors and other medical personnel who were responsible for Jim's treatment.

"Hello Dr. Fleming," Renee said. "Do you have any more information about Jim's condition? Is there any chance he might recover?" Renee's questions were those of the loved one who knows deep down the gravity of the situation but who still hangs on every thread of hope, no matter how slim.

"We're not sure what happened to your husband, Mrs. Donovan."

Dr. Fleming was clearly trying, without success, to hide his own puzzlement so as not to shake Renee's confidence.

"The closest I can come to a diagnosis is that Reverend Donovan's symptoms and condition appear similar to what is known as Locked-In Syndrome. This is a syndrome that often occurs as a result of a brain stem stroke."

"What does that mean?" Renee asked.

"Locked-In Syndrome is a condition that leaves a person completely paralyzed and mute, but he can still receive and understand sensory stimuli, like words and language, sight and smell. In other words, his brain is working, but he can't respond to anything. Sometimes a person can communicate by blinking or moving the eyes. But so far we've seen no sign of that capability from Reverend Donovan."

"Then how do you know he's not in a coma?" Father Ray asked.

"We're monitoring his brain waves and there is definitely activity and that activity increases, and even becomes somewhat frenetic, when there are people and activities around him. He is definitely receiving the stimuli. You'll recall, Mrs. Donovan," he said nodding towards Renee, "the significant increase in his brain wave activity when his mother first visited him. That was the most extreme example of the increased brain activity he is exhibiting in relation to stimuli, especially when people he knows visit him. The truly interesting part of that is that when it comes to family, like his mother and Mrs. Donovan here, the increase in brain wave activity, as well as his heart rate, seems to begin a little bit *before* the person who stimulates it actually enters the room. That's something we haven't been able to figure out yet. It almost seems like there is some sort of precognition but since that's not possible given his condition, we'll continue to monitor it and look for the real explanation. He also closes his eyes when he's sleeping and opens them when he's awake. We're fairly certain that this is not a typical coma."

"My God! How horrible!" Tears welled up in Renee's eyes as she reacted with shock and horror at Dr. Fleming's description of Jim's condition. "How could this happen?"

"Locked-In Syndrome is usually a result of a large stroke in the upper brain stem which severs the nerve connections between the brain and the body," Dr. Fleming explained. "The person may retain consciousness and be capable of intelligent thought, and possibly some eye movement. But otherwise he's completely paralyzed."

"You said this is *usually* the cause," Father Ray said. "Do you mean that's not the cause for Reverend Donovan's condition?"

"Well, that's the strange thing here. We've run all of the usual tests, the scans, the imaging, everything we would ordinarily do to identify and pinpoint the stroke. But everything comes up negative."

"What are you saying Dr. Fleming? That there's nothing wrong with my husband?" Renee was now completely confused and severely stressed.

"No," the doctor answered. "There's something definitely wrong with your husband, Mrs. Donovan. Something seriously wrong. What I'm saying is that we can find no physiological or medical cause for it."

There was a long pause. She looked at Ray. She was utterly disconcerted and dismayed. Ray put his arms around her in a comforting hug.

"I'm sorry I don't have better news or more complete information for you, Mrs. Donovan," Dr. Fleming said. "We'll do the best we can for your husband. We'll let you know if there is any change."

"Thank you doctor," Renee said gratefully as she delicately wiped her tears away with the tips of her fingers. "Are there any limitations on visiting him?"

"No, none at all. While it may be very frustrating for him, I'm sure there's a lot of loneliness when no one's around. And maybe it will help him to try to communicate with his eyes."

"Thank you again, doctor, for everything."

Dr. Fleming turned and walked away.

"Do you want to go in now?" Ray asked.

"No, I don't want him to see me like this," Renee said. She turned and looked up at Ray. "Father, I need to go there."

"Where?"

"To the house. To where it happened. I need to see it."

Please, no! Jim thought. *Don't go Renee. Don't go to the house. Please, Father Ray. Stop her! Don't let her go!*

"Renee, I wouldn't suggest that," Ray said, as if in answer to Jim's unspoken plea. "It can't do anything but bring you more pain."

"No, Father. I *have* to see it. I don't know why, but I just have to. Will you come with me? Please."

"Of course," Ray said, softly placing his hand on her shoulder. "Let's go."

Jim would have cried, if he could have.

Chapter 24

Norma Hutchins took her seat. The Paradise Community Christian Church's Women's Club Board of Directors was holding its monthly meeting in the large gazebo in the town park across the street from the church. The day was pleasantly cool for August and Norma, the chairman of the board, simply did not feel like meeting in the closed-in atmosphere of the church hall. It would be nice, she had decided, if the ladies brought their cookies and lemonade to the round table of the gazebo and enjoyed the sunshine, especially in such troubled times.

Norma called the meeting to order, but before she could even begin the discussion of business, the talk turned to what had happened to Reverend Jim.

"Had himself a stroke, I hear," said Fern Riggins, the baker's wife.

"Such a young man to be having a stroke," said Belle Ferguson. "Now if my Ned was to go and get himself a stroke, I'd have understood that. But not Reverend Jim. He's barely in his thirties."

"Poor Mrs. Donovan," chimed in Winnie Lowe. "With them two small kids and all. How on earth is she going to raise them kids herself? You can be sure they ain't got much money put away. And with Reverend Jim still being alive and all, she can't even go out looking for another man to help her."

"Now Winnie," chided Belle, "you shouldn't be talking like that. Long as Reverend Jim's still alive, there's always hope he'll come out of that coma he's in. Lord does miracles you know."

"And if anyone's deserving of one of God's miracles, it's Reverend

Jim," said Fern. "After all he's done for this town and the folks here. It'd be a downright sin if God didn't find some way of helping him and his family now."

"Heard the Widow Chievers was there when it happened," said Crystal Stevens, the beautician. "What do you figure she'd have been doing there?"

"Don't go believing every rumor you hear, Crystal," retorted Winnie. "No reason to think Mrs. Chievers would have been there."

"Well, where's she been then? No one knows where she went off to. And maybe she and the Reverend had something going."

"Hush your mouth, Crystal," Winnie said, emphatically slapping her hand on the table. "Don't you start spreading such mean things around town. Your flirting with Reverend Jim ain't been no secret. And he's done a pretty good job of staying away from you now, hasn't he?"

"Yes ma'am, he has. Was just harmless flirting though. Besides, much as I hate to admit it, I'm no Widow Chievers. And her being so much older than me. Lord, I don't know how that woman can look so good at her age. Anyway, I got it on good authority—straight from Chief Bruener—that Sandra Chievers was there when Reverend Jim had his stroke."

"Well, maybe it was just coincidence," said Belle. "They probably just ended up in the same place and ran into each other by accident. That would explain her being there when it happened. She'll be back any time now. Reckon she'll tell us then."

"Coincidence?" Crystal pressed on. "Both ending up way out there at the Outer Banks, in the same town, at the same time? And then her being with him when he has his stroke? Miss Belle, that's like saying it's a coincidence that it gets light at the same time the sun comes up."

"Now Crystal, you're just being mean-spirited," Winnie said not even attempting to hide her irritation at the young hairdresser. "Stop all this nonsense about the Widow Chievers and Reverend Jim having something between them. You know as well as I do the Reverend was devoted to Renee and those two darling children of his. And all the good he's done for all of us. Won't do having you spreading hateful things around like that. Won't do at all. The only Christian thing for all of us to do now is pray for a miracle for that man, and for his family."

"You're absolutely right, Winnie," Belle said. "That's what we have to do, all of us. We've got to pray hard for Reverend Jim and his family. So hard to figure though. Such a good man. So many people needing him. Why's he the one taken away?"

Fern Riggins stood up and walked over to the rail facing the church. "Well, you know what they say dear," she said, leaning on the support post. "God does work in mysterious ways. Who knows why it's Reverend Jim this happened to. Maybe he's being punished for the wrong he's done. We've all done wrong. Even preachers. Or maybe God's punishing Paradise. Taking our beloved pastor away. Or maybe it's just one of them things, part of God's will that stays a mystery to us little people down here. You know, something we'll only find out when we join Him in *His* paradise."

"*If* you join him," Winnie said, laughing.

"Now Winnie, don't be talking like that," Fern said as she and all the other women joined Winnie in her laughter. All, that is, except Norma Hutchins.

"Has nothing to do with us or the town," Norma said. Fern sat down and each of the women stopped their laughing and whatever fiddling and fussing they were otherwise engaged in. They stopped to listen to Norma. Norma didn't so much express opinions. It was more like making pronouncements.

"We all have our own score to settle with the good Lord. He don't tell us when or where it's going to happen. Or how. He decides. And when He does, we better be pretty darn sure we're ready. Reverend Jim ain't no different than the rest of us. He has his score to settle with the Lord. I reckon it's settling up time for him right about now. Hope he was ready. Yep, sure hope he was ready."

The other women looked at Norma Hutchins as she looked pensively out over the church grounds. From the beginning, Norma had feared this day would come. She just hadn't realized that her niece would be a part of it.

Chapter 25

As they pulled into the driveway of the wooden house at 114 Tidal Lane, Renee got her first glimpse of the house. Her first reaction was to ask Father Ray to turn right around and drive away. But she knew that as painful as it would be for her, for both of them, she needed to see the place where her life, as she had known it, had so cruelly been torn away from her.

Ray put Renee's minivan into park and shut off the engine. For awhile they both sat, neither one of them speaking, both gazing at the innocent looking vacation home standing before them as if staring at the house would make everything that happened there just a bad dream from which they would soon awaken. Now that they were there, she found herself secretly hoping that Ray would say "let's get out of here." But he didn't. Looking over at him, it was clear to her that even though he had urged her not to come, Ray too had wanted to visit the scene of that week's strange and awful events.

Renee finally broke the silence.

"I guess it's time. Let's go, Father."

She opened the passenger door and slid out. Following her lead Ray did likewise on the driver's side. He walked around the front of the minivan and joined her as she stood at the foot of the stairs leading to their destination.

"Are you sure you want to do this?" he asked her.

Now you ask, she thought. *One minute ago I would have said no. Too late now.*

"No," she said. "I'm not sure I want to. But I have to. And so do you."

Ray just nodded. He gently took her by the arm and together they slowly began the climb. At the landing they stopped. He looked through the screen door at the small, enclosed porch room that had served as Sandra's prison and sanctuary a few nights earlier. Renee took a look. She turned and watched Ray as he stared. She could almost feel him hearing Sandra's sobs of sorrow and seeing her fearfully crouching on the bare floor in a futile effort to hide from the powerful forces swirling around her. Renee could read Sandra's pain in Father Ray's face.

"Come on," he said to Renee, turning away. "Let's go."

They continued up the stairs. When they reached the top they stopped before actually entering the deck itself. Renee looked at it as if it was a place of historical importance, to be beheld with awe or respect before being entered. In fact, it was such a place—a place where history, her history, their history, had taken place in a way that would profoundly affect the rest of their lives.

The police had taken the boom box, tapes, air mattress and empty wine bottle as evidence. Otherwise, the scene hadn't been disturbed since that night. Renee looked at it trying to imagine the forces which could have caused what Sandra had described as having happened and Jim's otherwise unexplained condition. While Renee's beliefs, and Father Ray's for that matter, certainly allowed for supernatural causes, perhaps even demanded such allowance, logical human minds always sought more earthly explanations. But, as Detective Hall had told her, the facts as they knew them didn't easily lend themselves to logical or rational analysis. Nonetheless, the police had closed the file ignoring the unusual physical evidence and explaining Sandra's testimony as the shock-induced ranting of a woman whose lover had had a stroke in the middle of their lovemaking.

After a few moments of staring at the deck, Renee finally crossed the invisible boundary separating the life she had known from the genesis of the life she would come to know, and walked onto the widow's walk. Ray followed as she stepped to the eastern railing and looked out over the relatively calm sea.

"You know why they call these balconies widow's walks?" she asked.

She didn't wait for an answer.

"Sailors would build these for their wives so the wives could watch for the return of their ships. The wives would watch, and wait—watch and wait to find out if their husbands had survived the journey, so they would know if they were widows. I think I know how they must have felt."

Ray stood beside her and said nothing. Though she had come to see the place where Jim had met his fate, she avoided looking at the small enclosure of the porch itself. She kept her eyes fixed on the ocean, fearful of what might be revealed to her if she looked too closely at Jim's and Sandra's tragic love nest.

Ray comfortingly put his arm around her shoulders.

"Don't give up hope, Renee," he said. "He may come out of it. Just keep praying."

"No, Father," she said. "I fear he's never coming out of it. Not in this life anyway."

She looked up at Ray with grateful eyes.

"Thank you, Father. Thank you so much for being here. I don't know how I would have made it through the last few days without you."

As she looked into his eyes, Ray gripped her upper arms with his hands as if he was getting ready to pull her towards him for a comforting hug. He hesitated. She could see in his eyes that he felt great compassion and sympathy for her. They seemed to be expressing guilt. But about what? Guilt over Sandra having been Jim's lover? Guilt that he hadn't found Sandra in time to prevent what had happened? She wasn't sure. But the pain it was causing him was evident.

She continued to look at him, drawn by a sudden desire to see who he really was. His eyes were very expressive. They were eyes that seemed to say, "Welcome. Enter. There is so much we would like you to know."

She accepted the invitation. As Ray continued to hold her arms, neither drawing her near nor pushing her away, saying nothing, she peered deeply into those expressive eyes trying to see into this man's heart and soul. Why this had become important to her she didn't know. It just was.

"Renee," he said as he gripped her arms a little more firmly. "I'm. . . I'm sorry . . ."

"Shhh," she said, placing her index finger to his lips.

It happened without any further warning. The touch of her finger to his lips set off something powerful within her. One moment she was looking at Father Ray gratefully, expressing her appreciation to this religious man who had helped her through her time of grief. The next moment she was looking at a man who made her forget Jim, her children, her inhibitions, her morals, her principles. All she wanted was for him to hold her, kiss her, rip her clothes off and make violent, passionate love to her, there on the wooden floor of the widow's walk.

Images flashed before her eyes of the two of them making wild, primitive love, doing things she would never have done with Jim, things he had pleaded with her to do. They didn't seem wrong now. Not only did they not seem wrong, they seemed absolutely delightful, and she had to have it. Her body cried out for pleasure like never before.

Ray wanted it too. She could see it in his eyes. She could feel it in his hands and arms as they began to tremble, slowly drawing her closer to him. They embraced. The pounding of his speeding heart ran through her body like a raging river. The passion of his loins pressed against her abdomen burst through her like Fourth of July fireworks electrifying her senses from her toes to the top of her head.

It was too much for her, for any human being, to resist. She would wait only a few seconds more before taking matters into her own hands, ripping off his collar and ending his renewed vow of celibacy with glee and delight.

"Renee."

It was almost a whimper as he leaned his head down towards hers.

"Ray," she said longingly as she closed her eyes and parted her lips for the tender kiss that would transport her to a world beyond delight.

A loud, screeching, metallic bang startled the steaming couple. They looked behind them toward the direction of the cacophonous sound that had so rudely interrupted them. In front of the house next door a garbage truck was lifting a large dumpster of trash and depositing it into the pile of already collected refuse it was carrying.

They turned back and looked at each other. They let go of each other and took a step back. Fear filled both of their faces. A wave of embarrassment swept over Renee. Ray took her firmly by the arm.

"Let's get the hell out of here," he said.

"Yes," was all the shaken Renee could manage to say.

As they walked down the stairs to the driveway, she could feel the overwhelming passion she had just experienced dissipating ever more quickly. By the time they reached the minivan, what had just occurred on the widow's walk already seemed a distant, almost false, memory. Ray opened the passenger car door and Renee slid in.

What happened? she wondered as she pulled the shoulder harness across her body and attached it to the locking mechanism of the seat belt. She felt flushed. Perspiration continued to form on her forehead. Ray got in behind the steering wheel and looked at her. He pulled a handkerchief from his back pocket and handed it to her. She wiped her brow.

As she handed the handkerchief back to him she turned and looked directly at his face for the first time since they had left the widow's walk. It was pale, ashen really. While fear had mostly given way to embarrassment for her, she could see that that wasn't the case for Father Ray. Like her, he had been scared out of his wits, and still was.

He put the handkerchief back into his back pocket and fastened his seat belt. He started the engine. He kept his eyes focused on the steering wheel and the instrument panel as if he was intentionally avoiding looking at the house, or Renee. He shifted into reverse and slowly backed out of the driveway. During the entire drive back to the hospital not a word was spoken.

Chapter 26

There she was. He could see her, feel her. Right outside his door.
Sandra looked up and down the hospital hallway right outside
the ICU. She didn't want to be seen. She certainly didn't want to run
into Renee Donovan. Having reassured herself that the coast was
clear, she entered the ICU. He watched her slowly, haltingly walk
past the nurses' station towards the motionless, expressionless body
of her lover.

When she reached the head of his bed she looked down at his
face. His eyes were open, looking up at her. Her formerly rich, auburn
hair was now dull and interspersed with a significant amount of gray.
The bags under her eyes, which previously were only apparent in the
morning, appeared permanently affixed. And wrinkles now lined all
parts of her face. In a brief three days, he thought, Sandra had aged
at least fifteen years.

"I know you can hear me baby."

She spoke in a lowered voice so as not to be heard by the various
hospital personnel in the room.

"And I know that what you're going through must be hell."

He could feel her concern for his plight, and her fear.

"You saved me, and I should be grateful. But, what did you save
me for? And what did it cost you?"

Was she expressing regret, or just recounting the futility of what
he had done? For some reason, those feelings, those thoughts of hers,
weren't coming through to him.

"I'm going away Jim. And I won't be back. But I needed to see you one more time, to let you know how sorry I am."

She took his left hand in hers, raised it to her lips and kissed it gently, carefully avoiding the IV needles. His eyes remained fixed on hers, where they had been since she first arrived. She softly put his hand down, stroked his forehead and turned to leave. She immediately stopped in her tracks. Renee and Ray were just entering the ICU.

For Jim, the scene unfolding before him was like the ending to an old B-grade movie, with all the main characters gathered together in one room where the sly detective exposes the identity of the murderer and all the loose ends of the plot are finally tied together. And there he lay, not only as the chief protagonist in the story, but as the only member of the audience watching the ending unfold with the added blessing—no, the curse—of knowing and sensing every thought and feeling of every other character. He so much wanted to close his eyes and mind. He so much wanted to be able to get up and walk out of the theater. He so much wanted to die. He could do none of those things. He could only lie there and watch, listen and feel.

Sandra was uncomfortable seeing Renee. She was absolutely shocked to see Ray. On seeing Sandra, Ray quickly walked up to her, unthinkingly leaving Renee slowly walking behind him.

"Sandra, are you all right?" he asked her, taking her hands in his.

"Yes, I'm fine," she answered, glancing nervously over his shoulder at the approaching Renee, and then at Ray again. "What . . . what are you doing here?"

"I've been looking for you," he said. Sandra felt a pastoral kindness she had never experienced in him before. "I had a feeling you might be in trouble. I went looking for you, to help if I could."

"Well, I guess you called that one right," she retorted. "But you're a little late."

Renee stepped up and stood beside Ray. Ray and Sandra stood between her and Jim's bed. Sandra pulled her hands from Ray's and turned her head slightly and looked directly at Renee. Her look was one of resignation.

"I don't deserve your forgiveness," she said to Renee. "And I won't insult you by asking for it."

Even in these tawdry circumstances, Sandra managed to maintain an air of dignity. "But whatever you think of me, I want you to know, I didn't do this to Jim. It was . . . some kind of . . . of crazy . . ."

"I read the police report," Renee interrupted. "I know what you told them about what happened."

Jim could feel that Renee's emotions regarding Sandra were a jumble of contradictions. Bitterness, anger, the pain of betrayal, even fear of her. Yet, at the same time, she pitied this lonely woman who had so disastrously sought solace in the arms of a younger man and, no matter how hard she tried, would never be able to escape the consequences for the rest of her life. Renee knew that Sandra wasn't, and never had been, the real threat to her or to Jim. Her own experience on the widow's walk had confirmed that.

Renee's brief thought of the widow's walk flashed through Jim's mind. In an instant he knew what had happened and how Renee and Ray had felt. *Thank God*, he thought, *thank God they broke away before it was too late for them.*

"I think I should leave now," Sandra said.

"Yes, I think you should," agreed Renee, holding in all of the feelings which a less disciplined person would have let pour forth.

"Where will you go?" Ray asked Sandra.

"I don't know. But please, Ray, don't ever come looking for me again. Trust me. It'll be better that way."

She walked past Ray and Renee and headed towards the exit door. After a few steps she turned and looked again at Renee.

"Renee, I never wanted to hurt Jim, or you. I . . . I really loved him."

Renee looked intently into Sandra's eyes.

"It would seem, Sandra, that one way or another, you bring the men you love face to face with God."

Sandra said nothing more. She turned and left the ICU.

Renee looked at Ray and a solitary tear fell from her eye. He gently wiped it away with his curled index finger and nodded towards Jim, who had lain there seemingly all but forgotten.

As they stood over his bed, Jim's eyes remained fixed on Renee. For a minute or so, neither Renee nor Ray said anything as they both silently tried to fathom the state Jim was in. It was an exercise they both found overwhelming and futile. Not knowing what else to do or to say to comfort her, Ray crossed himself and prayed. He prayed for a miracle if it was God's will, for Jim's soul if it wasn't, and for Renee to be blessed with the strength and courage to survive this tragedy, to support her children, to continue loving Jim and to find forgiveness in her heart.

Thanks, Jim thought. *Thanks for protecting her, much better than I've been able to do.* His eyes followed Father Ray as the priest turned and left the room, leaving Renee to be alone with her husband.

As she looked at him lying before her in his vegetative state, she didn't know what to say. The pain of betrayal was still too fresh to offer her forgiveness, though she knew, as did he, that she eventually would. The pain of the loss of her husband was greater still, which made it unlikely she could say much without breaking down, something she didn't want to do in front of him. So, for several minutes, she just looked into his eyes, silently, having no way of knowing how much of what was inside her was making its way into his isolated consciousness. Finally, she put her hand on his arm and sadly told him, "I love you." She turned and slowly walked away.

As he watched her walk away, Jim could only continue to lie motionless and helpless in his bed. What he had seen and heard squeezed so mercilessly hard that he felt the pain in every nerveless and numb organ in his body, or so it seemed. He prayed for tears to run freely from his eyes to provide some relief from the unbearable situation he was in for what he feared would be the rest of his natural life. But none would come. As with the rest of his paralyzed body, his tear ducts were inoperative, and they would remain dry.

What now? he wondered. *What's to become of me? How long must I lie here, alive but not really alive, hearing, feeling, knowing every thought, every emotion, of those dearest to me, of those I've betrayed, and who I've abandoned?*

He had seen so much on that widow's walk. His soul was revealed to him in all its glory—his kindness, compassion, ability to bring the best out in others and minister to their needs to make their lives better—and all its depravity born of insecurity—his arrogance, his need for success and acclaim, his desire for vengeance against all who had slighted or wronged him, his deceit and pre-emptive strikes against being deceived, and his promiscuity, the fruitless search for nurturing, intimacy, and control. He understood clearly now the ultimate conflict and the final battleground.

But there was much he still didn't understand. *Am I in Hell?* he wondered. *If this is my eternal state, I must be. Oh God, please no! Don't let it be. Please, let this be just . . . just some sort of Purgatory, or penance. Please God, tell me. Talk to me.*

He waited. There was no sound, no thoughts conveyed to him, no words of comfort. He remembered how Melanie Leigh had taunted him about never really *hearing* God talk to him, not like she heard her guru, and not like he heard the voice of evil on the widow's walk.

He stared at the ceiling. *Voice or no voice,* he thought, *you must be there. Why else would I still be here, whether this is Hell or some way station to Heaven, or whatever the state of being with you is? How else to explain the resistance to the Other One, the fierceness of the battle over my soul?*

He waited. No sounds other than the occasional whispered conversations of the nurses. He waited some more. Then, a voice, a voice he recognized, talking to Renee, just outside the ICU door.

"Renee, I'm so sorry it took so long for me to get here. I came as soon as I heard."

Yes! Yes! It's Dr. Westin!

"Thank you, Dr. Westin," Renee said as they hugged. "Thank you so much for being here."

"I met a Father Chievers on my way in," Dr. Westin said. "I told him who I was and he explained everything, at least as best he could. Is there anything I can do?"

Yes! Thank you, Dr. Westin! Thank you for being here!

"I'm all right," Renee said. "I'll be fine. Right now, I think Jim needs you more than anyone."

Just like Renee. Always thinking of others. Always thinking of me.

"Of course," Dr. Westin replied. "Let me go in and see him. Will you wait for me in the waiting room?"

"Yes, of course."

Dr. Westin opened the ICU door, identified himself to the head nurse, and walked over to Jim's bedside. Jim hoped his mentor would see the joy in his eyes, but knew that he probably couldn't. All the same, seeing Dr. Westin, though creating embarrassment and pain, was, at the same time, a blessing.

Dr. Westin placed his hand on Jim's hand, being careful not to disturb the IV needle. He said nothing, but Jim could hear his thoughts and feel his emotions—the disappointment in him, the concern for him, but most importantly, the unconditional love.

Finally, Dr. Westin spoke.

"I can't imagine what you're going through, Jim. But keep your faith, and you will be forgiven."

The dry tears flowed in Jim's mind at his mentor's words. He tried so hard to lift his hand to take Dr. Westin's in it, but he couldn't. He wanted so much to ask Dr. Westin for *his* forgiveness, but knew it was fruitless. Most importantly he wanted to ask Dr. Westin to care for Renee and the kids, those who had loved him the most, and who he had hurt the most—not only in what he had done, but in how he had now left them alone.

Dr. Westin lifted his hand from Jim's. "Good-bye, Jim," he said. "And may God bless you." He turned and started to walk away.

Oh, please, Dr. Westin, Jim silently pleaded. *Please take care of Renee and the girls! Please be there for them!*

Dr. Westin turned and looked at Jim.

"I will, Jim," he said. "Don't worry. I will."

What? He . . . he heard me?

Dr. Westin smiled. He turned and walked out of the ICU.

A sense of peace came over Jim. It was accompanied by a sense of knowing. He came to appreciate the cruel irony of his plight, in a black humor kind of way. Now that he was finally beginning to understand the true nature of the life-long inner and outer battle for his soul, and the enormous price one may be asked to pay to obtain ultimate redemption, he could explain it to no one. There would be no more counseling of troubled parishioners, no more inspirational sermons. He knew what warnings to give, but couldn't give them. He knew the secrets, but couldn't divulge them. He had seen and experienced great mysteries up on that widow's walk, but couldn't describe them to anyone. It had all been revealed to him now, the truth as no mere mortal could ever understand it, and it would remain tightly locked within his knowing, yet disconnected mind, until it was time for the condition of that mind to be replaced by the fate of his soul.

Or would it remain locked up? *Dr. Westin heard me. I'm sure he did. And if he could hear me . . .* A single, wet tear formed in his right eye, spilled over his eye-lid and rolled down his cheek. Jim's eyes closed, and he peacefully went to sleep.

Chapter 27

"Yes, doctor," Jim heard the nurse's voice say. "Reverend Donovan is right over there."

Jim opened his eyes. Dread and horror filled his lifeless body.

"Good morning, Reverend Donovan."

Leaning over him and looking down at him with a sinister smile was Dr. Pe're, wearing a white coat with a name tag that identified him as a physician.

"And how are we this morning?"

Jim could only stare. He remembered Dr. Westin's visit and called upon all of the strength and faith he could muster.

Dr. Pe're leaned closer to him.

"I know you're a baseball fan," he whispered. "Just remember Yogi Berra's famous words. 'It ain't over till it's over.'"

At that, Pe're's face contorted into a grotesque, hideous form that sent chills throughout Jim's body. Jim could feel and smell the creature's hot, rotten breath as it stared down at him, black saliva beginning to drool from an ever wider-opening mouth that revealed no teeth, no tongue—only a cavernous black void.

Jim's mind was now as frozen and helpless as his body. He could feel himself being drawn into the void which had grown so large that it completely obscured any portion of the creature's sickening facial features that may have remained. Jim wanted to resist, but he couldn't move, couldn't think. He tried to pray, but his thoughts were nothing but random images, swirling into the vast nothingness of the creature's void.

There's nothing left to . . . Then, nothing.

Suddenly, a loud thud crashed into his consciousness. The room's lights, which had been snuffed out by the void, streamed into his eyes, momentarily blinding him. When they finally focused he shifted them back and forth to see what had happened.

To his left he saw the creature staggering up like a punch-drunk boxer who had been knocked silly by a perfect left hook and was trying to stand before being counted out. Jim looked to his right and what he saw shocked him even more.

There stood Norma Hutchins, gripping her raised walking cane in her two hands like it was Hank Aaron's baseball bat and he had just hit the homerun that broke Babe Ruth's record.

Oh my God! Norma Hutchins just clubbed Pe're! But, but how . . .

Before he could think another word, the creature leaped up and sprang over the bed. It had claws rather than hands and they were stretched out reaching for the old lady's neck.

With the dexterity and speed of a cat, Mrs. Hutchins stepped aside, spun around and took another homerun swing. She connected again, right between the creature's bulging eyes, and down it went again.

Jim looked at Mrs. Hutchins in total disbelief. She seemed neither tired nor old. Her features were those of the octogenarian he had known, and who had so clearly disapproved of him. But he could feel her spirit. It was young, and strong, and very caring towards him, even protective. She smiled at him and turned her head just as the creature made another lunge at her.

This time she didn't swing her cane like a bat. Instead, she quickly gripped it with one hand on each end and held it across her chest. Just as the creature's lunge brought it within arm's length of her, she pushed the cane forward to meet it.

As soon as the creature touched the cane another transformation occurred, and Jim was once more looking at Dr. Pe're. He stood before Norma Hutchins, her cane pressed against his chest. They stood silently, face to face, cane to chest, as if they were both taking the time to size up their enemy and plan their next move.

Behind the two combatants Jim could see the two duty nurses standing and looking as if they were engaged in conversation. But there was no sound from them, no movement. It was as if time, and existence itself, had stopped.

He looked back at his unlikely savior and the evil doctor.

"Do you really believe you're strong enough to defeat me, old lady?" Pe're snarled.

Mrs. Hutchins said nothing.

Another snarl, unintelligible, rolled out of Pe're's mouth.

Mrs. Hutchins remained silent and still.

Quickly, Pe're turned his face towards Jim. His eyes were a fiery red. Jim had seen them before—following him in the woods as the fifteen-year-old groped his way home in the dark, naked and humiliated. And in the eyes of the wolf that had frozen him as he drove along the dark and lonely North Carolina road just a few days before. They had been there throughout his life, following him, watching him, scaring the hell out of him. Those same evil eyes. And here they were again. They started to open ravenously wider and a smile started to crease Pe're's lips. But before he could complete the sinister smile Mrs. Hutchins pushed her cane so forcefully against his chest that he was flung mightily against the wall. On impact, the body that was Dr. Pe're crumbled to the floor into a heap of dust.

Jim's own eyes grew huge in amazement. They slowly moved from the pile of dust on the floor to the aged warrior who had felled the monster who had held a choke hold on Jim's life since he was a kid. She walked over to his bedside and looked down at him.

Thank you. Thank you so much, Mrs. Hutchins.

He paused a second to collect his thoughts.

I don't know how, or why you . . .

"Yes you do, Reverend Jim," she said, though her lips never moved. "You've always known."

She nodded over toward the pile of dust that was once Dr. Pe're, and more.

"You're forever free of him."

I am? Are you sure?

"Yes. I'm sure."

Mrs. Hutchins, will I ever, will I ever move again? Be able to say "I love you" to Renee? Hold my kids again?

Jim was desperate to hear her say "Yes, you'll be as good as new."

She looked down at him lovingly.

"In this life? That I can't tell you, dear. But you're free of the evil."
Then, she was gone.

"Did you see that?" Jim heard one of the nurses say. He looked in their direction.

"See what? " the other nurse said.

"He smiled!"

"Are you sure?"

"I think so."

"Sure enough to put it in the chart? That would be a pretty big deal, you know. Sure you want to raise false hopes for the family?"

"Maybe you're right," the first nurse said with some disappointment. "It was probably just the way the light reflected off him."

"Yeah, I'm sure that's it."

Jim smiled to himself and closed his eyes.

Norma Hutchins hung up the phone and took her seat in the rocking chair in the sitting room of her neatly kept home in Paradise, South Carolina. Cat jumped into her lap and purred.

"Well, my furry friend," she said as she softly stroked the feline's head. "That was Father Ray. Seems that the same Lord that he left Sandra for has brought them back together."

Cat meowed softly.

"Yes, yes Cat. He'll take care of her. I've no doubt about that," she said to the balled up lump of fur in response to the question only she could have heard or understood. "He's a good man."

Cat meowed again.

"What's that? Will Reverend Donovan ever be truly free in this lifetime?" She chuckled softly. "In due time, my friend. In due time."

With that, Norma slowly drew her hand over Cat's face closing her companion's eyes.

"Our work here is done, Misty Velvet Cezanne the Third," she whispered.

Norma closed her eyes.

"Our work here is done."

Both Norma and Cat took two more breaths, and breathed no more.

At the same moment, in a hospital one state away, Renee Donovan held Jim's limp hand in hers and looked down at her sleeping husband.

She dismissed the first sensation of his strengthening grip as wishful thinking. But then, his eyes opened, looked deeply into hers and welled up with tears.

"Baby," he said. "I'm . . . I'm so . . ."

As tears flowed from her eyes, she put her finger on his lips.

"Shhh," she said, and laid her head on his chest.

"Shhh."